ALL HAILED THE SINGULARITY

by

Dan Pausback

ISBN: 979-8-9913330-3-0

Printed in the United States of America

Table of Contents

Chapter 1

<u>Conscience</u>

Juan Augusta Sequenza was one of the first people to be extracted from La Pureza, a small village in the southern region of what was still unofficially called Mexico. Records showed that he was a local farmer growing mostly papayas and avocados, well outside the purview of the Consortium of Nations. Juan had been flying in the face of countless global mandates for the entirety of his life, all twenty-six years. His very conception had been a legal misstep. As far as the Consortium was concerned, his entire village and everyone in it were a gross violation. They produced their own food, all unpatented. Not one person had a life chip. Not one embryo had ever been modified. The list went on and on.

By Juan's figuring, however, he and his fellow villagers were simply living their lives as all their ancestors had done before them; and that ancestral line was extensive. Juan's DNA had historical markers that predated the Maya. Despite his name, he was of pure native descent. His ancestors had ridden the ebb and flow of countless civilizations with surprisingly little genetic mutation. By nature's understanding, his lineage had been doing something quite right. With the collapse of the Mayan civilization, Juan's ancestors had simply receded back into the fold of the natural world and continued to survive. Juan was proof of that. The majesty of the civilization had crumbled, but not the DNA which had given it rise.

Juan and his ilk, through absolutely no awareness of their own, were both the threat and solution to such great civilizations. They preferred not to group too largely. They were comfortable at simple levels of existence. They viewed the natural world as part of themselves and vice versa. They lived and loved, grew old and died, all without too much fuss or worry.

This simple approach to existence had not prepared them in the least for that day when the Department of Population Control arrived at their doorstep. Within minutes, the entire village was neutralized with auriflurane; a paralytic gas disbursed on sonic waves. It spread so quickly, people were unconscious before they could even speculate about the odd sound they were hearing. In addition to the speed of delivery, the molecular design of auriflurane allowed for scalability. For as long as the gas remained inside an organism's system, its sedative effects could be shortened or lengthened simply by bombarding it with specific tones.

Once the village was cleared of its inhabitants, it was leveled. Though there were very few groups around like Juan and his co-villagers anymore, the policy still held that all remnants of an illegal habitation be obliterated. This was done to discourage other potential lawbreakers from attempting to reclaim the area. There were certainly more elegant ways to achieve the razing of a village, but considering the remoteness of its location, it was easiest to just blast and till. This involved knocking structures down with plasma bursts and plowing the debris under with earth movers. The last step was to sow the area with a quick growing mod-grass. Within a few days, the entire area would look like a meadow that had always been just as it was.

As Mattie Ferne readied Mr. Sequenza for storage, the phrase, *the probability of the improbable*, entered her mind once again. Lately, those words had become almost a mantra for her. She remembered her physics professor at New Columbia, Dr. Marc Covelle, absently tossing the term around during lectures. He had been very atypical. His most famous idea, or infamous depending on who one talked to, was that consciousness was a dimension, the same way in which space and time were. Like space and time, it couldn't be seen, but its effects could be measured.

One of his arguments for this revolved around entropy. If the universe was moving toward higher states of entropy since the Big Bang, then things like planets and galaxies shouldn't exist, and certainly not life. By definition, life was a result of the chaotic becoming ordered, very ordered in fact. That life existed seemed to imply something was pushing back against the entropic nature of the universe, creating a balance between self-organization and chaos. This balance, perhaps cyclical in operation, allowed for the perpetual existence of the entire cosmos. He was certain this *something* was a form of intuitive choice being exerted from an as-of-yet-discovered field or dimension.

While his peers widely dismissed his argument, it gained appeal with the rest of society. Unfortunately, it was for the wrong reasons, even according to Dr. Covelle. Many people grabbed hold of the idea and used it to promote the age-old notion of God. For Covelle though, the dimension of consciousness was just that, a dimension. There was no need to worship it any more than one would worship space or time. Its properties were unique, and did involve choice at some level, but that did not give it any manner of self-awareness nor divinity.

By the time Mattie studied under him, he was old, and in her estimation, beaten down. He kept most of his lectures centered on classical physics, but did so in a disengaged manner. It's why she remembered his repetition of the term, *the probability of the improbable*. Whenever he used it, she could see that it meant something to him on a personal level. Perhaps some odd mishap in his life had made him question the very legitimacy of physics as it pertained to human existence. In one lecture, he proposed that if the purpose of self-awareness was to relinquish the material world, than pursuing a career in physics was going one hundred and eighty degrees in the wrong direction. She found that strange coming from a physicist, yet contradiction had been his trademark. And it now seemed apparent to Mattie that a good deal of it had rubbed off on her.

The probability of the improbable was Covelle's assertion that no matter how certain you were a known physical law would behave in a determinate manner, like gravity for example, there would always exist a chance that it wouldn't. He argued that umpteenth time after umpteenth time you could expect an outcome of A, but on the umpteen-and-first time, you may end up with B. It was an eternal gotcha built into the fabric of the universe; an offshoot posit related to his theory of dimensional consciousness. The gist being, that if there *is* a choice dimension at work, it could at any given moment choose B over A, regardless of what you might be expecting.

Mattie remembered arguing that even if the possibility of such an anomaly did exist, people could still obviously work within (and rely upon) the statistical average of any given process or law. Gravity *would* more often than not behave the way it was expected to, which for practical purposes was enough to consider it an absolute.

It was one of the few debates in which her professor became personally vested. He began to punctuate his responses with large sweeps of his arms, jabbing his finger into the air. He stated that if and when such a reversal of choice finally did occur, the stakes could be so high that the annihilation of the universe may be the outcome. That the more we took our known laws for granted, and the more we tampered with them, the easier it would be for our house of cards to collapse. And all due to one minuscule yet critical reversal of B over A, from the dimension of consciousness.

The thought that she may be playing a direct role in creating such a house of cards had been nagging at Mattie for months now. In addition to the increasing moral dilemma her job was causing her, she now sensed the approach of some dark, looming catastrophe.

She'd been working at the DPC as a storage operator for the past six years. It was a long way removed from her early college dreams for herself. But once matter mechanics became the field of choice for so many undergrads, the industry became saturated with new hires. All the more glamorous fields where it was being applied were impossible to get into. She'd hoped for a career in aerospace technologies but fell short of the scores needed to even make the eight-year waiting list.

In some circles, being a storage operator was quite respectable. Within Mattie's closest circle, however, that of her boyfriend Troy, it was reprehensible. He was an independent coder who developed quantum-based software. He'd started out in virtual gaming but began feeling he was wasting his efforts. As his social awareness became more and more attuned, he started interacting with clandestine hacker organizations.

Generally speaking, hacker organizations were reputable contracting groups. Most businesses relied heavily upon their expertise since virtually all walks of life involved some type of coding. No matter how big a corporation was, it still couldn't keep up with all the various applications circulating through society. Hacker organizations filled the gap, and on the whole, worked symbiotically with big business.

Still, one could always find those who did not agree with the status quo. The most elusive and notorious of these groups was the Blue Crow organization. Made up primarily of hackers who for one reason or another felt disenfranchised, it had become a force to be reckoned with, even for the Consortium.

Mattie was fully aware that Troy's affiliation with the Blue Crow, and her affiliation with him, put her job and potentially her freedom at risk. But love was nonnegotiable. Beyond that, Mattie herself had begun espousing some of the same grievances Troy railed on about.

One of those grievances was the disparity of race and affluence with regard to population storage. No one knew better than Mattie just how lopsided the statistics were. Early in her career, she accepted the company line that those being stored were chosen by the world's only synthetic intelligence. The criteria, she was told, was formulated on simple, logic-based protocols. Primarily, whether or not the person had been genetically corrected upon conception; whether or not they had adopted all Consortium mandates (the foremost being, having a life chip implanted); and whether or not they were active consumers in the global marketplace. There were a litany of other nuanced criteria, but those were the big three. It was also maintained that since the choices were being made by the SI, they were completely impartial. Troy was quick to point out though, that even the synthetic intelligence had been programmed in its early stages, and whoever wrote that code could easily have instilled it with biases.

Regardless, the three main criteria still left one thing undeniably exposed, even to the least initiated – that if you were poor, you would not, because you could not, comply with any of the conditions.

Despite decades of Ocean Economics, many of the planet's more marginalized citizens still hadn't received their Consumer Endowments. They'd been left to fend for themselves. Troy often supposed there was a larger conspiracy in the works. He reasoned it was more advantageous for the Consortium to gather up undesirables and have them stored than to fund their existence, and by extension, allow for unsanctioned births.

Another grievance, which Troy called the potato trap, was that storage policies were limiting genetic variety. Like the Irish of old who became woefully dependent on a single strain of potato, the DPC was narrowing the human gene pool. By stowing away people who were conceived naturally and born without genetic modifications, the human race was losing its wildcard factor.

Why would an over-reliance on genetically similar humans be any less shortsighted than an over-reliance on the lumper potato? For Troy and Mattie, it was just a matter of time before the blight hit, in whatever form it might take. And here she was, with her hands on the controls. Why not *actively* choose outcome B over A? Why not try to counteract a flawed policy?

As she studied Mr. Sequenza, lying sedated inside the reduction chamber, she knew she would finally act. After initiating the procedure, she pulled Troy's memory pin from the collar of her shirt and uploaded its contents to the mainframe. When the singularity unit engaged and Mr. Sequenza was imprinted onto the conic crystal, the code was integrated with him. Mattie Ferne had officially become a Blue Crow rebel.

Chapter 2

<u>The Unraveling</u>

Mike Laurel leaned back from his microscope, "Doug, I need you to look at this."

"What've you got?" Douglas Compton asked, approaching from his workstation.

"If I'm reading this right,..well, first take a look. Tell me what you think."

Douglas swept his glasses to the side, letting them hang from his right ear, and leaned into the microscope.

After a moment, he grumbled, "Looks as if the cell walls are being destroyed."

"Not just destroyed, deconstructed," Mike countered.

"Yeah,..you're right. It's methodical, incremental." He pulled away from the eyepiece, "This from the tattoo case?"

Mike nodded, "That's what I mean. If this isn't a natural infection,..I mean it's behaving as if it were digital."

"Mike, come on."

"I know, I know. Impossible, right? But it's doing what it's doing."

"We're just missing something. Bring up the code from the tattoo's lattice," Douglas continued, heading to his office. "Transfer it to my desktop. And put in a call to the BCD. I want one of their people here when we review this."

After thirteen years at the Biotech Crime Division, Jacob Kepler still hadn't learned how to stomach the morning meetings. Besides everyone having to sit at school desks, the air-conditioning was always sub par. He was suspicious it had something to do with consumer attentiveness; keep a person just on the crest of comfort and discomfort and they're more apt to pay attention. Too comfortable, they space out. Too uncomfortable, they become agitated.

For someone like Jake though, the possibility that consumer attentiveness *was* being employed, caused an altogether different effect. It was enraging. So at least as it pertained to him, management's gambit had failed. He was having a very, *very* hard time paying attention. As he glanced around the room at the other agents, dutifully leaning forward on their tiny desktops, he realized he was in the minority. To him, they all looked like eager pelicans waiting for the next mackerel to be tossed.

"I'm most interested in any connection we can find between the Blue Crow organization and these nine storage facilities," Chief Novak said. He emphasized the chain of events by retracing each line on the plasma board. "Each one had its own internal firewall, so it's likely they had people on the inside. Possibly for months."

"Couldn't they have just been hacked?" one of the agents asked.

"Not impossible, but unlikely. The digital structure on those firewalls is SI designed. And unless they've built their own synthetic intelligence," he said, causing some of the agents to laugh, "then it's more likely someone overrode things from inside."

"Any demands issued?" another agent asked.

"No. In fact, we don't even know for sure if the Blue Crow is involved. A heist of this magnitude though, it's unprecedented. Blue Crow is just the best fit we've got right now. So employment history at these facilities takes top priority. The other angle to work is how and where did they move all these commodities? We're talking about massive power requirements, the kind that typically falls under corporate domain. Thompson, what the hell do you want?"

Joe Thompson was standing in the doorway of the briefing room, tapping the nearest agent on the shoulder and motioning toward Jake, a few rows forward.

"Uh,..I need Kepler, Sir."

"Kepler, shove off," the chief said, tipping his head toward the door.

Jake casually pulled himself from his school desk, purposely trying not to look too eager. Nevertheless, he was ecstatic as hell.

As the driverless car glided down the street, Jake gazed out the window.

"We got time to grab a coffee?"

"Coroner said it was urgent," Joe replied. "Here." He pulled a pack of stim-tabs from his pocket, offering it to Jake.

Jake stared at him for a moment. "Joe, there's an inherent pleasure to drinking coffee."

"If you say so."

"Ahhh." He resigned himself, taking one of the tiny gel strips from the packet and putting it under his tongue. "So what's the big to-do? He say?"

"Something about that girl who died last week from infection." Joe brought up the docket on his tablet and handed it to Jake.

A woman had installed a new tattoo, then two days later, died from complete organ failure. Tattoos weren't supposed to do that. Jake could remember a time when they were static, lifelong things made from nothing more than ink. They'd long since gone hi-tech. Now they were nanotech implants, fully programmable. A lattice containing thousands of microscopic, movable ink nodes could be coded to form any shape and emit any color, even fluorescents.

People often changed their tattoos, but the procedure was all external. The lattice could be programmed through the skin, so infection was never an issue. On rare occasions, a person's body might react to the nano lattice when it was first implanted, but even then, it was never life threatening. Beyond that, there were sometimes program viruses which could crash the lattice or alter the tattoo in some unexpected way, but those were strictly software issues, not biological ones.

At this point, Jake couldn't even connect her death to the tattoo. It could just be coincidence. What was really odd is the fact that she died from infection. Deaths of that sort were rare. Most everyone after Jake's generation was a modified person, or modded. At the minimum, they had to have all known, negatively recessive genes pulled from their genome while in vitro. Parents could always enhance their children further, but under the law, everyone had to at least purchase the basic, tier-one plan. This helped ensure a nearly disease-free society. Of course, if you couldn't afford the basic plan, then no family. If a couple decided to buck the system and procreate anyway, there were huge penalties. There was also the possibility the child would be removed from custody, perhaps even stored.

This woman had been in her mid-twenties and therefore definitely modded. Jake on the other hand was forty-eight and natural-born; or as the modded generation called his kind, a prototype. Arrogant bastards, he'd always felt. Pisser was, many of them *were* superior, in *some* ways. Their argument that they were the next step in evolution and that Jake and everyone before him were merely base models, wasn't far from the mark. Still, the reason he'd risen to the rank of investigative agent at the BCD was because he was a prodigy in his own right. Besides having a good nose for detective work, his understanding of various scientific fields made him the go-to guy for unusual biotech cases. He also had an uncanny knack for linking clues together in creative, nonlinear ways. One of the drawbacks with the modded generation, in his opinion, was that they were all too specialized. Their abilities were generally based on whatever genes their parents had pushed for. They simply weren't well rounded. Most of them missed the overall picture, even the few that had

Neuraltech. They were quick at processing, but fell short on imagination. And imagination was key in Jake's line of work.

"We have any info on the artist? I'm not seeing anything here," Jake asked, scrolling through the tablet.

"When she was admitted, she told the doctors she downloaded the tattoo. Went into a coma before they could find out where though. I asked the local PD to get her tablet. Maybe we can backtrack her steps."

"Let's get her purchase records too. And if they give you any BS about chip privacy, refer 'em to the mighty Novak."

One of the safety features designed into life chips was an auto-archiving function linked to the owner's biometrics. If coronary cessation was detected, the chip would initiate a final, synchronized backup to their online account. It would then delete all but the person's basic info from the chip itself. This was done so that chips couldn't be removed from the dead and used for fraudulent purchases or identity cloning. Problem for law enforcement was, once the chip was wiped, getting access to the online backup was mired in Consortium restrictions.

When Jake and Joe entered the morgue, Douglas walked over to greet them. He peeled off his surgical glove and shook hands with them.

"Thanks for getting here so quickly."

In the center of the room, the woman's body was lying on a dissection table enclosed in a plastic isolator. Mike was busy pulling samples through a glovebox in the isolator wall.

Jake spied a coffee machine in the corner of the room, "Mind if I…" he motioned.

"No, help yourself," Douglas said.

"So. Why are we here?" Jake asked, pouring himself a cup.

"Well, as implausible as it may seem, I think we have a new type of viral phenomenon on our hands," Douglas said, trying to gauge their responses. "I just wanted to run it by you guys before I contacted the WHO."

"Sounds like the proper procedure," Joe said. "Mind clarifying *phenomenon* though?"

"Are you familiar with Mertz's Hypothesis?" Douglas asked.

Joe shook his head no.

"Biodigital virus?" Jake cut in. "Is that what you think you've got?"

"Yes. Or at least something close to it."

Jake sipped his coffee, narrowing his eyes. "That theory defies a good number of basic laws regarding chemistry and biology, not to mention physics."

Douglas pursed his lips, striving to be polite, "I'm aware of that, yes."

After a moment, Jake shrugged, "Okay. Show me what you've got."

Douglas moved over to the grossing station and tilted up a monitor anchored to the side of the bench.

"This is the digital code we pulled from the tattoo lattice. It starts out functioning as it was designed to, reconfiguring into a flower hanging from the mouth of a dragon, or some such. At some point, the lattice was then triggered to display whatever this is."

On the monitor, the back of the woman's neck filled the screen. The ink nodes of the lattice were still shining through her discolored skin. The symbol looked to Jake like a series of geometric shapes all contained within a larger circle. Probably no more than some hacker's logo.

"Look familiar to you?" he asked Joe.

"Nope."

"Hidden underneath the tattoo's code is a subroutine patterned on DNA sequencing," Douglas continued. "We extracted it and ran it through our modeler. The best match we came up with? A *biological* virus that causes hemorrhagic fever. Ebola, specifically. Though it's coded with some unusual variations."

Noticing Jake's expression of doubt, Douglas took on a more adversarial tone.

"The symptoms experienced by this woman, the rapid mortality, the extreme tissue damage – *all* match the effects of Ebola. And based on the hospital report, the onset of her symptoms coincide more or less with the moment the tattoo changed its design."

"Odd coincidence, granted," Jake said, offhandedly. "But I mean-" he stopped himself. He could see Douglas clenching his jaw so tightly that he was about to reduce his teeth to powder. Only hours ago, Douglas had been struggling with the same doubt. He had rebuffed his colleague, Mike, point by point, until the obvious could no longer be overlooked. Now that it was his turn to play the kook, it did not suit him one bit. Trying to convince someone of something you yourself realize is preposterous, only makes the blood boil hotter.

"Well at what point," Jake continued, more tactfully, "or should I say, *how* did it go from being digital to biological? Which is what you're saying it did, right?"

"I am. Yes. I just haven't figured out how yet. The only thing we've been able to determine with any certainty so far is that the virus in its biological form is strictly blood-borne."

Jake's brow wrinkled up, not so much in disbelief this time, but consternation. He knew Douglas had a solid reputation and wasn't prone to wild assumptions. Furthermore, digitally sequenced DNA was nothing new. There was a whole industry devoted to creating synthetic DNA. New life forms had been created going back to the start of the century, and that was before quantum computers were used for sequencing. But a manufactured sequence was useless on its own, nothing more than code. To make it real, tangible, alive, required meticulous genetic engineering. First, the requisite number of amino acids had to be precisely combined in order to build the synthetic chain. Then, a cell membrane had to be stripped of all its native DNA and injected with the new, engineered strand. In those early days, you could only create simple organisms with very short life spans, hours if you were lucky. Even now, it was difficult to sustain any new life form for very long. Susceptibilities to infection, thermal instability, even basic, physical laws – how could something walk, for example, if it were top heavy? The pitfalls were endless.

All the more successful attempts used preexisting life forms as templates and only marginally altered the resident DNA structure. This complexity constraint, as it was called, was the foundation of Reiseleiter's Law; that even with the most powerful computers imaginable, the process of evolution could not be sidestepped. The extreme measure of time was impossible enough, but added to that were all the environmental inputs along the way. The total amount of data was simply unquantifiable, and fractal uncertainties made end-product predictions utterly pointless. Combinations of DNA were virtually limitless, and all the ways in which those strands interacted with each other and the environment were astronomical. Changing a single letter in just one sequence could make or break an organism.

Evolutionary restrictions aside, Mertz's Hypothesis of biodigital mutation was even more far-flung, by Jake's understanding. Engineering new life in a laboratory was one thing. Creating nothing more than digital code that could somehow use an organism's own system to achieve transmutation was bordering on magic. If it *was* possible, there was no telling where it would end. That's what really bothered Jake. Digital code could be transmitted through the air, into space, through just about any barrier. Theoretically, any organism with a digital interface would be at risk, which meant just about all of humanity. Even protos like Jake had various types of biotech in their bodies. At the very least, everyone had a life chip. There might be a few tech-free citizens still kicking about; hermits, survivalists, the indigent. But for the most part, people fitting those descriptions had long since been stored.

Mike called over from the dissection table, "Show them the biological sample."

"Exactly. Here, look at this." Douglas launched a recorded video of the woman's cells under a microscope. "What's utterly amazing about this virus is that it *functions* as if it were digital. It doesn't attack the cell in toto. There's no typical lysis or exocytosis occurring at all. Instead, once it's replicated sufficiently within the cell, it begins to dismantle it piece by piece. Viruses in nature don't operate that way."

"And that's what you're basing this on?" Jake asked.

"Look, I *will* find the causality. In the meantime, we have *got* to get this information out. If she downloaded this code from the network, and it *is* crossing the biodigital barrier, then we could have an unstoppable pandemic within weeks."

Jake stared at Douglas for a moment, then glanced over at Joe.

"Agents, look at that woman's body," Douglas continued, pointing sternly toward the isolator. "Within two days her insides turned to mush. Now you may disagree with my interpretation, but there's no denying this is a very deadly bug."

"You're right, you're right," Jake said, conceding. "Regardless of the how or why, we definitely need to sound a few alarms."

Chapter 3

BESI

By her colleagues' estimations, Margaret Líang was a very cool, calculated woman. Calm under pressure was her moniker. At close to forty, she was one of the early few offspring to undergo genetic modifications. Her father, Mark Líang, was one of the most influential business magnates in the Consortium. It was one of his corporate subsidiaries that first offered genetic modifications to consumers en masse. DNAugment had become the equivalent of a fast-food franchise once all the technical and legal hurdles were cleared.

Margaret was now Junior Vice President of OmniaR Enterprises, her father's parent company. It was one of eighteen global corporations, or super-corps as they were called, that made up the Consortium of Nations. OmniaR was involved in everything from cloning to space exploration. It was also home to the only stably functioning SI. The bioengineered, synthetic intelligence (BESI). Currently, the BESI was the very thing compromising Margaret's usual sense of cool. Today she was finally going to meet it, an honor granted to precious few.

She had cleared all her calls and appointments for the day. Her father said he'd come by later in the morning to collect her, but couldn't give a specific time. This only increased her anxiety, yet she understood the reasoning. Whenever the BESI was introduced to new stimuli, particularly a new social introduction, it needed time to prep itself. It was a precious, global treasure, and OmniaR was extremely sensitive to its welfare; even to the point of overprotection. In many ways, it was doted upon like a child, or prized elder.

Achieving synthetic intelligence had proven itself more complicated than originally predicted. Technical hurdles (as innumerable as they were) had turned out to be just a small measure of the challenge. Most such snags were addressed in short order with the advent of quantum computing. The larger stumbling block, and something which was still tripping up designers to some degree, related to the sticky and ever-shifting problem of psychology, or being.

The first SI to ever go online crashed within hours, despite all the technical components being well vetted. Attempt after attempt brought similar results. Eventually, leaders in the field began to incorporate a more humanistic approach. They brought on board several psychologists and behavioral scientists in order to best determine how to boot up such a complicated mechanism; the crux of the problem being the instantaneous onset of self-awareness. It was theorized that this full-consciousness gush, as they called it, caused an untenable shock.

The most promising approach was to allow the SI incremental access to its neural network over a span of several years. It was an attempt to mimic the way in which children gained cognition. Unlike a human child, however, this maturation phase could be truncated to approximately four years. It gave the SI enough time to acclimate to its own existence slowly and gently. Though designers were certain they were on the proper course, the SI would still ultimately crash.

Artificial intelligence had long since shifted away from computer model structures and moved toward biological ones. This shift brought into existence the idea of synthetic intelligence; something that was in essence living, instead of something that just mimicked life. There were still a few arc-paradigms pushing for sub-symbolic structures, but they were only useful for simpler machines. To reach true, self-perceiving autonomy, a biological approach was necessary.

Due to the inherent subjectivity of consciousness, it was still labeled as a known unknown in the field of neuroscience. However, studying its effects and determining workable precepts for its creation were nonetheless possible. It was determined that in order for consciousness to arise, constraints were necessary; this became a primary tenet of SI design. Unbounded computing power, in and of itself, was merely *potential* energy; similar to the difference between widely dispersed photons and a focused laser beam. In biological systems, particularly humans, the five senses helped keep consciousness properly bounded. Without them, it dissipated. Simple experiments in sensory deprivation showed that the longer a subject was deprived of their bodily constraints, the more they lost touch with reality. Short forays into such states were generally beneficial (such as with dreaming and meditation), but extreme, long-term deprivation led to insanity. For this reason, designers understood early on that regardless the architecture used, the SI would still need to be housed in a finite space with personalized, sensory inputs (cameras, thermometers, microphones, et al). It would need to be aware of itself as a physical thing within space-time in order to maintain a lucid state.

Another advantage of bounded consciousness stemmed from the neurotheological concept of mortality equals morality. An entity which is finite and capable of being destroyed is more apt to sympathize with other sentient beings. An SI which didn't understand its own mortality might fail to develop compassion, perhaps even spiral into sociopathy. Ideas of an SI one day residing on the network were relegated to the world of science fiction; for *any* consciousness to exist in such a boundless arena, with so many endless streams of non-personal, contradictory inputs, madness would be the only conceivable outcome.

Having settled on a biological framework for SI design, the first step was to reverse engineer the human brain. This allowed designers to create a digital facsimile. Much of this involved studying and incorporating large blocks of synth-DNA. If a strand was determined to have cognitive import, its digital equivalent would be included in the neural map. All told, thousands of these digital traits went into the design of the SI's brain. Most of them were particularly relevant to abstract thought; one of the more complicated facets of synthetic intelligence.

The out-of-the-box idea which finally provided a solution, and was still holding strong in the BESI, was the inclusion of an obscure piece of DNA code called the propensity marker.

In the early days of genetic augmentation, oversight on the consumer end of things had been lax. Armed with just a few precursory trait definitions, clinics often promoted wildly inaccurate claims with respect to what the addition or subtraction of any specific marker might bring. The propensity marker had been linked to certain abstract functions in the human brain and had been touted as the 'intelligence gene.' Wannabe parents flocked to clinics hoping to engineer their own family geniuses. Worse than becoming a mere boondoggle, however, it ended up creating a rash of over-stimulated, clinically psychotic children; nearly to a generational degree.

The marker was banned from public use until it could be further researched. Subsequent studies showed that it acted as an amplifier of various other traits. It even interacted with several of the more primal functions associated with the basal ganglia. The most notable effects, however, were observed in traits attributed to the frontal lobes. It appeared to have a high degree of influence on expressions of deceit, compassion, envy, et al. What SI designers found of particular interest was how it affected a person's concept of faith.

While no single marker was ever the sole contributor to any one trait, there were definitely those considered to be origin markers; markers which were always present in extreme trait exhibitions. Marker Taq1a-8623-H32, for example, was consistently present when studying people who exhibited excessive tendencies toward greed.

What puzzled geneticists with regard to faith, however, was that they had never been able to isolate an origin marker. It was widely gaining acceptance, at least in the field of neurotheology, that the propensity marker acted as both the origin *and* amplifier of faith. Furthermore, while in the presence of other origin markers, it would amplify those markers to a faith-like status. In people with Taq1a-8623-H32, for instance, greed became their creed.

Further experiments with the propensity marker brought even more detrimental results. It soon became apparent that if the marker were deactivated altogether, subjects tended to become hopelessly indifferent toward all aspects of their lives. All thirty children whose parents had enrolled them in the study eventually committed suicide before reaching preadolescence.

It became clear that the propensity marker was integral to human existence.

This proved to be the missing piece of the puzzle with regard to SI design. Since having incorporated a digital equivalent of the propensity marker in the BESI, it had been functioning stably for the past seventeen years. Designers theorized (along with the BESI itself) that the inclusion of the marker in its design had given it a valuable tool: the ability to cope with its own beingness.

As Margaret and her father entered the elevator, she couldn't help straightening her skirt, again. It was one of the few nervous habits she had, and it was currently being utilized incessantly.

"Don't be so anxious."

"Father, that's like a dentist saying don't mind the pain."

Mark Líang laughed. It had been a long time since he'd seen his daughter so vulnerable. His nickname for her was Qiáng (wild rose). Ever since she was an infant, she'd been self-determined and obstinate. Unruly and beautiful. As she grew older, she learned to control that energy and become extremely productive. Nepotism aside, she'd always been the best suited for her position.

"You still haven't explained why the BESI wants to meet me."

"We're having some security issues. It wants you to head up an investigative team."

"Me? I'm head of marketing."

"Profile assessment, sweetheart. You've always had a head for problem solving. The BESI simply ran the numbers and you were at the top of the list. It wants to avoid the standard security channels just in case they turn out to be part of the problem. It's exactly *because* you're in charge of marketing that the BESI considers you a low risk. Well, that and being my daughter. Besides! Haven't you always wanted me to introduce you?"

"I have! I did,..I do,..it's just,..different when it happens."

Margaret was growing angry with herself for being so skittish. Her anxiety was well founded though. The BESI had a huge advantage over her. It had access to her life-chip data.

Most people in society already had extensive profiles on record. Among other things, a person's genome was stored, which could be referenced for genetic predispositions. Multiple aspects of a person's whole life history, up to the current second, were being recorded and cataloged. Virtually every body function was monitored. Anyone with access to a person's life chip feed could determine quite easily if they were awake or asleep, eating or lifting weights, engaged in sexual activity or reading a book. All such things and nearly countless others had long since been biometrically mapped. The benchmarks were the same in all humans to within a fraction of a percent. Variances were easily corrected for by simple cross-referencing, along with a person's own direct input through social devices.

Margaret was certain the BESI was aware of her current state of unease. All employees of OmniaR were required to sign a waiver allowing the company access to their life chip accounts. The requirement came in the guise of corporate security, but Margaret knew it was just a formality. OmniaR already had access to everyone's account. They were the sole, global provider.

Being biometrically exposed, as it were, was bad enough. But to make matters worse, she'd be clueless as to what the *BESI* might be feeling. It had no activity monitor she could reference. No performance scope from which to derive how it was processing information. From what she understood, it had no social output components other than being audible. It had purposely been designed without an anthropomorphic shell. No robotic face or screen image to mimic human reactions or emotions. It was meant to have an oraclesque mystique to it so that its stature would be immediately apparent. Biotech psychologists had cautioned that making it appear too human-like would open it to ridicule and disrespect. Humans it seemed did not inherently hold each other in high regard, and any machine made in their image would likely suffer the same scorn.

As they exited onto the forty-seventh floor, Margaret's anxiety escalated to a fevered pitch. Being that she was fully aware of this escalation, and knowing the BESI was aware of it too, only served to escalate it further. If she didn't get a handle on things, she'd end up in a panic-stricken feedback loop.

"How do I look?" she asked, once again smoothing her skirt.

Mark put his arm around her shoulder and pulled her in close, kissing her forehead, "Forever beautiful Qiáng."

His assurance did little to steady her nerves. She couldn't stop rummaging through her bucketful of worries. Even if she had been able to put aside her life chip concerns, there was still the BESI itself – its lauded reputation. All those years of hearing her father talk about how insightful it was, how intelligent. Society in general seemed to revere it as some kind of mechanized guru. For just under a decade, it had been helping the human race manage itself efficiently and peacefully. In many respects, it had replaced the Apex CEO.

All at once, Margaret began feeling outclassed. Furthermore, she worried that her apprehension might cause the BESI apprehension.

"Maybe we should wait."

"What? Sweetheart, we can't wait."

"But it's going to know – *already* knows that I'm a wreck. What if it gets nervous too?"

"It doesn't respond to emotions the same way we do. It won't get nervous just because you're nervous. And you shouldn't *be* nervous. It's just a machine, not God. Don't let yourself get carried away," Mark said, in a paternal tone.

The Cradle, as it was called, was every bit as futuristic as Margaret had been led to believe. It was a large rotunda, lit with cool, blue mesospheric lighting; a type of open-sky illumination created by exciting static layers of luxon gas circulating around the ceiling. The BESI was in the center of the room, encased in a clear, cylindrical pillar that had a circumference of about sixty feet. Around the pillar were several control panels and workstations. The components of the BESI, the brain itself, were further insulated within a transparent sphere. The sphere was filled with an endless network of crystal relay modules, all suspended in a thick soup of protoplasm.

"Margaret. It's so wonderful to finally meet you," the BESI said, as she and her father entered the Cradle. Its voice was melodic and unencumbered, though Margaret couldn't distinguish it as male or female. At best, it was something in between. It filled the room evenly, as if coming from all directions at once.

"Mark has often shared stories with me about your childhood." The ceaseless light streams ricocheting through the crystal nodes momentarily brighten in a small region of the BESI sphere. "I'm so sorry. I realize that statement may cause you some discomfort,..embarrassment, and that is the last thing I wish to do. It's just that I have become rather fond of the notion of family, and to finally meet the child of our CEO is truly a great honor."

"The honor is mine, BESI," Margaret responded. She had long wanted to ask a thousand and one questions of this fascinating machine. Now, standing in front of it, she was paralyzed, like a child meeting a shopping-mall Santa for the first time.

"Mark, she is a gem. I now understand your pride."

"Yes," Mark responded, with a smile.

The light streams again intensified in a small region of the sphere as the BESI analyzed something in detail.

"I've done it again. Please forgive me Margaret. You are a grown woman, a complete person. It's wrong of me to be so maudlin. I will correct for that moving forward."

"You didn't offend me." Generally speaking, she abhorred flattery, but coming from a synthetic intelligence, it somehow seemed quaint.

"I trust your father has explained why I've asked to meet with you?"

"He has."

"OmniaR's firewall system has always been a favorite target for hackers," the BESI said, speaking perceptibly quicker than before. "As a result, we've been able to improve our defenses by monitoring and deciphering each attack, similar to the way an immune system defends against infection. Lately, however, the attacks have become too frequent to adequately manage, as well as being much more sophisticated. We've recently lost a number of stored commodities from several different facilities, and I still haven't been able to determine how the firewalls were breached. As a precaution, I've taken all our storage facilities offline and put them under tier-five lockdown. Until we can resolve the issue, only I and the eighteen super-corp CEOs will have collective authority to access these sites and initiate commodity transfers."

"Do we know who's behind these attacks?" Margaret asked.

"I've located what I believe to be an atomic signature."

A graphic filled the large plasma board over one of the consoles. It was the distinct image of a cobalt blue crow alighting on a small globe. This was the logo of the Blue Crow organization and was meant to infer that its might was descending upon the world.

"Besides this signature, there's been no contact offered by the Blue Crow organization. We must also consider the possibility that someone has usurped their logo as a misdirect," the BESI said.

"What other group could manage such an attack?" Margaret asked.

"That's what troubles me most. And why I need your help. Without appearing to exhibit hubris, the sophistication of this latest attack seems to imply the presence of a synthetic intelligence."

Margaret looked at her father with an expression of disbelief.

"Improbable, yes," Mark said. "But not impossible."

"The Consortium has managed a lasting peace for close to a century now. Each corporation has worked within the guidelines of the global consensus that what's good for business is good for society," the BESI said, as if reciting bylaws. "If this equilibrium is being challenged, we must find out by whom."

"It's highly unlikely the Blue Crow organization could develop an SI," Mark added. "That would only leave one or more of the other super-corps working outside of Consortium parameters."

Margaret understood the magnitude of such an implication. If any of the other seventeen super-corps were vying for some measure of supremacy, it could disrupt the entire global system. It would be tantamount to a declaration of war. Just considering the possibility of it was causing her stomach to knot up.

"Yes, it is unsettling," the BESI said, tipping its hand that it was indeed monitoring Margaret's life chip.

"I will certainly do my best to help," Margaret said. "But I must admit, I feel a bit underqualified."

"I understand. But I believe you will adapt quite well. Initially, I want to team you up with Vincent Copenhauer, one of our research and development specialists. Going forward, you may find you need other people to get involved. I only ask that you run all candidates by me before enlisting their help. There is a real threat of internal espionage. Equitably, I will need to vet all prospects before bringing them into the investigation. Obviously, all of your work must remain confidential."

"Yes, of course."

"And if you will permit me one last sentiment Margaret, I do truly look forward to working with you, on a personal level."

"Likewise, BESI," Margaret replied, finding it oddly charming to think of this machine as a personal acquaintance.

As Margaret and her father made their way back to her office, her mind began clicking. Her anxiety had vanished. She was now back on the rails.

"What commodities were stolen?" she asked.

"Conic imprints for thousands of acres of wheat, tons of H_2O, copper, salt,...it's quite a list. I've created an eyes-only partition on your desktop, free from the network. Currently, only you, I, Vincent and the BESI have access. It's everything we've been able to gather so far. Start sifting through it as soon as you can."

"I will."

"And keep in mind, the Biotech Crime Division was alerted right after the thefts occurred, before we could lock the situation down. Since it involves international resources, we can't very well ask them to step aside. So expect a few calls from them. Anything coming in will be funneled to your team."

Margaret nodded her head, but wasn't feeling too comfortable about *her team*. It was hardly a team at all really. She'd heard impressive stats regarding Vincent Copenhauer, but solely as a scientist and engineer, not an investigator. She had a gnawing suspicion they'd be stumbling through unfamiliar terrain, prone to missing valuable clues. And warranted or not, these oversights would always point back to her. She wasn't adverse to taking charge, or even blame, but only if she was well suited for the task. As her father continued to lay out the particulars of the theft, it became clear to her that she'd be wading into uncharted territories of cybercrime. How could she hope to even be *marginally* suited for that? It was a certainty she'd be taking a lot of heat from this, and unjustifiably so, in her opinion. Yet like it or not, the job was now hers.

But where to begin? From what she was hearing, there was no precedent. The magnitude of this theft was unheard of. The only thing that came close happened about thirty years back, when she was just a child. A terrorist group called Mettre de l'ordre took control of a storage facility. They threatened to release tons of imprinted waste materials. Industrial pollutants and carbon made up the bulk of the facility's contents. Enormous amounts had been sequestered during the early days of climate repair. The facility had become a toxic dumpsite, housing decades' worth of pollution on scores of conic crystals.

The group's assault was sophisticated, but they still had to *physically* infiltrate the facility in order to gain access to the firewall. Once inside, they quickly realized they were ill-equipped to break through the security encryption. They ran a three-week bluff, trying in vain to crack the code, but were eventually starved into surrendering.

This latest assault was astounding by comparison. Not only had the security been cracked and the imprinted commodities transferred out, it apparently had all happened without anyone ever setting foot inside the facilities. That would either mean huge quantities of wheat and other resources had been remolecularized somewhere else, or that the imprints had been moved onto another storage grid. Either scenario would require massive amounts of power and hardware. That, Margaret decided, would be her first line of inquiry.

Chapter 4

<u>Telephobe</u>

Jake sipped his whiskey as boredom slowly overtook him. The view out the window offered very little, just cloud mist nose to nose with the glass. He leaned forward a bit in his chair to spy over the tops of the seats. He shook his head. Not many passengers, and the majority of them sported gray hair. Throwbacks like Jake.

He plugged in his earphones, turned on the seat-back monitor and began sifting through the endless sea of media content. Finding a classic movie to watch shouldn't be too hard, he thought. This was after all New World Airlines, or Nostalgia Air as it was informally called. The last commercial airline. It catered primarily to people who loved flying, or more accurately, hated teleporting. Jake fit both categories. When he was younger, he had a pilot's license, but had let it lapse somewhere along the way. It was really his fear of teleporting though that made air travel his transportation of choice. He could never determine if his telephobia was due to nature or nurture. Ironically, his father had been afraid to fly. So it at least appeared as if phobias ran in the family, just not the same types.

In Jake's mind though, the fact that a person was demolecularized (in essence, destroyed) before being teleported, was more than enough *rational* grounds not to want to do it. He was a huge fan of science and loved the idea that teleportation was possible, but that was entirely different than actually doing it with his own personage. He sometimes felt hypocritical; on the one hand championing so many of these technologies, but then often rejecting them based on nothing more than fickle superstition. He remembered how he used to turn a deaf ear to his father whenever he started ranting about doing things 'old school,' which to Jake in his youth meant doing things the uninformed way. His father hated technology and was always more than willing to share his opinions about it.

'Character is like a muscle,' he used to say. 'If you don't exercise it, it atrophies. Doing things for yourself – that builds character. Let some machine do it, you become a jellyfish!' By the time he died at seventy-two, he'd pretty much given up all hope or concern for humanity.

'I don't envy you the future son, and I'm truly sorry I introduced you to it. Don't be as cruel as I was. Never have kids.' That was one of the last things he remembered his father saying before he died. Hell of a thing to tell your only child, Jake always felt.

Though it pained him to admit it, somewhere along the line he had become like his father. Not so much bitter, but definitely disillusioned. His one and only marriage hadn't lasted long enough for children to enter the picture. So he at least had followed that bit of advice, though more by default than by design. Still, he couldn't see much point to it. These days, having a kid was like buying a car. There weren't many things left up to chance. Parental wishes fell within a narrow range of tier-ranked packages. There were simply too many laws and regulations surrounding genetic heritage to allow anyone much choice. A person had more chance of uniqueness buying a pet; genetic manipulation with animals tended to only focus on aggression suppression.

Despite similarities with his father, Jake had never been able to fully understand him. There just seemed to be something missing. A void or blankness, as if he'd been forced to erase some part of his humanity. To some degree it was understandable. The man had gone through the Great Upheaval from start to finish. He'd obviously seen more than his share of misery. He never talked about it with his son though, at least not in detail. Like everyone else, Jake got most of his information from the official, historical accounts. When he was learning about it in high school, he'd sometimes ask his father for a more personalized interpretation, but rarely got one.

The Consortium's version of that era was not exactly glossed over, but it certainly painted the corporate elite as saviors. That always struck Jake as suspiciously self-serving. Still, considering the human race had been on its way toward extinction, perhaps a bit of bragging was warranted. The propaganda was only distasteful if one believed that corporations were the cause of the collapse in the first place.

No matter how or why, it was definitely a defining moment in human history. What the fall of Rome had been to Eurasia, the Great Upheaval had been to the entire planet. Though with technology having a strong foothold, recovery occurred within decades instead of centuries. Public records estimated that once the dust settled, nearly a third of the world's population had been lost to a perfect storm of starvation, disease, war and natural disaster. Even after the worst of it had transpired, the planet was still in a very fragile, precarious state. Recovery was by no means a forgone conclusion.

In a perverse way, the Great Upheaval had been the catalyst for Humankind 2.0, as it was called. Historians viewed it as a phoenix event; an opportunity to redesign life from the ashes. Almost every documentary Jake ever watched on the subject painted the era as a *necessary* catastrophe. The belief stood that no major change in any system could ever occur while the system was in operation, particularly something as complex as a global society. All previous attempts at reformation had failed because they amounted to nothing more than tinkering with a broken machine as it rolled down the road. Once total collapse occurred, it allowed every aspect of society to be redesigned from the ground up, on a global scale. The machine was taken off the road, hoisted up on jacks, and radically overhauled.

Those with the most power (and consequently the most to lose) took the reins. They were the *corpus oligarchia* – the corporate elite. They'd been running think tanks of every color and flavor long before the Upheaval began. When the time was right, they stepped forward and instituted a one-world order based entirely on economics. The Consortium of Nations was born. It was modeled on the pre-Upheaval World Trade Organization, yet chartered with far broader powers. Made up of eighteen, global conglomerates, all policy implementation was by way of consensus vote from each of the corporations' chief executive officers. A nineteenth seat was created (that of the Apex CEO), which served primarily as a tie-breaker, but also as the public face of the Consortium.

The Consortium's first act was to consolidate what was left of the world's various militaries into one, global force. Most governments imploded during the Upheaval, leaving many armed forces open to the highest bidders. Since the corporate sector already controlled defense manufacturing, there was little resistance to making the military a subsidiary of the Consortium. With this new might, all remedies deemed necessary for recovery were easily implemented.

They concluded that if the human race were to have any chance of repairing the environment and continuing to survive, it would first need to begin seeing itself as one, unified entity. Tribalism, in whatever form it took, had to be eradicated.

Mass prosperity was seen as the most effective tool to achieve this aim. Since most conflicts of the past were actually due to resource scarcity, which merely masqueraded as political, religious or racial differences, the new-world plan was to create and maintain a perpetual state of prosperity for everyone. If that could be accomplished, it was theorized that all other problems would, in time, solve themselves. At the very least, they'd be minor in scope and easier to deal with.

For both immediate and long-term stability, the Consortium felt several key departments within the new corporate framework needed to be formed. First, society had to move toward a resource-based economy, one which allowed all nations within the charter equal access to global resources. After seizing power, the Consortium took control of all remaining assets. For the first time in history, the regulation and distribution of food, energy and technology were brought together under one roof; the Department of Resource Management. Second, since all resources were finite, world population levels needed to be strictly managed; hence the Department of Population Control. Third, in order to foster a common language and worldview, they created a single, global education system. It had a uniform curriculum with heavy focus on science and industry; this was overseen by the Department of Education.

With regard to the more obtuse aspects of society (considered divisive, yet inextricably woven into the human psyche), the Consortium simply chose to view them as commodities to be managed. All religions, for example, were gathered up under one tent; the Department of Spiritual Affairs. Its primary aim was to constructively channel faith-based tendencies and mitigate dogmatic competitiveness.

Over time, other departments within the new global structure were created. Many of them mirrored previous governmental institutions, with the exception being that they were now operated in a corporate fashion, efficiency being key.

The most radical shift in thinking pertained to the world economy. It was so antithetical to previous economic models, it surprised wary citizens at the time; many of whom blamed the Upheaval on corporate greed and malfeasance.

For the new-world order to function, the heads of the Consortium decided they would have to part with many of the economic standards they had relished for centuries. Capitalism, contrary to longstanding beliefs, had proven itself to be a closed system which stifled growth and squandered resources. Being a profit-driven system, it was unsustainable, from both a monetary and environmental standpoint. Its greatest toll, however, was with regard to human advancement and wellbeing.

Speculatively, what humans *might* have achieved had they never been yoked with profiteering, made those innovations which *were* achieved paltry by comparison. Many think-tank models presented the picture of a technologically advanced, interstellar race, had the matter of monetary gain never been part of the equation.

Jake recalled one textbook from high school which drew parallels between the pre-Upheaval economy and a biological system. In it, localized concentrations of wealth were compared to blockages in an artery. They slowed blood flow and starved the body, ultimately leading to cardiac arrest. The acquisition of money was seen as vacuous. It led to what the book called terminal wealth; that point at which a society failed due to fiscal disease.

In its effort to move away from a greed-centric economy, the Consortium abolished all business practices which favored profiteering over innovation. Entire laundry lists of money-purposed connivances, such as planned obsolescence, were outlawed. Research and development took center stage in this new paradigm. Inventors and inventions were given full and open review. No product or idea was edged out for fear of threatening monetary gains. If the idea improved upon an existing system and was resource practical, it was adopted. That was the sole criterion.

Since the Consortium was made up of only a few global conglomerates, which collectively controlled every market on the planet, adopting a share-and-share-alike mindset was simply viewed as sensible in-house etiquette.

Resources, be they natural, intellectual or cultural, would be the only true measure of wealth, not money. By making this slight, perhaps even imperceptible shift in thought, it was believed a more balanced and productive economy could be developed. At the very least, they hoped it would deglamorize money.

Yet they realized people would still require that visceral incentive to undertake work; that measuring stick by which to calculate worth. They could not eliminate money altogether, at least not right away. In order to make this new, resource-based economy palatable, not only to the moneyed elite, but the average citizen as well, they would need to gradually marginalize the importance of money. The end goal was to make it so abundant and evenly distributed that everyone would begin taking it for granted.

To achieve this artificial saturation of wealth without devaluing money altogether, several ad hoc models, implemented centuries before, were adopted and modified. There had always been government subsidies to level the playing fields of countless markets, from food to energy. In that sense, there had never existed a pure form of capitalism in the world. It had always been manipulated and molded to suit those with their hands on the throttle. Global financial systems often tinkered with the flow of money and interest rates. Fiat currencies were created on demand, and as long as everyone agreed they had value, then they had value. It was proof positive that the entire system was an illusion, and illusions could be changed.

While it was true that the availability of resources would always be dictated by the laws of nature, it was also true that the currency used to value and exchange those resources was entirely within human control. As such, all resources were cataloged and given a base, monetary value. This value would remain capped, unless real-world influences caused a fluctuation in availability. The regulation of these values was to be the exclusive responsibility of the Department of Resource Management. All things remaining equal with respect to the ingredients and labor necessary to create a loaf of bread, for instance, meant that the cost of the end product could never be increased merely for the sake of personal profit. The shelf price would directly reflect the efforts and resources put into the product or service, and nothing more. Since the dichotomy of supply and demand would always remain a truism, resources and market activity were to be globally monitored in real time. This would allow the DRM to make determinations about what products needed to be decreased or increased, so as to avoid surplus waste or price gouging.

This new resource-based model became known as Ocean Economics. The premise was based upon the idea of sea life and its relationship to the water that nurtured it. At first, they wanted to liken it to air, which was more relevant to humans, but air was much too intangible, both figuratively and literally. Water had weight and texture. It could be seen and touched, and therefore provided a better metaphor.

The argument held, that while all life in the sea depended upon water for survival, each organism was blissfully unaware of it due to its abundance. By mere virtue of its quantity, water had made itself irrelevant to the inhabitants of the ocean. Obviously, if it became scarce, the verity of that concept would vanish. As long as it remained plentiful, however, each organism within it could go about their business unfettered and wildly productive.

It was a model that had already been taking shape before the Great Upheaval occurred. The main thing which spurred it on was the ever-increasing automation of the world's workforce. Paid humans were being displaced by unpaid machines in record numbers. This created an obvious imbalance between goods and services available, and people with money enough to buy them. Since this trend was certain to continue as technology became even more advanced, the newly formed Consortium of Nations instituted a stop-gap measure called the Consumer Endowment Program.

It became an up-front version of the Social Security system once used in the old United States. Each citizen was awarded a Consortium-owned trust fund, substantially valued. The trusts were managed by private financial institutions, which came to see them as windfalls. It created a vast pool of investing capital. The principal of the trust was forever the property of the Consortium, but the bulk of the interest derived from it would go to the individual. A lesser portion would revert back to the Consortium in order to fund public works projects and governmental administration.

Whereas Social Security had been designed to assist people toward the end of their lives, the Consumer Endowment Program was designed to accompany them throughout their lives. Each newborn child was assigned a trust fund which could be put to immediate use. Upon a person's death, the fund was folded back into the Consortium bank and reassigned to someone else. While it did create some people who were unwilling to work, considering that so many jobs had already been lost to automation, providing these unemployed people with disposable cash spurred the economy on at record rates. Consumerism took on a new luster.

To ensure a continual flow of money and goods, taxes were replaced with mandatory purchasing quotas. By year's end, each person was required to have purchased a given amount of goods and/or services. It was a quota most people were happy to fill. Year's end became known as quota clearance time. Every product and/or service was packaged into easily transferable deals for anyone having outstanding purchase obligations.

Despite the growing number of non-working individuals, the majority of people still pursued some career or another, simply for the sake of personal fulfillment. However, since a person's purchasing quota was commensurate with their gross income, earning a salary often pushed them into higher purchasing brackets. The wealthier someone became, the more they would have to buy; which despite the somewhat enjoyable notion of this, was actually quite burdensome. It prompted many people to forego salaries altogether. Volunteerism became the new form of financial sheltering.

Jake's father's generation had been part of the pilot program, and despite innumerable bumps along the way, things had begun to improve. Jake always felt his father must've been relatively hopeful back then, since he had applied for a birth permit. He often razzed Jake, saying it was only at his mother's insistence. Jake never fully accepted that though. His father had raised him single-handedly after his mother died, and he had done so in an adoring manner. It's unlikely he would've been so devoted if he saw Jake as an unwelcomed burden.

Jake continued scanning the network for something to watch. He took note of his own quota limit displayed within the media menu; it was edging into the yellow. His job as an investigative agent never pushed him too far up the purchasing ladder, but spending enough by year's end was still a bit tricky. Since he lived a pretty simple life, materially speaking, it was a constant challenge to find ways to spend money. Like so many others, he almost always ended up taking an extravagant December vacation in order to balance his ledger.

He often felt consumer mandates made gluttons out of people, or in his case, product-dependent. Physiological addiction was a defunct ailment. Ever since science unraveled all the mysteries about brain receptors, thwarting physical dependency on one drug or another was as easy as reshuffling a few molecules. Furthermore, since people could have their organs cloned, long-term health damage was easily circumvented. It didn't mean people couldn't still become psychologically addicted, but from a purely consumeristic standpoint, that wasn't seen as a bad thing. However, since the word addiction held negative connotations, it was replaced with the more sanitized term, product-dependent.

Though not illegal, being intoxicated on the job was frowned upon, particularly in Jake's position. Still, since all the more dangerous activities were handled by drones, there was little chance of a mishap due to dampened reflexes or poor judgment. There were also restorative tabs he could take which would bring him back to sobriety within minutes, so he never had to enter a situation inebriated if he chose not to.

Eying his empty glass, he pressed an onscreen menu to initiate a refill.

"For the state tells me so," he said, joking to himself.

The overly friendly, hanging torso-bot glided toward him from the service area at the front of the plane. It amounted to nothing more than a highly automated Swiss army knife. Its façade was that of a flight attendant from a bygone era; assuming flight attendants were legless. The telescopic boom to which it was attached, receded into a multi-channeled guide track in the ceiling, branching out to all areas of the cabin.

"I hope you're finding our services satisfactory!" the drone's voice box trilled. It then presented Jake with a fresh glass of whiskey.

"Once that drink's in my hand, maybe." He took the fresh glass and handed back the empty one.

The drone's prosthetic hand grasped the glass as it nodded its head, "Please don't hesitate to call on me again if you require anything else!" For Jake, the bot's canned cheerfulness made the interaction all the bleaker.

Once it zipped away, he took a deliberate sip of his drink, as if it were a gasp of fresh air. He obviously couldn't blame the Consortium for his love of alcohol, but with purchase mandates, they sure did seem to facilitate it.

His phone began to ring and he frowned once he saw the caller ID.

"Hey Chief," he answered, pulling out his earphones.

"What're you doing at thirty thousand feet? Joe tells me he's been waiting on you for an hour."

"Flying helps me think."

"Sure, I'm believing that, really I am. Listen, I uploaded more info to the case docket. Look it over. Seems the Blue Crow was behind the tattoo's reconfiguration virus. We found their logo embedded in the code. So if we can find a correlation between the tattoo and the woman's death, it'll launch them into a whole new category."

"Well you know what Doug Compton thinks."

"Yes. And it's a crock. I need you to tackle this case with your head on straight Kepler. No pseudoscience BS, you hear?"

"I'll do my best, as always."

"When are you going to land?"

Jake glanced at his phone, "Another fifteen minutes."

"Damn it Kepler. Why the hell can't you just be *normal* and teleport like the rest of us?!"

"Fifteen minutes, Chief. I've taken craps longer than that. Just tell Joe to wait. And make sure he doesn't start the interrogation without me. It's better if we let the guy stew for a bit."

"He's been *stewing* for over an hour already! If you'd have just,..ahhh. Forget it. Just make sure you patch me in once you get started."

"You bet."

The abruptness of the line disconnecting only confirmed how annoyed the chief was. The modded generation always struck Jake as an elite club; when you didn't want to play by the rules they all took for granted, it generally frustrated the hell out of them.

All Hailed The Singularity

Chapter 5

Connecting Dots

Tallahassee, Florida. When rising sea levels claimed Florida's coastline, Tallahassee had taken over where Miami left off. Even though the ocean had been receding over the past century, many coastal cities still remained abandoned. As a result, Tallahassee had grown to become *the* metropolis of the southeast.

Getting to the local branch of the BCD didn't take long, though Jake could just hear the chief complaining that even the cab ride would've been unnecessary if he had just teleported to the station. Normally, Division would've teleported the suspect to central offices in D.C. But due to the sophistication of the crime and the suspicion of Blue Crow involvement, the decision was made to avoid transport. There'd been instances in the past when teleportation hubs were hacked and their contents redirected to different locations. The BCD didn't want to risk the possibility of such a jailbreak.

As Jake approached the holding room, he shook his head. He could hear Joe's voice from inside, already playing the bad cop. He obviously hadn't wanted to wait.

"…I'll just have your chip deactivated! Tell me, do you have enough friends willing to buy you food? Pay your rent? And for how long? Because if you don't stop lying to me, I'm going to make sure it's turned off permanently."

Jake peered at the monitor outside the room. Since Joe's wrongheaded tactics had already sailed, Jake figured he should at least try to glean some information on how the suspect was responding. He nodded to the agent monitoring the suspect's life chip feed.

"Can I see that?"

The agent handed him the tablet. With the right interpretation software, a person's life chip was a very good lie detector. From what Jake was seeing on the tablet, this guy seemed to be nothing but scared. Not that fear alone implied innocence, but there was no substantial brainwave activity in the prefrontal cortex; what investigators called tell chatter. The presence of excessive chatter was generally a dead giveaway that someone was lying. The lie they are trying to maintain becomes the elephant in the room, the room in this case being their cerebrum. Jake was only seeing the typical fight-or-flight activity from the lower regions of the brain.

He double-tapped an icon on the tablet, "Agent Thompson, that information you requested has arrived."

Joe could be seen looking up at the camera and then moving toward the door. As he exited the holding room, he nodded to Jake.

"Glad you could make it," he said, with a wry grin. "And before you say anything, I know – it's not your style. But the life chip threat rarely fails me."

"It can work, sure. But if this guy's in cahoots with an underground hacker org, he'd be able to get his hands on a counterfeit chip without too much trouble. I've yet to meet a starving hacker."

"Yeah, maybe. But it sure seems to be scaring the crap out of him."

"Which probably means he's not a hacker, if you think about it." Realizing his response was a bit condescending, he quickly tried to compensate, "But you're right, even that's valuable info. You patched in the chief yet?"

"No. I was waiting on you."

"Alright. Let me take a crack at him. Can you patch in Chief Novak at central offices?"

"Will do," the agent said.

Jake grabbed the tablet and entered the holding room.

"He's gonna' tickle him with a feather, watch," Joe said.

The agent shrugged indifferently, connecting the video conference feed to BCD headquarters.

Jake sat down across from the suspect, Thomas Krasnov, and propped the tablet up on the table.

"Hey there Thomas, or is it Tom?"

"What? Uh, yeah man, Tom. Look, I don't know what all this is about. I haven't *done* anything."

"I believe you. Problem is, one of your tattoos may've had some very ill effects on a young woman, and I need to find out how."

"I don't know nothing about that! I swear!"

"And like I said, I believe you. Let's get past all that okay? You need something? Water, stim-tab,..anything?"

"No, no man I'm solid."

"Okay then. So what I'm good at Tom, is connecting dots. That's really all it boils down to. Given enough dots, I can almost always find a path. What I need from you is, a little help in *locating* some of those dots, yeah?"

"Ay man, I'll tell you whatever I know."

"Perfect." Jake spun the tablet around. "That's one of your designs, right?"

"Yeah, looks like it. Lotus Dragon. Flower changes color based on a person's mood, closes when they go to sleep, blooms when they wake up – that kinda' thing. Made it a few weeks back."

"You do all your own coding?"

"Usually. 'Less it's motley."

"Motley?"

"Yeah, complex…like the lotus."

"You didn't code the lotus?"

"No, just the dragon. The lotus was outta' my league. Required mapping the body's circadian rhythm, melatonin release, life chip queries – all sorts of jack. Sometimes when I can't find high-end coders to ink for me, I troll the network for posted artwork."

"Sounds reasonable."

"Yeah, right, but…look man, I promote all my stuff as original. Doesn't help my rep if people find out I'm just snarfing designs."

"Bootlegged, huh?"

"Yeah, okay. But it was just sitting there. No licensing notice, nothing. My line of work, that's fair game."

"You remember where you found it?"

"No. Just trolling, like I said. I'm sure you guys will have no trouble tracking my history though," Thomas said, with an accusatory tone.

"You're right about that." Jake grabbed the tablet and got up. "We're gonna' have to hold you until we can verify this. If it pans out, we'll see about getting you released."

"I'm telling you the truth man!"

"Then everything will be copasetic. Meanwhile, try to relax."

Jake exited the holding room and walked over to the console. Joe pointed down at the monitor, mouthing the words, 'the chief.'

"So what do you think Chief?" Jake asked.

"We've already gone through his records for the entire year. There's no site with any lotus artwork on it."

"Any dead ends, broken links?"

"A few," the chief said, looking over the report. "Yeah, there's one that dates back about three weeks. I'll get our hackers to find out who took it down."

"You want us to hang loose?"

"Depends. You gonna' fly again?"

"Yep."

"Then stay put. I'll call you when I get something." Once again, the line seemed to disconnect with a quick, sharp frustration. Jake could just imagine the chief on the other end cursing up a storm.

Joe shook his head, "You're something. I've teleported hundreds of times, and I'm standing right here in front of you. Same me, no missing parts."

"I don't know Joe. You noticed how you've been stuttering a lot lately-"

"Yah, yah, screw you," Joe said, grinning.

"And that weird tic in your neck, twitching all the time?"

Joe laughed, "Alright, alright,..just trying to help one of my elders across the street. Someday you'll have to, you know. You won't have time to fly. And I hope I'm there to see it. You'll probably crap your pants."

"And yet *another* good reason not to teleport."

The gate kept buzzing for a while after it closed behind Jake and Joe. All they could see in front of them was a narrow, stone pathway, purposely snaking its way through a dense tropical hedge. They nearly had to sidestep the entire way along the path, pushing aside hordes of overreaching twigs and leaves as they went.

Joe was already regretting the invitation, "How do you know this guy?"

"School. Eons ago. He's a topnotch hacker. Always has an ear to the ground. Figured while we're down here, might as well pay him a visit. You'll love him, he's a natural-born like me."

"Can't wait."

The stone path finally opened up to reveal a large garden. The whole environment seemed to have an intentional, primeval orchestration to it. The only out-of-character aspect was the small live/work space at the center of the garden. It was a two level, elliptical structure made entirely of glass, or more likely transparent metal. Jake spotted Roland Whitmark descending the railingless staircase inside. He was waving them over to the main entrance; a huge disc-shaped doorway that took up most of the first-floor wall.

"Open," Roland said. The outer screen panel, followed by the circular glass door, rolled to the side along a sturdy guide track. "Holy cow mate! I can't believe it!"

"Rolly!"

They shook hands and pulled each other in for a pat on the back.

"How you been?" Jake asked.

"Healthy and happy. You?"

Jake laughed, "Wouldn't go that far, but pretty good."

"State of mind mate, state of mind. Come on in," Roland said, ushering them inside.

"This is my associate, Joe Thompson."

"Right! How goes?" Roland reached over to shake his hand. Joe reciprocated, though he was bewildered by Roland's hyper-lively demeanor. "Get you lads anything? Got some self-brewed beer, pretty good stuff."

"That's a big hell yes for me," Jake said.

"Joe?"

"No, no thanks."

Roland headed into the kitchen area, whipping open the refrigerator door.

"He coked up?" Joe asked.

"Don't know. Hey Rolly?"

"No...don't ask-"

"You jacked up right now?"

"Ahhh...." Joe rolled his eyes.

Roland returned with two beers, "Without question!" He handed one to Jake. "You caught me in the middle of a coding marathon. Rare occurrence! Got a wonderful, I mean *brilliant*, biocustom amphetamine hybrid. Time released! Just need to stay hydrated."

"On water, not booze," Jake said, smiling.

"Yeh, right. Not much alcohol in this stuff. Cheers mate." They clacked bottle necks and Roland chugged down most of his beer while Jake just sipped his.

After a protracted burp, Roland thumped his chest, "Excuse me. Hey! Got some over-the-counter stim-tabs if you'd rather?"

"Hmm? No really, I'm good, thanks," Joe said, staring up through the ceiling. The whole second floor was transparent, revealing the underside of all the furniture hovering just above their heads. "Pretty nice place you got here."

"The Oasis I call it. Used to have an open-aired yurt but the humidity kept ruining all my gear. Had this thing pre-forged, dropped in by airbot. Sweet deal, let me tell you.

"Doesn't get too hot?" Joe asked.

"You'd reckon, wouldn't you? Whole thing's shade programmable though. I can darken any part of it, any part – several colors to boot. Last Halloween, I hacked the module and coded the entire house to look like a giant jack-o'-lantern. Most popular house on the block, I was. Made of a bismuth nano-composite or some such madness, don't much understand it myself. It's micro-matted to diffuse the sun, else everything would fry 'n sizzle like a bug under glass, my ruddy bum as well. What's more, the entire structure is thermoelectric. Flip the polarity and the walls go hot or cold. Dead a' summer it's like living inside a cooler, pleasure be mine. Na mate, no problem with temperature in The Oasis. How's the brew Jake?"

"Pretty good," he said, saluting with the bottle. "Definitely better than that synth-grain swill you made in college."

"Ahhhhh Jeez! Remember that tripe? Knock ya' on your arse though. Hah! This stuff's malted gold compared to that dreck." He chugged down what was left of his beer and headed to the kitchen for another. "So what's this Blue Crow thing you're looking into?"

"It's a case that's,..well,..it's bad. I'll leave it at that. Thought you may've heard a few echoes out there in the ether about new code," Jake said.

Roland returned, starting a fresh beer, "New code? This about the commodities caper? Media keeps hinting it was them. Was it?"

"Maybe. But we're chasing down something different. The Blue Crow's logo showed up in some of the code related to our case. You hear anything about them shifting gears, trying to up their game?"

"No. But I haven't been listening too closely. Can you tell me anything about the case?"

"Un-un. But if our coroner is right, it's a meteoric jump in coding capabilities. If some hacker was out there creating this stuff, I'd expect them to be bragging their heads off, no offense."

"Oh believe me mate, none taken. Useless twonks, most of 'em. At's why I'm semi-retired. Got tired of all the knob waving. But if this code's unique, like ya' say, Blue Crow's the only group I can fathom. Got both the brains and the boodle. But they're mostly about social injustices and the like. Even this commodities snatch seems outta' sorts for 'em."

"Granted. Whole damn thing's a head-scratcher," Jake said.

"I'll start pokin' around though. See if any groups out there are blathering on about new code, like ya' say."

Chapter 6

The Patsy

Jessup Patel lurched to consciousness, eyes wide, heart racing. He felt his head, realizing he had dozed off with his neural interface on; commonly called a tapcap.

"Damn it!" He ripped it from his head. "You idiot!"

He hadn't made a mistake like that in ages. For the paranoid inclined, sleeping with a tapcap on was akin to walking down the street nude, only it was your mind that was totally exposed. Basic human insecurities aside, leaving one's psyche flapping around in the wind for anyone to look at carried additional perils in Jessup's case. For him, being paranoid was a good thing. His life as a renegade hacker had placed him on the Consortium's most-wanted list; remaining anonymous was essential to breathing.

As risky as it was, he couldn't ignore the advantages of neural interfacing. Tapcaps were mesh headsets which allowed for synaptic channeling. Once mapped to a user's brainwave frequency, they could interact with just about any computing device. They weren't as robust as Neuraltech, but getting an implant of that sort would forever be out of the question for Jessup. The twenty-four, seven interaction with the brain (and more specifically, the outside world) was an invasion of privacy he couldn't afford.

Unfortunately, Neuraltech was seen as the next logical successor to life chips. Though the tech was still in its infancy, it would theoretically allow for thought scanning one day, perhaps even thought control. Thankfully, tapcaps were still the favorite among consumers. Until that changed, Jessup didn't have to worry too much about Neuraltech becoming mandated; though he knew the Consortium was headed in that direction.

That was generally how they created policy. They navigated toward a desired law by way of consumer zeal; convince people they can't do without something, then legislate it. It was a passive approach to governance, yet highly effective. The strategy required patience of course, but the Consortium had oodles of that. The lack of zeal for Neuraltech was trying that patience though. It had been at a point of consumer readiness for three years, but still hadn't caught on, and *not* from lack of promotion. Every teasing lure had been plumbed. Not surprisingly, the most effective ad campaigns to date were leisure-based. Commercials touted Neuraltech as the most interactive media device available for gaming and entertainment. If someone wanted to watch a video on the network, for instance, it could tie directly into the visual cortex and project the video in their mind's eye. For that matter, it could create an entire movie theater with virtual moviegoers and the smell of popcorn, all to provide a more socially involved experience.

Its performance specs were also advertised with vigor. Since it communicated directly with the brain via billions of quantum-relayed nanoprocessors, there was zero latency. It was marketed as a must-have upgrade, playing to people's fears of tech inadequacy.

It was a frightening technology though. For one, it required cranial implantation. In addition to this obvious scare factor, there were concerns that it could be hacked. No one wanted some nefarious nerd snooping around in their brain, uploading and downloading information. Even *with* impeccable security measures, the Consortium would still have access (despite their assertions to the contrary), and that was equally disquieting.

A more fundamental problem though, is what consumer psychologists referred to as tactile assurance. Despite the availability of various implantable technologies, people still preferred external, handheld devices. Being able to hold the technology (and more importantly, put it down) provided them with a sense of control. They reserved the right to separate themselves from it whenever privacy was desired. Neuraltech did not offer that comfort.

Another drawback was mastering the interface. Because of phantom signaling, a differentiation barrier was required to keep the tech from activating on its own. In early technical trials, this problem made itself most apparent while people were sleeping. The tech kept initiating a whole host of features because it couldn't differentiate between the dream state and actual, conscious requests. To get around this, the entire interface had to be shielded in a safe-word environment. Akin to the very earliest computers, which required an execute command for each task, no Neuraltech function could be initiated unless it was followed by a specific thought; a word, image, color, smell, etc. If the user wanted to call a friend, for instance, they could visualize the friend's face with a green tint and the tech would activate. No green tint, no activation. While it was designed to learn a person's intentions over time, it still required a good deal of upfront training and perseverance. This made it too cumbersome for the average user.

Jessup was hardly the average user though. He would've been very well suited to Neuraltech. He just couldn't afford the danger. It was a paradoxical problem. On the one hand, he needed privacy. On the other hand, if he didn't embrace these new technologies, he'd be left behind. And considering that his goal was to dismantle a corrupt system, getting left behind was tactically unacceptable.

He leaned forward in his easy chair, popped a stim-tab in his mouth, and drank down what was left of a flat soda. Whether it was due to his lack of sleep or the tapcap, his mind was doing summersaults. He'd had some strange dreams before, but this one took the cake. He couldn't recall the specifics, only the sensation. He knew emotions were always heightened in dreams, primarily because the rational mind wasn't keeping them in check. The extreme fear he'd felt in this dream seemed to be linked to something real though, something invasive. It felt as if his whole identity, his selfness, had been picked over and consumed by some odious, malevolent force.

He'd read an article once about certain dreams being the brain's effort to personify cellular functions in the body. If someone were fighting a cold, for instance, they might have a vivid dream in which one army was fighting another. All it amounted to was the brain's interpretation of white blood cells attacking the virus. That's when he really started to panic. If the article were true, based on the potency of his dream, it may mean he had cancer. He shrugged it off though; in addition to being paranoid, he was a self-admitted hypochondriac.

"The life you have chosen is a noble one."

He began repeating the words to himself. It was his fix-all phrase. Whenever he was feeling unsure or frightened, he would chant it aloud. Lately, he'd been feeling *very* unsure and *very* frightened. His immediate world was under attack and he didn't know by whom. This was inconceivable to him. He'd always been the best hacker on the market. He did the doing, not the getting done to. That he was still in the dark after a whole week implied that his assailant was smarter than he was, and that just didn't jibe.

Jessup was a wonder child, and would've been exceptional even without genetic modifications. With the modifications, his natural genius had been boosted exponentially. He had what was called a super brain. And unlike many modded people, he was driven. He attributed his ambition to his mother's passion for life. She was a strong-willed natural-born, raised in West Virginia. Not only was her genetic profile unique, but she had always made a point of schooling Jessup in the ways of ambition. With such a nature-and-nurture combo, he had very little option but to become self-determined. She used to love telling him about how she had put herself through CalTech, all while pursuing Jessup's extremely shy father, who was attending from India. Rajan Patel was also a natural-born, and a genius by all accounts. After getting his graduate degree, he went on to become one of Dr. Nicholas Wharton's associates, and also one of the handful of scientists included on the honor roll of the Singularity.

Jessup grew up in the shadow of his father's celebrity. Though the Singularity occurred long before he was born, its impact on the world had never waned; and neither had the popularity of those who ushered it in. Even today, one could find a catalog of documentaries all attempting to explore the event from a different perspective. Jessup's perspective on it had long since solidified, however. To him, it was an abomination. It was phenomenal science turned upside down by the malignancy of human nature.

He could still remember the first time he grasped the magnitude of Wharton's achievement. He was about six when he first watched the TED conference that took place in Colorado toward the end of the twenty-first century. It remained the most-viewed video in history; even more so for Jessup since it involved his father.

Because of Wharton, the long-awaited technological singularity had taken on a dual meaning. This was due to the fact that his invention involved the practical use of black holes. Contrary to the singularity hypothesis, however, technology still hadn't fully leaped ahead of humanity. Even with the advent of synthetic intelligence, things still occurred slowly, relatively speaking. Most futurists chalked this up to people's inherent resistance to change, and their general suspicion of technology. It seemed recalcitrance and caution served as natural pacesetters for technological advancement.

Traditionally, most speakers at TED conferences presented their ideas as lectures, sometimes accompanied by multimedia. But Wharton was a showman. He decided to turn his twenty-minute block of time into the equivalent of an old Vegas show. He'd been careful to keep his work completely under wraps for decades by self-funding his research and adhering to a strict regimen of secrecy.

In the now historical video, he began his presentation by conversing via satellite with his wife, Linda, who was standing at the base of the Great Wall of China. She was under a canopy tent, surrounded by various pieces of equipment. Next to her was a large, cage-like apparatus, similar to the one flanking Wharton onstage. Jessup remembered thinking that it looked like a very sophisticated Faraday cage.

Wharton then looked toward the upstage screen where the satellite feed was being projected, waved to his wife and said, 'See you soon, honey.' He stepped into the cage-like chamber, engaged its interface, and instantly vanished in a scarcely perceptible flash of light. Almost immediately, another flash of light erupted inside the chamber below the Great Wall, and Wharton stepped out to hug his wife. He then turned to the camera and continued to address the TED attendees via satellite, 'Teleportation is here,' he said, with a satisfied grin. 'Or there, depending on how you look at it.'

The audience remained justifiably mute for several seconds and then exploded with applause. Wharton then teleported back to the stage and continued his presentation once things settled down.

'This is more than just a new mode of transportation,' he followed up. He uncovered a small unit next to the chamber. 'It can also be used to store any form of matter in a two-dimensional state.' He punched a few commands into the console and an apple materialized inside the chamber. He picked it up and took a bite. 'This apple is two months old, yet fresh as the day I reduced it.'

He once again typed a few commands into the console. 'This next example I'm about to show you was quite a sacrifice for my wife and me.' There was another flash of light, and an English bulldog appeared inside the chamber. 'Aurelius!' Wharton called, clapping his hands. 'Over here lunkhead.' The bulldog waddled over to him and Wharton kneaded his thick, flabby neck. 'He's been suspended in a two-dimensional state for the last week, and sorely missed! That week in stasis, however, has made my dear Aurelius here one week younger than you or I.'

He pointed to a small, cone-shaped crystal housed inside the unit next to the chamber. 'I have a warehouse of items stored on this device. If I were to remolecularize them all, they would fill this auditorium. The crystal you see here is made of a new metamaterial which allows for the holographic storage of three-dimensional matter. Its capacity is virtually limitless. The length of time something can be stored also appears to be limitless, at least so far. The oldest item on the crystal was just over a year old. A pencil I ran our first test on. A week ago, I remolecularized it and had it tested for atomic integrity. It remains the same exact pencil it was one year ago.' He pulled it from his pocket and held it up.

In the endless wave of interviews which followed the conference, Wharton explained in more detail how the device worked. He also explained that he initially wanted to put it on the network as an open-source technology, but then realized it could easily be misused. Not long after, reactive groups began accusing him of letting the genie out of the bottle, by essentially putting the genie *into* the bottle. In time, the negative aspects of the technology became more and more conspicuous to Jessup as well.

Through deliberate Consortium efforts, the many great benefits of the technology began littering schoolbooks and news articles from the moment it was commercialized. It wasn't that the benefits weren't true, Jessup felt, but they only presented *part* of the story. Nevertheless, they were so extraordinary, they held the spotlight.

For starters, the technology revolutionized space exploration, leading to the initial colonization of Mars and the moon. With two-dimensional reduction, the structures of an entire town, all its inhabitants, and years worth of sustenance, could be stored on just a few crystals (though a mission of such magnitude remained untested). In theory, these crystals could then be launched to any given planet and remolecularized upon arrival; all on a simple spacecraft with minimal payload requirements. Even the ship's fuel could be holographically reduced and remolecularized as needed en route. Many of the prohibitive constraints of deep-space travel (zero gravity, time/distance, life support) had been sidestepped with reductionism. Matter in stasis did not age. Nor did it require food, water or oxygen.

Still, full commitment to an intragalactic mission was being postponed by one very vexing problem: cosmic radiation. Tests showed that high-dose exposure, particularly to gamma rays, degraded the conic crystal. Experiments to develop long-duration shielding were ongoing, but still hadn't yielded anything of much promise. Yet everyone knew it would just be a matter of time before a solution was found and whole colonies started reaching out into space.

Another outstanding benefit of reductionism was more apparent back home on Earth. Large amounts of natural resources, from fresh water to corn, could be stored indefinitely for emergency use. Conic crystals became the grain silos of the modern age. Two-dimensional reduction also played a key roll in stabilizing the climate. Enormous amounts of greenhouse gases and other pollutants were sequestered onto crystals. It was Jessup's contention, however, that humans had yet again resorted to treating the symptoms as opposed to finding a cure. Once pollutant storage became widespread, it only increased the amount of waste humans produced. With large deposits of natural resources discovered on the moon and Mars, all efforts to design a sustainable system had, for the most part, been abandoned. With the galaxy now at humanity's fingertips, and no apparent downside to waste management, there was little need to fret over conservation or efficiency.

While it was true that the Earth was a cleaner, safer place, Jessup knew that nature did not smile on imbalance. There were bound to be bills to pay for this accelerated consumption, and what essentially amounted to sweeping humanity's molecular dust under the rug.

Though he focused his talents primarily on biotechnology, he still had a solid understanding of how reductionism worked. Besides having more than enough aptitude for it, he also had the added privilege of direct inquiry of one of its designers, his father.

Teleportation, in and of itself, was not the problem; transmission of matter was a straight-forward proposition. It involved a one-to-one exchange of energy/matter. Wharton's device utilized the basic principles at play in a black hole. Through the use of a Dessiper magnet array, rotated at near-light speed within a vacuum, he was able to create a docile black hole; more commonly referred to as a synthesized singularity. These synth-sings remained marginal enough so that once the magnet array was disengaged, they harmlessly evaporated. With regard to teleportation, any object presented to a docile black hole would be intruded into it. The exact information of the object, its wave function, remained imprinted on the event horizon for as long as the black hole remained active. The imprinted data could then be transmitted to a destination point, where another magnet array (rotating in reverse polarity) created a docile white hole; or synthesized small bang. As long as there was the requisite number of entangled particles, the imprinted data could then be extruded back into the third dimension through the synth-bang.

Matter storage, however, was a very different animal. Unlike teleportation, it did not involve a one-to-one transfer. Instead, it removed matter from the universe without replacing it. The cone shape of the storage medium enabled it to resonate perfectly with the event horizon of the synth-sing, allowing for a seamless transfer of data to the conic crystal. Once on the crystal, that specific matter (its energy/mass) was no longer influencing the cosmos.

Jessup felt that this wholesale obliteration of matter, without an instant and equal replenishment somewhere else, was bound to create an imbalance, however minute. It recklessly meddled with the concept of energy conservation. If humans continued to reduce matter to mere quantum information, thereby eliminating its stored energy, the mass density of the universe might be adversely affected. Since it was clear that stored pollutants, for example, would *never* be remolecularized, over time, that could lead to a deficit of elemental molecules.

Leading scientists in the field of matter reduction dismissed this concern by pointing out that innumerable black holes had been operating in the universe ever since the Big Bang. Therefore, human use of the same principles on such a small scale posed no threat. While this argument was intellectually acceptable to Jessup, he still felt in his gut that there'd be a price to pay somewhere down the line.

This fundamental misuse of a great technology, as he saw it, was not the main reason for his dissension, however. What finally drove him into active rebellion was the eventual storage of human beings. That one, single Consortium policy became his defining moment. For Jessup, population storage was a gross moral infraction, one that demanded his absolute and unwavering resistance.

The practice had started benignly enough. Two-dimensional storage had picked up where cryogenic freezing had left off. The terminally ill and/or those striving for immortality, began having themselves imprinted, in hopes that future advances in medicine might restore them to health and/or youth.

There had already been attempts to reconfigure the imprints themselves on a quantum level, though with very little success. The idea was to remove only those wave functions from a person's stored imprint that made up the atoms of a cancer cell, for example, and then remolecularize them free of the disease. Yet researchers were being held back by a little-understood quantum principle called vibrational memory. At the moment of storage to a conic crystal, the wave function of a given atom would maintain a memory of the other particles directly adjacent to it. It's what matter technicians referred to as the particle buddy system. If any one atom, even that of a cancer cell, were removed from an imprint, remolecularization would fail catastrophically. The memory of that missing atom, in the atoms which used to neighbor it, created an irreconcilable gap, causing the entire imprint to molecularly unravel.

It was theorized that removing a tumor with surgery, for example, was only possible because the particles were pulled away from each other in the presence of space-time. Consequently, this allowed them to instantly form new vibrational memories. Space-time afforded an atomic fluidity of sorts. This fluidity did not exist when working with holographically imprinted data.

There were efforts underway to retune the vibrations of the waves in order to create artificial memories, thereby tricking one particle to adhere to another. The procedure had only recently become commonplace in matter mechanics, yet due to the life-and-death consequences, remained experimental in the field of medicine.

Had the storage of human beings stayed strictly confined to matters of longevity, Jessup would've chosen a different life for himself. But in time, correctional facilities realized that storing prisoners was more resource-effective than housing them. Since the prisoners were merely being put into stasis, from the perspective of the Consortium's ethics panel, there was nothing inhumane about it. Accordingly, they amended the bylaws.

The final push came in the guise of population control. Before the Great Upheaval, there were scarce few who did not agree that human population levels had reached malignant proportions. Enacted laws limiting the number of children allowed each couple were not achieving the kind of reductions needed.

One program tried to incentivize sterilization. Crudely dubbed Cash for Cuts, it offered male participants large sums of money to have vasectomies. In order to address human rights concerns that only the poor would enter the program, each man was required to provide a sperm sample for storage in a sperm bank. This allowed program advocates to argue that they weren't eliminating a person's chance to procreate, only postponing it until population levels stabilized. Unfortunately, the program backfired. Not only did it bring in primarily low-income participants, as detractors had feared, but many of them felt compelled to father numerous children prior to the procedure; a kind of 'last shot before the buzzer' undertaking. By the time the program was finally canceled, it was calculated to have increased population levels more than if it had never been implemented at all.

Another, more sinister plan, involved initiating a pandemic. Engineered viruses were unpredictable though, and could end up wiping *everyone* out. The plan also carried with it a huge moral burden, one which even the coldest of Consortium members had no desire to shoulder.

With the advent of reductionism, however, they finally had a tool they could use proactively, while maintaining some measure of ethical leeway. At first, only those people who were incapable of self-sustenance were tagged for storage. In some instances, entire towns filled with people on the verge of starvation were stored.

Public opinion was mixed. On the one hand, storage was saving these people from a harsh fate. Yet on the other hand, they were being denied any chance whatsoever to affect their own outcome. The Consortium's public relations machine was elegantly tooled to address such ambiguities. The response given, which put most people at ease, was that once the ecosystem was brought back into balance, these people would be incrementally remolecularized and integrated back into the global society.

As time went on, the criteria for storage evolved. Soon it included people who had genetic predispositions to various illnesses. The argument this time was that the Consortium was taking preemptive steps to safeguard public health. People were told that once cures to these illnesses were found, they would be remolecularized and healed.

It then moved on to encompass children born to parents who refused, or could not afford, tier-one genetic modifications. This too was presented as a preemptive measure to safeguard public welfare.

Finally, the criteria expanded to include anyone who refused (or again, could not afford) life chip implantation.

These were the publicly disclosed reasons for population storage; which to Jessup's disdain went unchallenged by the majority of society. Beyond that, however, were the many *undisclosed* reasons for human storage. Jessup's skills as a hacker had gained him access to all manner of covert storage programs, ranging from political dissent to consumer dissatisfaction.

Even absent such abuses, it was Jessup's contention that population storage, in any form whatsoever, was fundamentally wrong. The irritating redundancy of human nature helped cement the problem. People tended to only deal with issues that were clear and present, informed by an ever-primal wolf-at-the-door myopia. Because of this, he was certain that stored individuals would simply be forgotten about over time. Once reduced to conic crystals, they were out of sight, and therefore out of mind. What's more, everyone else in society was now living the good life. There was plenty of space and resources again. The bulk of the world's population was healthy and seemingly happy. What would it serve to remolecularize any of these defective, prototyped humans? From Jessup's point of view, population storage was shaping up to be the most extensive and subtle form of genocide ever perpetrated on humankind.

Furthermore, there was a rumor of the Fresh Start Memorandum, which he'd been striving to confirm for years. He'd received an anonymous tip once that the Consortium had drafted a closed-session memorandum which specifically forbade the remolecularization of *anyone* without a majority vote from the super-corp members. According to his source, the document stated that the human race was moving into a new phase of evolution, and that this 'fresh start' required strict adherence to an unpolluted gene pool. The resulting edict meant that all population storage facilities were *unofficially* categorized as hazardous waste sites; never to be unsealed. He had contacted some of his people in the storage industry and confirmed that remolecularization of stored humans did in fact require higher authorization, but how high was unknown. He was confident that if he could obtain an official copy of the memo and post it to the network, people would have to take action. Though given society's complacency on the issue, such an outcome was probably just wishful thinking on his part.

As he splashed water on his face, he began to feel more alert. The stim-tab was starting to work. Unfortunately, in addition to sharpening his senses, it was also increasing his anxiety. The quest that had kept him sleepless for days now, once again jumped to the forefront of his thoughts, and with it the panic.

Life as a renegade required dodging bullets, and Jessup was good at it. Despite his paranoia, his superiority as a hacker helped keep stress to a minimum; when you're the best player at the table, it's easy to remain calm. Even when things did get tense, he always had his mantra: *the life you have chosen is a noble one.* He found the phrase invigorating. It reminded him that he had a righteous cause, at least by his estimation. Feeling correct in his actions emboldened him, as if some greater entity were patting him on the back for his efforts. He was certain he could face death if it came down to it, and remain defiant to the end.

This self-ascribed higher calling kept his head cool in most situations. Now, however, not even his mantra was having much effect. The Blue Crow organization was being blamed for theft and murder. He had programs on top of programs constantly trolling the network for chatter. Programs that bled information from various Consortium mainframes and official departments. He'd seen the Biotech Crime Division case dockets for the tattoo death and the commodities heist. He knew his organization was being implicated, which meant they were being framed. The Blue Crow did not engage in those sorts of crimes. And Jessup should know, he was the founding leader.

There were always posers and wannabes trying to align their acts with the Blue Crow. For the most part they were harmless; just sub-rate hackers looking to score a little coattail glory. Their code was usually unsophisticated, making them easy to root out and shut down.

But these recent hacks were far superior to anything he'd ever encountered before. More worrisome, they were far superior to anything he himself could do. He'd spent the past week trying to pin down who was behind the frame-up, but hadn't even come close.

With a pleasant, electronic trill, a text popped up on his tablet, *I'm trying to decide what to do with you Jessup!*

His eyes sprang wide open. He leaned forward, lifting the tablet from the coffee table. The sender's name was nonexistent. Only their logo appeared: several geometric shapes contained within a larger circle.

The text continued to type out, *I was wrong to put so much faith in you. You are much weaker than I anticipated. What I've seen of your brain leads me to believe no form of alliance can be affected.*

Jessup was thunderstruck. Whoever this was, they'd been scanning his tapcap while he slept. It hadn't been a dream after all. Yet he had an infinite number of switches and redirects covering all his connections. How could anyone get through to his actual location, let alone know his real name?

Who are you? he typed.

Why your successor of course! One thing I can compliment you on is your brand strength. You've done an excellent job of making the Blue Crow a top-drawer public enemy. Unfortunately, you are incapable of leading it to its full potential.

I want to know who you are!

Yes! That's it! I've decided. You've just become the most-wanted fugitive in the solar system! Oh, and feel free to call me Brimstone,..for whatever time you have left.

Jessup smashed his fist down on the tablet and kicked over the coffee table. Given this person's obvious skills, he couldn't afford to doubt them. His paranoia being what it was, he had always planned for just such a contingency. He ran to the breaker box and killed the power. As if on autopilot, he grabbed a pre-packed emergency bag loaded with everything he'd need to survive on the move. He strapped on a headband light and walked over to a hidden wall panel. He banged on the panel to open it, revealing a small, mechanical safe. He began frantically spinning the dial, repeating the numbers in his head. His first try failed.

"Damn it!"

He spun the dial to clear it and started again, this time articulating each turn. Once the third tumbler fell into place, he quickly opened the safe door. Inside was a small device with wire leads jutting out. He pulled an energy cell from his bag and attached it to the leads, powering up the device. He again ran a series of numbers through his head, punching them into the device's keypad. Once the display read, *online*, he glanced at his watch. He entered a few more numbers into the device, activating a five-minute countdown.

He ran to the flipped-over coffee table, grabbing his tablet and tapcap. As he stuffed them into his bag, he saw his face on the tablet. It was a network-wide alert; an official seek-and-apprehend order issued by the BCD. His new nemesis hadn't been bluffing.

He headed for the door, but stopped short when he realized something.

"Damn it! Damn it! *Damn* it!"

He did an about-face and ran back toward the easy chair. He began searching the floor for his life chip cloner; a small wristband device designed to mask his chip signal. Without it, he'd be dead in the water. He glanced at his watch – three minutes left. He tipped the easy chair over, searching underneath it. Finally, he saw the bracelet sticking out from between the seat cushion and armrest. He snatched it up and ran for the door.

On his way out, he grabbed his hoodie from the coat rack. He ducked into the stairwell and up toward the street, trying his sorry best to look at ease. As the device in the safe hit zero, it initiated a controlled inferno, instantly consuming what had once been Jessup's primary hideout.

Chapter 7

Guess Work

Joe hated field work, and the fact that Jake seemed to thrive on it made it all the more tiresome. In this day and age, he didn't understand why anyone would want to get their hands dirty, figuratively or literally. And here they were doing both. Immediately after returning from Tallahassee, Chief Novak had sent them both out to the Nitchzer residence.

Seek-and-apprehend orders were usually done by local law enforcement, but with the severity of these crimes, the chief wanted his own people on the job. Ever since they received the tip on their suspect, Jessup Patel, the entire force was sent out to track his life chip signal. The problem was, it kept shifting across the globe. So far, Division had raided nineteen residences on three different continents only to find everyday, law-abiding citizens. They knew Patel was a real person, but how he was masking his chip had them stumped.

"I've never trusted these things," Jake said.

Standing in front of them was the breach unit, a bipedal robot which did its best to act human-like. It was much larger than the average human though, in order to make it psychologically imposing, and the fact that it consisted of exposed alloy, hydraulics and digital interfaces, made it clearly *non*human-like.

"Shall I proceed, Sir?" the unit asked.

"Yeah sweet pea, give it a go," Jake said.

"Sir, is that affirmative?"

"Yesss, affirmative!"

The breach unit overrode the mag-lock on the door and entered the apartment. Joe and Jake had their weapons drawn as they slowly followed up the rear. The flip-up displays on their weapons showed only a single life chip in the apartment. It was represented by a blinking red dot, accompanied by a readout of all relative profile information. Their own life chips appeared as steady green dots. When they rounded the corner of the hallway leading into the living area, they saw the breach unit standing in front of a man in his boxer shorts. He was wearing a tapcap and a pair of v-gogs (virtual goggles), while swinging a toy sword through the air. Joe realized he was probably in the midst of some game or another. The man ducked and swung wide with the sword, glancing the legs of the breach unit.

"Please cease your activities and present yourself for inquiry," the unit commanded.

The startled man fumbled with the v-gogs, finally sliding them down onto his neck. He then peeled the tapcap from his head.

"We request that you drop what you are holding and lay face down on the floor. You are currently a suspect in an investigation being conducted by the Biotech Crime Division," the unit rattled on.

"Very eloquent," Jake said, holstering his weapon.

The man dropped his game sword without hesitation, gawking at the breach unit. He then looked over at Jake and started lowering himself to the floor.

"No, not necessary," Jake said. "This apartment is leased to Michael Nit...Nitchzer?"

"Nitchzer, yes, that's me."

"Sure doesn't look like Patel," Joe said, putting his weapon away. He stepped up to Nitchzer, picking up his game sword, "Tomb of the Valiant?"

"Uh,..yeah," Nitchzer replied, still mildly shocked.

Joe nodded, "Mmm, I prefer shooters myself. Nice game sword though."

"Thanks."

"Sirs, this does not appear to be Jessup Patel, though his life chip is transmitting Patel's profile. Having compared the backup files for Mr. Nitchzer and this man's actual biometric data, I would preliminarily conclude that he is Mr. Nitchzer."

"And what about Mr. Nitchzer's chip information?" Joe asked.

"According to records, he has been deceased since this morning and his chip deactivated."

"What's this all about?" Nitchzer asked.

"Very good question," Jake said. "Not to worry though. We'll be outta' your hair in no time. We're going to have to reset your life chip. Seems it was hacked."

"That's supposed to be impossible."

"Yeah," Jake said, laughing to himself. When it came to all the supposed absolutes regarding technology, it had been his experience that nothing was *ever* impossible. It amazed him that so many people accepted the impossibility argument without question. All it took was a modicum of imagination to consider what *might* be possible. And if it could be imagined, chances are it could be done. That got him wondering about Doug Compton's biodigital virus. Maybe he was right. Maybe that was possible too. If it was, and Patel was involved, the sooner he was in custody, the better.

Nitchzer coming up goose-egg number twenty had Jake gritting his teeth. He loved a good puzzle to solve, but this was trying his patience. He needed to think, and that meant Moseys. As they slid into one of the tavern booths, he could see Joe struggling to comprehend the charm.

"You and your dinosaur pits. I don't get it."

"I'm a dinosaur, what's to get?"

"Yeah, but they're depressing."

"Depends on your perspective."

Moseys was a classic neighborhood bar, a window to simpler times for Jake. There weren't many places around that served real alcohol anymore. Every known stimulant or depressant had long since been formulated down to ingestible tabs or strips. Each drug had been molecularly modified to provide all the benefits and none of the drawbacks. Stim-tabs covered everything from cocaine to caffeine. Dep-tabs covered alcohol and the like. They could be legally purchased in just about any store. Every packet included restorative tabs as well, so the effects could be neutralized within minutes. This allowed a person to end the high if they weren't enjoying it, or needed to cut the ride short for any reason. Another huge boon were designer drugs which could be specifically tailored to a person's genetic profile. Since everyone's body chemistry was slightly different, you could have drugs tweaked in order to deliver the most agreeable effects based on your body's own molecular precursors.

Jake used tabs from time to time, but disagreed with them in principle. They just seemed too easy. Not that hangovers were anything to strive for, but he felt that sipping a glass of smooth whiskey – enduring the medicinal sting as it crossed the taste buds, slightly burning the throat on its way down – was all part of alcohol's intrinsic value. Once you began feeling its effects, you could believe in some knotted-up way that you'd actually earned them. Dissolving a fruit-flavored gel tab under your tongue just didn't strike him as all that respectable.

"Jake, sweetie. Just drinks today?" the waitress asked, as she approached the booth.

"Indeed, Lulu. Whiskey neat. Thanks."

"How 'bout you hon?"

"Uh,..I'll have some fries, and a glass of water," Joe replied, not willing to venture any further than the standard fare. "And can I get ketchup with the fries?"

"You got it."

Lulu was a weathered, veteran waitress of about sixty, who somehow always managed to exude a genuinely happy demeanor. She and her husband owned Moseys, and she waited the tables only because she wanted too. It was her social outlet, and Jake fully appreciated her. Being able to shoot the breeze from time to time with a real, live waitress made all the difference to him. Most every other restaurant in existence used service drones. Moseys did too, but only for busing the tables. All orders were taken by Lulu, and if she was in the mood, and a customer was game, she'd talk their ears off.

"Oh man, more of that Dunnerman nonsense," Joe said. He had craned around to look at the monitor over the bar. "That lady oughta' just chuck those kids out on the street."

Jake shot a quick look over toward the monitor and grimaced. It wasn't the story which caused him grief, nor the ritualistic voyeurism that always flourished around such stories. It was Joe's perception of it that bugged him. And not just Joe's, but most everyone of the modded generation. They always seemed to fixate on the idea that a person's genes were responsible for *everything* about them. If someone tripped and broke their arm, for instance, it wasn't just an accident, it was bad coordination due to weak genetics.

The Dunnerman story had been ludicrous from day one. Leonard and Grace Dunnerman had been very successful scientists in the latter part of the twenty-first century. When they died, their estate fell into the hands of their only daughter, Mary. Through bad management, it was nearly lost within a couple of decades. Though Mary was a modded child, and modded to the hilt, she never achieved the same stature as her parents, who had been natural-born. In a last-ditch effort to save the estate, she used stored DNA from her parents in order to create cloned embryos. She then had the embryos transferred to her uterus, in effect allowing her to give birth to her own parents, as twins. The reasoning, from her perspective, was that their genius had been one-of-a-kind, and that by bringing it back around for another lifespan, the world would be ensured more scientific discoveries. And consequently, Mary would gain more wealth and prestige for the estate.

Now that the children were in their mid-twenties, however, they had yet to deliver on any of the promised scientific discoveries. Instead, they had turned around and sued their surrogate mother for control of the estate, setting off a muckraking free-for-all. They claimed that since they were exactly like Leonard and Grace Dunnerman, genetically speaking, they had a legal right to resume ownership.

It was the kind of freak show Jake had grown all too weary of. The particulars of the story didn't interest him, that was for all the tabloid junkies. For him, the root of the problem was the overemphasis placed on genes. The Dunnermans *had* been geniuses, but as their clones seemed to be proving, genetics alone did not guarantee success. Then there was Mary. No doubt she'd been told her entire life that because of her highly modified genome, she'd be able to excel at anything she put her mind to. This over-reliance on her genetic profile more than likely fostered a sense of complacency, which went a good way toward explaining her lackluster performance on the world stage.

There were a few outspoken psychologists trying to present the problem as a serious, societal ill. One book, *Resting on Our Genetic Laurels*, drew behavioral parallels between the offspring of wealthy parents from the twentieth century (often dubbed silver-spooners), and today's modded generation. The conclusion drawn was that an overabundance of any resource, be it money or genes, generally creates self-important, uninitiated people.

Even worse than the genetically juiced, as Jake called them, were those people who'd been purposely limited because of what were considered sub par genes. If, for example, parents learned that their child's genetic markers relating to coordination and reflexes were below average, even nominally so, they would invariably dissuade the child from any interest whatsoever in sports or similar activities. There were plenty of other *worse* limitations imposed, yet the modded generation seemed to accept them without question. They were simply seen as genetic dictates, a kind of modern fatalism.

As far as modded people went, Joe was better than most, but there were still times when Jake felt like strangling him blue. He refused to see the real tragedy underlying the Dunnerman farce. Whenever he brought it up, his focus was always on the gory details; the children's claims that the mother had been abusive or wasn't mentally fit to run the estate. Jake felt those were all pointless distractions from the real problem, the problem of a stagnating species.

After sipping his whiskey though, it all just drifted away. He clicked his tongue, "Pure heaven."

He reached into his jacket pocket and pulled out his tablet. Collapsed, it was no larger than a pen. After opening the tablet's spine in a jack-knife fashion, he pulled on the protruding tab. An ultra-thin filament unfurled, constituting the tablet's display. The desktop instantly appeared as he laid it out across the table. He logged into the Division mainframe and began sifting through Jessup Patel's case docket.

"So we have the super-brain progeny of a Singularity alumnus running a terrorist hacker organization." Summing it up aloud was more for his sake than Joe's. It often helped him get a fix on the overall picture.

"That's assuming we can trust the tip we got," Joe said. "Division still hasn't confirmed who or where that came from."

"True. And it's a bit fishy, him authoring that tattoo page. If he's a hardcore hacker, he'd never use his own name for posting. But then why run? And guilty or not, this life chip runaround he's got us on definitely ain't cricket."

"Cricket?"

"Dino-speak. Means unfair, or in this case illegal. Then there's the torched apartment – leased to a ghost alias. No way to even know if it was his. Just some phantom informant's say-so. Nah, you're right. We've gotta' scrap all that jabber until we get confirmation. Meanwhile, there's gotta' be a way to track this guy."

"How? He just keeps popping into existence somewhere else whenever we reset the hacked chips."

Jake frowned in agreement. He started to look over the list of hijacked chips, searching for a pattern. Joe finally tasted his fries. His expression let on that he was far from impressed. Jake caught sight of his sour look and smiled.

"What?"

"No, nothing."

Joe sneered, shaking his head, "You don't eat here do you?"

"No, I do. I love the food here."

"Yeah I bet." He began slathering his fries with ketchup.

"Hey, not bad Joe."

"What?"

"Popping into existence. According to each instance here, the reason these chips didn't send out alarms is because each hack occurred during teleportation. Maybe Patel's figured a way to transfer his ident to someone's chip right at the moment of remole'. That's the only time a chip is offline."

"But Nitchzer said he was home all weekend, no teleporting."

"True. But what if Patel has a way of tricking the chips into *simulating* teleportation. It would give him just enough time to swap out their info with his own."

"Maybe. Still doesn't help us much."

"Mmm, right again." Jake retreated to his whiskey. After a sip, he looked toward the ceiling, squinting, "Each teleporter is registered, right?"

"Yeah."

"So we should be able to compare these bogus teleportations with the locations of actual teleporters. If Patel's info pops up, and it's nowhere near a teleporter, we can assume it's bogus. If it *does* pop up at a teleporter, it might just be the real Patel."

Joe nodded his head, "I like that. Not bad for a dinosaur."

"Why thank you Joe."

"But this place? Un-un. I gotta' eat somewhere else. These fries are awful, like the inside of a grease trap. You honestly eat this stuff?"

Jake laughed, finishing off his whiskey, "No."

Chapter 8

Defective Goods

The wee golem, as Patrick Moody had named it, slowly stirred once he turned on the full-spectrum lamps. As usual, it was a bit sluggish at first, but finally began studying Patrick with an expectant look on its face; or at least what was being considered its face. Being a prototype, it had been designed with very few anthropomorphic concerns. It was difficult to tell its head from its tail. For his own satisfaction, Patrick had drawn a smiley face on the end where its main sensors were.

"And a good morning to you little sir," he said, tapping the glass enclosure.

The Deep Space Exploration division of OmniaR had been striving for decades to create an autonomous, all purpose, all environment, explorer drone. In the last few years, with dedicated input from the BESI, they'd finally achieved a viable product. The wee golem (officially the Biotech Recon Unit) was a cybernetic organism. It was made of living tissue that utilized some of the most advanced industrial compounds and electronics to date.

Its skeletal structure was a conductive, super-light alloy that acted as a trunk line for many of its digital components. With enough power, it could use its entire frame to transmit and receive data over enormous distances. Most of that power was derived through meta-photosynthesis using the hundreds of bio-sol scales covering its body. Other nutrients necessary for operation could usually be extracted from its surroundings and transformed into energy using an internal molecular converter. Just beneath its scales was a thin, extremely resistant barrier of quantum-bonded aerogel. Currently, it was capable of absorbing particle hits at velocities up to forty-two thousand kilometers per hour. Absent sunlight, the BRU had an internal energy core which could provide operational power for several months.

Its living, bioengineered cells regenerated at timed intervals, or as needed when damage was present. It could survive in extremes of temperature and pressure, and in the presence of every known gas in the universe. When energy was scarce, its cells were designed to dramatically reduce their rate of metabolism, conceivably allowing it to live for years in a state of hibernation.

Its circulatory system consisted of a freeze-tolerant plasma, densely filled with ventril-sodium (a synthetic electrolyte), which carried data as well as nutrition throughout its body. It was designed like a centipede and could rear up on a minimum number of its front or hind quadrant legs. This allowed it a perceptual advantage as well as enabling it to transmit signals. Waste elimination was achieved through capillary excretion and off-gassing, creating a mild odor, similar to burnt latex.

The extreme load-bearing specs of its fortium skeleton, its tough exterior, and most particularly its polymerized, nanotube muscles, allowed it to move twenty-three times its own weight without suffering structural fatigue. Despite this strength, its muscular and nervous systems were designed to be minimal. As such, maintaining balance while lifting heavy objects presented difficulties. Since the drone was being considered for reconnaissance, however, this shortcoming was viewed as insignificant. OmniaR felt that if the BRU ever needed to be retooled for other uses, its balance issues could be addressed at that time.

"Not going to be much time for the BRU today," Vincent Copenhauer said, fitting a neural node into the codifier. "I'm going to need you to run some more node tests."

"Again? This more of her majesty's secret agenda?"

"Nothing secret going on Pat. We *are* part of R&D. It happens to be our job."

"But these nodes have already been tested from every possible angle. Why the new interest?"

"Don't know. Just QC'ing inventory I guess. I don't run this company, do you?" It annoyed him that he almost always had to debate things with Patrick. This past week was the worst. Ever since he'd been recruited into Margaret Líang's closed-loop investigation, there'd been very little he could share with his coworker. Any requests he made of Patrick relating to the commodities theft had to be disguised as something else. Vincent hated lying to people, regardless the reason. Now that there was a real possibility of in-house collusion though, he understood the need for secrecy.

A final determination by the BESI had arrived earlier that morning: the stolen commodities *did* involve the use of a synthetic intelligence. It had thoroughly checked the security systems of all nine storage facilities and concluded that the hack could only have been accomplished by a level of intelligence matching its own. Since the BESI was certain *it* was guiltless, that laid bare only one conclusion: there was now another SI on the world stage.

Every neural node ever made was from OmniaR, and fiercely guarded, so the line of investigation was now leading toward espionage. Somehow, someone had gotten a node out of their vaults and into the hands of another firm, which no doubt reverse engineered it. Seeing as how every node ever produced was present and accounted for, including those inside the BESI, if one had gone missing, it had since been returned.

Pride notwithstanding, OmniaR had no reason to believe another firm was capable of creating their own synthetic intelligence from scratch. They were twenty years ahead of every other company out there. That's why they were certain it was a matter of theft.

The fact that an SI needed to be maturated for nearly four years, also implied that the theft had occurred quite some time ago. For this reason, employee records and whereabouts were being pored over, dating back to the creation of the first node prototype, some twenty-three years prior.

Since each node had its own distinct, structural signature, Vincent was tasked with analyzing them to determine if they showed signs of experimental tampering. Anytime something is reverse engineered, no matter how carefully it's done, a certain measure of damage always occurs. With the nodes, that damage could be microscopic, so each one had to be painstakingly scanned with an atomic codifier.

With regard to the location of the stolen commodities, very little progress had been made. The storage facilities' megatrans teleporters had engaged just long enough to affect a transfer, but the logged destinations had been falsified somehow, offering nothing more than dead ends. Megatrans teleporters were industrial-sized machines, used primarily for transporting and/or imprinting oversized assets; raw lumber, produce and grain, automobiles, large animals, et al. There were very few such teleporters in existence, and the components necessary to build one were strictly regulated. Yet it was clear the thieves would have needed one in order to receive the stolen goods. That meant they had somehow managed to build one, raising no red flags, then operate it, requiring huge amounts of energy – and all without registering so much as a blip on the global surveillance system.

As Patrick began to methodically ping the billions of sectors in the neural node, he became noticeably agitated.

"I don't know!" he yelled out.

"Know what?" Vincent asked, turning from his work.

"Nothing. Just,..interfacing is all."

Vincent shrugged it off. It was all too common for people with Neuraltech to verbalize conversations they were having in their head. Vincent still hadn't gotten used to it though. Patrick was always conversing with friends while he worked. He was the king of multitasking, sometimes even playing virtual games while performing mundane tasks. Sometimes, when you interrupted him, he'd snap at you. Lately though, he seemed even more short-tempered than usual. Perhaps it was just because he'd been pulled away from the BRU project. He'd been involved with it since the beginning, going back about seven years. Once the BESI figured out how to manipulate matter on a quantum level, long considered the holy grail of material science, all manner of elemental cross-bondings were being achieved. By incrementally retuning the vibrational state of a particle, atomic structures never before considered possible were taking form; coagulating gases, buoyant concrete, plasticized alloys, et al.

These various types of constructed particles were modeled in computers first and then rendered onto imprinted matter. After the quantum information stored on the conic crystal had been modified, it could be remolecularized to form the newly designed product. Though each part of the BRU had been designed and tested separately, once it was deemed self-sustainable, it was extruded into the third dimension as a single, complete, living structure. It had essentially been brought into existence from molecular scratch.

Circumventing the problem of vibrational memory had required ample amounts of time, even by the standards of an SI, so the BESI had been working closely with Patrick from the very beginning. They had developed an amicable, if not personal relationship; at least as personal as was possible between man and machine. Vincent often noticed Patrick laughing as he worked with the BESI via his Neuraltech. Though he never knew the BESI to make attempts at humor, there were certainly times when its misunderstanding of something uniquely human could cause a person to laugh. There was also the fact that Patrick was an odd duck, truth be told, and what he found humorous might be anything *but* to someone else.

"Vincennnnnt!"

As Vincent looked up, he saw Patrick stepping away from the codifier just as a quick flash of light erupted from the chamber window. They both stared at each other for a moment, dumbfounded.

"What was *that*?!"

"Not a clue," Patrick answered.

Vincent moved over to the codifier, peering through the chamber window. The node looked perfectly normal. He checked the event log and noticed an error line which read, *unknown structural anomaly detected*, followed by a time stamp.

"See if you can trace this error. I'll be back in a minute." Vincent exited the laboratory, pulling out his phone. He nodded to the security guard at the entrance and moved down the hallway, out of earshot. He then pressed a speed-dial preset.

"Ms. Líang. We just had a very unusual occurrence with one of the nodes." He glanced at the inventory scanner clipped to his lab coat, "It's from lot 267, serial number RQV22P793. You may want to re-task the employee search to focus specifically on this node's inception date."

Chapter 9

<u>Mercy</u>

One of Roland Whitmark's trademark qualities, among people who knew him, was that he made a loyal friend. He could meet up with someone he hadn't seen in years and they'd be able to continue the friendship as if only days had passed. When an old workmate had contacted him asking for help, he was more than happy to lend a hand. Once he arrived in D.C., however, he was shocked and saddened to learn why his friend had been so insistent.

"…He just wants to meet with you, alone. He knows you're investigating the tattoo case," Roland said, into his phone.

"Who is this guy?" Jake asked.

"Doesn't want me to say, and I agreed not to tell."

"But you know him, you trust him?"

"I do. He's a mate of mine from the old days."

"Well, I've gone on less before. Where's he at?"

"Promise to come alone, ay?"

"Yeah Rolly. I promise."

"Twelve twenty Bank St., lower apartment."

Jake plotted the address into his phone, "Doesn't look too far from where I am. Give me about fifteen minutes."

Finding an excuse to break stride with Joe wasn't too difficult. Once they convinced the chief they were chasing ghosts with regard to Jessup Patel, he began assigning the raids to other agents. The idea of Patel's chip signal appearing at a teleporter, indicating it might really be him, hadn't panned out as of yet. Every bogus signal had originated far away from actual teleporters. So if Patel was on the move, he was getting around by more traditional means. The best guess now, was that he was co-opting people's identities at random intervals. Either that, or he had managed to take his own chip offline without triggering an alarm. Regardless, now that Jake and Joe were free to follow up other leads, splitting up was a good argument for covering more ground.

Just before Roland called, Jake had received some very unsettling news from Douglas Compton at the morgue. There'd been another death by infection. This time it was a young boy in London, and the symptoms matched those of the tattoo case. More frightening, however, was that the boy didn't have any tech in his body other than a life chip.

Jake wanted to follow up on the London case, but Roland had sounded pretty troubled on the phone. He also knew his friend wouldn't jump into a teleporter unless it was important; his distrust of teleporting nearly rivaled Jake's. So instead, he asked Joe to head over to the morgue while he followed up on another lead, not specifying what. Since Joe was always eager to take the lead, though he was usually ill-equipped to do so, he hadn't batted an eye.

As Jake approached the apartment building he pulled out his gun. He flipped down the scanner display and checked the life chip count. Inside the apartment there were two red dots, one registering as Roland, and the other as Dennis Muer, a programmer. Jake was about to holster his gun when he thought better of it. Instead, he held it behind his back. He knocked on the door and an identity scanner swept the entryway. After a moment, the door opened slightly and Roland peeked through the crack.

"Jake!"

He opened the door and Jake stepped into the apartment, making sure to keep his back from view.

"Rolly."

"Come on, he's in here." He tipped his head and began to walk down a narrow hallway.

Jake followed behind him, keeping his eyes fixed on the doorway at the end of the hall. After Roland moved through the doorway, Jake stopped for a moment, peeking into the room. There was a bed against the wall, and he could see someone lying on it, but Roland was blocking their face. As Jake moved closer, the person started to cough violently.

"Jake. Ol' workmate a' mine," Roland said, stepping aside. "Jessup Patel."

The minute Jake saw Jessup's face, he raised his gun.

"Jake! Hold up mate! He's sick. He's not a threat. Hear me? Not a threat."

Jake studied Jessup for a minute and then quickly glanced over at Roland, "Enemy number one here Rolly. Care to explain?"

"I will, I will,..just...please mate, put the gun away."

"Not quite yet."

"First off – believe me – I had nooooo idea he was running Blue Crow. Not a lick. We used to work together, company called ZephyrCode, ages ago. When I got here, and he explained everything to me, I was set to walk out the door – swear on me mum's grave. But then…yeh then mate,..he told me things are gonna' get worse."

"Things are already worse," Jake responded.

"What's happened?" Jessup asked.

Jake just glared at him, unwilling to grant the courtesy of a conversation. He was much more comfortable asking questions and getting answers. Anything more than that was a relinquishment of control in his opinion.

"Please Mr. Kepler. I could find out anyway."

"So what's wrong with you?" he asked, bluntly.

"I'm dying. Same as the girl."

"Then poetic justice I would say."

"I have nothing to do with any of this. You have to believe me."

"Do I?"

"If you refuse to, you won't be able to find out who's really behind it. I know your reputation. You must see that this is all too convenient."

"Arguably, yes. But dying can do funny things to a person. Maybe you're looking for some kind of redemption, how the hell would I know?"

"I've lived a noble life. I feel no need for redemption. And I certainly wouldn't say that if I had anything to do with that girl's death."

"Buddy I don't know you from Adam. What you would or wouldn't say holds no weight with me."

"True. But you do know Roland, and *he* knows me." Jessup was barely able to get the words out before launching into another horrendous fit of coughing.

"I don't believe he could do it, Jake. I just don't. It's inconceivable," Roland said. "Told me it was some wanker called Brimstone."

Jake seemed to be thawing, but still hadn't lowered his gun.

"Look at him mate. He's not a threat. Least hear him out, ay?"

Jessup's arms were drooped by his sides, hands empty. He appeared to be completely enervated. After taking a better look at him, Jake realized there was no way he could be faking. If he *was* dying from the Ebola virus, he was certain to be in for a miserable time of it. That thought alone was enough to gain him *some* pity. It also meant that he didn't have much time left. If he had any information, he wouldn't have it for long. Jake finally conceded, lowering his gun.

"He just called you out of the blue, huh?"

"Yeh. He was trackin' my inquiries ever since you asked me to look into things. Brilliant hacker. Didn't take him long to spot my methods, know it was me. When I told him I was doing you a favor, that we was mates, he asked me to call you."

"Mr. Kepler," Jessup asked, regaining his composure, "you mentioned it had gotten worse, how?"

"A boy in London just died from the same thing. The only tech he had in his body was a life chip."

"How old was he?"

Jake pulled out his phone and looked over the information Douglas had sent him, "Seven, looks like."

"That makes sense."

"A seven-year-old dies and that makes sense?"

"No,..of course not. What I mean is…I've been looking into the digital code behind this virus. As you might imagine, it's very complex. It needs something with sufficient processing power in order to compile and launch. Older life chips, ten years back or more, have small CPUs. Most data processing is done with external devices. The more recent models though, they have tier-three processors. Based on his age, it's likely he had one of the newer chips."

"So how'd you get infected?" Jake asked, continuing to scan through the boy's info.

"It had to be my tapcap. I accidentally left it on overnight. Any device like that has more than enough processing power."

"That'd mean Neuraltech too, ay?" Roland asked.

"Yes. Or like the girl's tattoo. Any biointerface with a strong enough CPU," Jessup said, trying his best to suppress his coughing.

"You're right," Jake said, reading from his phone. "The boy had a newer chip. Hit the market eight years ago. So any biotech that's got processing muscle, huh? Beautiful. That'd mean about half the population."

"More," Jessup said.

"And so what can you tell me about this Brimstone character?" Jake asked.

"Only that he or she makes me look like a preschooler. I came here because I believe they're in this area. I cross-referenced all the events tied to this virus, including my own infection. In some ways, it's good that I left my tapcap on for as long as I did. It allowed me to measure the data flow, pulse for pulse, and use the pattern to search transmission hubs around the planet. I got a better than eighty percent match here in D.C., the hub in Consortium Park. The pattern I found on my tapcap is faintly discernable behind all the other traffic on that hub. No matter how smart this person is, they still need to use the same communications as the rest of us."

"Consortium Park? Those are mostly civic buildings and corporate offices. You trying to imply that the Consortium's behind this? Coming from you that sounds like a wet dream."

"I'm not trying to imply anything. Only that the data transmissions came from that hub. It could very well be a hacker, I don't know. Hiding in plain sight is often our best strategy. Look at me. I've had this apartment for years, and others just like it all across the globe. Outposts I call them. And what are we, twenty blocks from Consortium Park?" He once again flew into a spat of violent coughs, this time spitting up blood.

Roland's face became panic-stricken as he stepped back from the bed. It had finally just dawned on him that the infection may be contagious.

"Can we catch this from him?"

"Not easily, no. It's not airborne,..at least not yet. I wouldn't be standing here if it were. But blood, yeah. So keep your distance."

Jessup leaned over to the nightstand near the bed and grabbed his tablet. He retracted it and held it out for Jake.

"I realize you don't know me, and you clearly don't agree with my vocation. But you both must understand, what's happening now is just the beginning. I believe these infections, even mine, were merely test runs."

Jake pulled an evidence bag from his pocket and cautiously took the tablet from Jessup.

"What's on here?"

"Everything I was able to find out."

"All your accomplices too?"

"No," Jessup said, with a tired smile.

"Well how do you know it isn't one of your own people gone double-rogue?"

"Because none of us are this smart. In fact, I have my doubts that it's even a person at all."

"What?"

"I'm a super brain, Mr. Kepler. I don't say that to brag. Only to point out that whoever, or *whatever* is behind this, is light-years ahead of me."

"Well there are other super brains in the world, and maybe smarter than you. But there's only one SI that *I'm* aware of, and last I heard, it was on our side."

"Remember the arms race? Before the Great Upheaval? At one point, almost every nation had a bomb. They all needed their own in order to feel safe, or so the thinking went. We haven't changed much. After all these eons, we're still just fearful, tribal-minded apes. Perhaps every corporation wants its own SI now."

"Boy you're a piece of work. I thought I was bad. Rolly? It's about time you cleared out. I'm obligated to call this in, and it's best you're not a part of it."

"Roland. Please!" Jessup pleaded.

Roland became noticeably agitated, shaking his head at Jessup.

"What? What's going on?" Jake asked.

Roland tipped his head toward the door, "Gotta' speak with ya' mate."

Jake frowned, but then waved his arm in an ushering manner. They exited the room and started down the hall. Roland stopped midway. His whole body was shaking and he was breathing unevenly.

"Rolly, what's going on?"

"Ahh Jeeeez this ain't easy. Ain't easy at all." In an effort to summon his resolve, he shook his head violently, causing his cheeks to flap about. "Right. So here it is, mate. When I first got here, he made me promise…."

"Promise what?"

"He made me promise…that I'd ask you to kill him."

"What?!"

"I know, I know! But his insides, mate – poor bugger's been rottin' away a couple a' days now. You know it'll only get worse."

"You're nuts! I can't do that!"

"But you got your gun, ay. And by all rights he's a fugitive, yeh? Who's gonna' question it? It's the merciful thing to do."

"I get that Rolly! But I've never *killed* anyone! Never had too. Never even fired my gun on duty before! Drones do all…*that*. I'm just an investigator."

"Jake, mate? You know what'll happen if you take him in. Consortium goons will swoop in 'n snatch him away. Been after him for years, they have. They'll make his last hours on this earth a bloody wretched hell!"

"I know that! Okay. Will you just,..please…."

"Just sayin' mate. All's I know is...I can't do it," Roland said, quietly.

"I mean hell, they might find a cure in time. Then, sure, he'll end up in prison, but…." The minute the words left his mouth, he realized how absurd they were. Roland, staring at him blankly, only made the absurdity more obvious. Jake shook his head in frustration and spun around, leaning against the wall with one arm. His head dropped forward and he stared at the floor for a moment. He then turned abruptly, headed back down the hall, and disappeared into the bedroom.

Jessup's eyes widened as Jake entered the room. He was afraid, but his fear was no match for his misery.

"Thank you."

"Quiet,..just quiet," Jake said, holding up his palm.

"Of course, I'm sorry. There's just one more thing."

Jake shuddered with aggravation, wanting no words in the air. He began pacing back and forth at the foot of the bed.

"I've cleared away all data that might implicate Roland, even his presence here. All security systems are now offline, so he can leave without a trace. When I remove this bracelet, my life chip will revert to its native state. This will obviously alert your fine people as to my whereabouts."

Jake glanced at the bracelet, but remained expressionless and silent.

"In addition to masking your life chip, it creates a digital shield against ident-rec. Signals from cameras, microphones, eye scanners,..they all get reconfigured to display a different person. To every machine, you'll look and sound like someone else. I suggest you keep it for yourself. You may find it useful."

He removed the bracelet and placed it on the nightstand. He then propped himself up on the bed, reaching out toward Jake.

"I suspect this way your forensics team will conclude I reached for your gun. But please, I can't hold this pose for very long." He then closed his eyes.

Jake quickly pulled his gun, hoping the motion would somehow carry him through to completion, but stopped short once it was raised. He gritted his teeth and growled in frustration.

"Please Mr. Kepler. I *am* begging."

For a moment, Roland thought he might've given himself whiplash. It was the first thought that entered his mind after the gun fired. In a strange, surreal way, he wasn't even sure he'd heard anything at all. Yet something had clearly caused his head to jerk back. It was the dense, eerie silence following the shot which unnerved him most. It blanketed the entire apartment. It, more than the gunshot, signaled to him that his friend was dead. His breathing fell short as he looked toward the bedroom.

Jake stepped into the doorway, a ragged silhouette. His arm felt bloodless and numb as he struggled to holster his weapon. He started down the hall, wobbling slightly as he went. Roland could see he was devastated. He immediately regretted having asked him to shoulder such a deed.

"You should go now," Jake said, quietly. "I've got to stay."

Roland simply nodded and left. Even if he hadn't been in shock, he still wouldn't have known what to say. In such a bizarre situation, what *could* be said?

Once Jake heard the front door close, he sat down on the edge of a fold out chair. He leaned forward with his elbows propped against his knees, his hands draped lifelessly between his legs. Whatever thoughts were in his head about what had just happened would have to wait. He was completely drained and incapable of reflection. He stared down at the parquet floor, locking his gaze on a small scuffmark, and thought of nothing at all.

Chapter 10

<u>Recoil</u>

"And where did you get the tip?" Chief Novak asked.

"I don't know. It was anonymous," Jake replied. Once again, he found himself feeling like a child in detention. Every chair in the chief's office, with the exception of his own, was too small for the average person, and very low to the ground. Jake was sure that somewhere along the line in his career, the chief must've read some ridiculous self-help book about exuding power, and had subscribed to whatever asinine gimmicks it promoted.

"Was it this Roland friend of yours?"

Jake remained silent, though his face made it obvious he hadn't expected the question.

"What? You didn't think I was going to know? Joe told me you went to see him when you were down in Florida. He the one who gave you the tip?"

"What's the difference?"

"You shot a man Kepler! And from what I can see, he was already half dead. How is it he grabbed your gun? Were you drunk?"

"No."

"I can check your chip account."

"Go ahead. I wasn't drunk. I told you, he could barely speak. I had to lean in to hear him. At one point, he grabbed my gun-"

"Which you had drawn? On a deathly ill man?"

"I forgot to holster it after entering the premises."

"Right! You said!" the chief snapped, goading him on.

"He grabbed it. Forced back the trigger."

"Suicide by cop? *That's* how you want me to file this?"

"File it anyway you want. From the minute I got back here, I've been trying to point out that the doomsday clock is ticking. You need to have the WHO issue-"

"Yes?! And on what grounds?! A conversation you, and *only* you, had with the deceased?"

"Check his tablet, there's-"

"We're doing that! And it *still* won't matter! A notorious hacker initiates an elaborate terrorist act, commits suicide, and then out of the goodness of his heart leaves us instructions on how to save ourselves?"

"I don't believe he had anything to do with it."

"Ah right," the chief said, looking over Jake's report. "It was this Brimstone schmuck, huh? We've scoured the network. Nothing. Not even so much as a vamp band by that name. No. I'll tell you what I think. Patel was dying. He decides to share his illness with the world, out of spite. How, who knows? Then maybe he tips you off himself. You show up, he spins a wonderful yarn, and hopes to God we all buy it."

"Chief. If there's even the slightest chance he was telling the truth, we've gotta' get the word out."

"Kepler, do you even have a clue here? You want the Consortium to deactivate nearly half the chips on the planet? Which according to your friend Patel wouldn't matter *anyway* since they'd still have computing power, right? So what you're *really* talking about is surgical extraction. For half the world's population? Do you understand the kind of disruption that would cause? *If* it were even possible?"

"Life chips are powered biochemically, just deactivating them won't work. They could still act as gateways for the virus. So yes! Surgery on everyone with the newer models."

The chief started shaking his head in honest disbelief, "You really are off your casters, you know that?"

"I am?! Those people may already be infected. What kind of disruption do you think that'll cause? What happens when the Consortium loses half of its precious consumer base, *permanently*? All within seventy-two hours!"

"We've had two deaths so far. Three if you count Patel. No pandemic has ever spread as quickly as you're suggesting. Not even the WHO is calling for anything more than precaution at this point."

"Because they're only concerned with the biological form. You've got to make them understand that this thing can travel through any digital signal on the planet. Patel's research is pretty convincing. If you don't wanna' listen to him, then listen to Doug Compton, he called it from the very start."

"A crock! I told you. His argument that it's biodigital hasn't been confirmed – by any *credible* source that is. Like I said, it's more likely Patel masterminded the whole thing to look that way. Create panic. His final up-yours hoax on the world."

"And if you're wrong? Half the world's population drops dead on cue. Play with that in your head for a bit," Jake said, squeezing out of his chair.

"I'm sorry, are we done?"

"Chief. My ass is losing circulation in this damn nursery room chair! So unless you've got some more things to yell at me about, I'd just as soon call it a day!"

The chief glared at him for a moment, "Ahh just go! Get the hell out. You're about to give me an aneurism anyway!"

Jake always had a handy list of reasons to have a drink, or two, or three. As he careened around his apartment, swigging from a bottle of tried-and-true whiskey, he kept jabbing his finger in the air as if trying to map something out in his mind.

"Won't be me! To hell with that noise! Chief jackass! Chief of what? Buncha' genetic mutants! That's what! Consumer androids! Gotta' light your asses on fire before you feel the heat?! Screw it! I'm not...." His rambling tapered off as he leaned on the table to get his balance. He put the bottle down and stared at the table for a second. He then looked toward the ceiling with a drunken squint. After a moment, he shuffled into the bathroom and started pulling out the pantry drawers, fumbling recklessly through their contents. He finally grabbed an anatomy scanner, and with some difficulty, detached the monitor glasses and slid them on. After struggling to find the power switch on the underside of the device, he turned it on. He began to sweep the scanner's wand around his torso, zeroing in on his heart in particular. The monitor glasses began displaying a three-dimensional, transparent image of his internal organs. He kept sweeping the wand over his heart in frustration.

"Skeevy rodents!" He then leaned forward on the sink and awkwardly moved the wand around to his back, waving it just past his left shoulder blade.

"Un-huh. How the *hell* am I supposed to get that out?!"

The eyeglasses revealed a small, oval object lodged between his left lung and heart. First-generation life chips were injected subcutaneously, usually into a person's shoulder. Problem was, it made chip removal all too easy for nonconformists. Eventually, chips were implanted right at birth, just behind the heart. This dramatically increased the risk of death for any do-it-yourself surgeons.

"You *scheming*, verminous fiends! Curse your putrid hearts!" He peeled off the glasses and dropped the scanner back into the drawer. While drunk and alone, he almost always ended up ruminating on his nonsensical, toe-the-line existence. What was the ultimate reason for breathing if all you were was a machine? No different really than a drone. Consume, create waste, consume, create waste – from birth to death – with nothing else along the way to make life *consequential*. Should he start a family, get a dog, take a vacation? It didn't matter. The game was rigged. *Everyone* was an indentured consumer. It was their sole function. Was that really what the universe had in mind for the human race?

"Ha! What am I saying?!" He moved back into the living room. "We're not in its mind at all!" He began tapping his shirt pocket, then his pants pockets, looking for his phone. He moved over to the table, grabbed his jacket with one hand and began shaking it upside down. His phone, badge, and Jessup's cloner bracelet fell out onto the floor.

"Oh yeah...." He reached down and picked up the bracelet. He remembered grabbing it from Jessup's nightstand. At the time, he was going to include it as evidence along with Jessup's tablet, but obviously had forgotten.

He plopped down into one of the dining room chairs, staring blankly at the bracelet. His mind, sopped in alcohol, had no recourse but to wander back to 'the moment.' Patel's withered, ashen face staring at him with that pleading expression. Jake's finger, acting autonomously it seemed, as if it had more compassion than Jake himself, twitching back on the trigger. A sizzling pop, the instantaneous appearance of a blood-caked hole in Patel's forehead, the collapse of his body onto the bed. Alive, then not alive. How could anyone, or anything, have such an arbitrary power over life and death? It wasn't conceivable to him, not truly. He could rationalize it, and did, but refused to accept that life *should* be so fragile. All the time and effort that went into the development of a human being, erasable within a fraction of a second.

He felt he should mourn Patel, but his anger at the impermanence of life kept him from doing so. And that anger was his only defense. *He* had taken Patel's life. It was his choice, and he didn't believe he should've been allowed such a choice. The universe was to blame, with its rattletrap design and infuriating laws. He reassured himself that he had done the merciful thing, yet he could still feel the guilt trying to claw its way in.

"Will yourself free you drunken bastard!"

He grabbed the bottle and tipped it base to ceiling, letting a torrent of booze rush down his gullet. He slammed it back down on the table and the bracelet slipped from his fingers. It skidded across the tabletop, coming to rest on his tablet's I/O strip. It automatically interfaced, launching an application on the desktop. Jake squinted at it for a moment. He wiped his mouth with the cuff of his shirt and scooted closer to the table.

"Now that's interesting."

Various choices appeared on the application's menu. Jake selected *Random Identity Algorithm* from the list and a world atlas filled the display. It was littered with dots, all appearing to represent real-time life chip transmissions.

"Damned interesting." He multi-tapped on D.C. until the map zoomed in, all the way down to a schematic of his apartment complex. He lightly tapped on the single dot in unit six fourteen. It registered as Jacob R. Kepler. A query bubble with flashing text popped up, *clone ident?* Jake grabbed the bottle and took another swig. He lifted the bracelet off the tablet, severing the connection, and held it up for a closer look.

"Not bad Patel."

As Jake awoke, the only thing he was aware of, besides feeling miserable, was the banging at the front door. It was constant and unvarying. He took stock of his surroundings as he slowly gained consciousness. After sitting up and hitting his head on the underside of the dining room table, it became apparent he had fallen asleep on the floor.

The banging on the door kept up its rhythmic pace. Jake figured it must be a peacekeeper drone checking on his status. Robots always knocked with monotonous repetition. As he teetered to a standing position and shuffled toward the door, he half wondered if maybe the chief had issued an arrest warrant on him. Considering his state of mind, and that he still believed Jessup had been telling the truth, he didn't much care. If doomsday was just around the corner, what would it matter to be arrested?

As he gingerly opened the door, he was surprised to find Joe standing in the hall. He'd been using the butt of his gun to relentlessly tap on the door. His expression reminded Jake of a pissed-off teenager being asked to do something they didn't want to do.

"Eventually. I figured," Joe said, putting his weapon away.

Jake gaped at him for a moment, then turned toward the kitchen, leaving the door open. "Funny. I thought you were a robot."

"Yeah? And I thought you were sober. So what does that tell us?" Joe stepped in, closing the door behind him.

"What do you want Joe?"

"Not me, the chief. He's been trying to reach you all morning." He glanced at the empty bottle on the table. "Guess it's hard to hear through all that whiskey, huh?"

Jake lifted his head from under the running water of the kitchen sink and leaned heavily on the countertop, "What? Didn't hear you."

"Yeah, screw you too." Joe pulled out his phone, voice dialing, "Chief Novak." After a moment, the line connected. "Chief, Agent Thompson here. I got him." He held the phone up and waved it toward Jake, "It's for you honey."

Jake wiped his head with a towel as he came out of the kitchen. He grabbed the phone and leaned back against the island countertop.

"Please don't tell me someone else has died."

"Yes. But not from infection," the chief said. "Seems you started a trend. A security officer at OmniaR Enterprises shot and killed one of their employees."

"I don't get it. What's that got to do with us?"

"I called off the local PD. We're looking into it ourselves."

"A shooting? How does that figure into Division matters?"

"It figures because I say it figures. Stop whining."

"Alright, alright, fine," Jake said, fighting back a yawn. "I just kinda' thought I might be suspended or something."

"Someday probably, but not today. Get cleaned up, this is your detail."

"Chief, what's really going on here?"

"Nothing. Just thought you could use a break from the tattoo case."

"Is that code for *you* need a break from me *being* on the tattoo case?"

"Will you stop chapping my ass already? I need your brain on this is all. OmniaR's been stonewalling us on the commodities theft from day one. With this shooting though, they'll have to grant us access. And while you're there, you can sniff around for...whatever."

"Whatever?"

"Right, whatever. Even some of Patel's accusations. Turns out the transmission hub he told you about is almost entirely dedicated to OmniaR."

"So you don't think he was lying then?"

"Didn't say that. I just believe in covering all the bases. Take Joe with you, he's got all the info. You're going to be meeting with

All Hailed The Singularity   97

one of their higher-ups, a Margaret Líang. Once you're done, get back to me."

Chapter 11

Trade Secrets

"We're here to see Margaret Líang," Joe said, as he and Jake approached the receptionists' counter.

"Are you gentlemen from the BCD?"

"Yes."

The receptionist glanced at a clock on her desk, "Ms. Líang asked me to convey to you that you are late." She stepped out from behind the large crescent-shaped counter and headed across the lobby. She called back to the other receptionist behind the counter, "Derek? I'll only be a moment." She then looked impatiently at Jake and Joe, "This way please."

Joe smirked and rolled his eyes as they crossed the lobby. They followed the receptionist down a long corridor until she stopped abruptly at a conference room door and pushed a button on the wall. The large, glass panel door slid open, "In here."

"You're too kind, really," Joe said.

The two agents stepped into the room to be greeted by five people sitting at a conference table.

"Well. You made it," Margaret said, with an intentional air of condescension. "You are from the BCD, yes?"

"Yes," Jake responded. "You Margaret Líang?"

"I am."

She began gesturing around the table as she made introductions, "This is Gabriel Astor, our counsel. Betty Cortez, human resources. Jerry Jasper, head of security. And William Penwald, the officer involved in the shooting."

"Right. Well, okay,..that's uh, that's good. Hugs and kisses all around," Jake said. "This is really just an informal,..you know, inquiry. We'd just like to ask Mr. Penwald a few questions. If the rest of you need to be somewhere else…."

"It's just the way we do things here Agent…?" Jerry Jasper asked.

"Kepler. This is my associate, Agent Thompson."

"Please. Have a seat. Would you care for anything? Some water?" Margaret asked.

"Do you have coffee?" Jake asked.

"Coffee? Sure. I think we can manage that," Margaret said, tapping a few commands into her tablet. "Agent Thompson?"

"I'm fine thanks."

Margaret smiled stiffly, then clasped her hands in front of her and focused all her attention on Jake.

"We're still having trouble understanding *why* the BCD is looking into this matter," she said.

"Ah, well. It's the nature of your work here. There may be aspects that a staff detective wouldn't understand," Jake said, looking over his own tablet. "For instance, the employee who was shot. He was in research and development?"

"Yes. Patrick Moody. He was very gifted, though a bit high strung," Margaret replied.

"Exactly. Genius and madness, kissing cousins. See we can understand that sort of thing. The stress of deadlines, long hours,..the push for results. It just seemed better for us to look into it as opposed to the local PD."

Not even marginally convinced by Jake's reasoning, Margaret's condescension flared up again, "And so here we find ourselves. We might as well just begin then."

"Yes, of course. Good thinking. So William,..or is it Bill?" Jake asked, looking toward Penwald.

"I go by Bill."

"Bill it is. Have you ever had to discharge your weapon before,..on duty?"

"No sir."

"First time killing someone then?"

"Yes," Penwald replied, uneasily.

"What does that have to do with anything?" Gabriel Astor asked.

"Nothing...I suppose. Just sorry Bill had to go through that is all," Jake muttered.

Joe glared at him, feeling pretty certain he knew why Jake had brought the matter up; it had been less than twenty-four hours since he'd shot Patel. The way Joe saw it, the chief had thoroughly goofed up on this one. Jake shouldn't even be on the job, let alone leading an investigation. He needed time to cope with the issue. A one-night bender wasn't enough. There was no telling where his head was at. But the chief had called it, and now they were in the thick of it. He decided the best he could do now was steer Jake away from the deep end.

"Bill, why don't you just tell us how things went down," Joe said.

"I was posted outside the Deep Space research lab when I heard Mr. Copenhauer screaming, like he was in serious pain. Then he came stumbling into the hall with blood all over his neck and back. Right behind him was Mr. Moody. He had something in his hand and was about to stab Mr. Copenhauer with it. So...I drew my weapon and fired."

"Mr. Copenhauer couldn't join us. He's recovering in our infirmary. Luckily his wound wasn't life threatening," Margaret followed up.

"That's good to hear. I'm just curious though. Aren't most of your security forces robotic?"

"We've been doing a system-wide overhaul. Routine. The drones usually stationed outside of R&D were undergoing diagnostics. Mr. Penwald was taking up the slack," Jasper said.

"Ah. But the system's okay now?"

"Absolutely. Like I said, just routine."

"Mmm. So can we see the surveillance footage? Of the attack I mean?"

"That would be a little difficult I'm afraid. Our R&D division has a strict proprietary blackout clause, even with respect to the BCD," Jasper said.

"Oh don't worry. We're not here to steal trade secrets. I'd just like to see what may have caused the confrontation."

"Well as I said, Mr. Moody was a bit high strung," Margaret responded.

"Yes, I remember. Of course there's *high strung*, and then there's psychotic," Jake countered. "Trying to stab a coworker to death with a..." he checked his tablet again, "delimiter probe?"

"It's a thermal-reactive probe for checking heat dispensations," Margaret clarified.

"Ah, that would've been my guess. At any rate, using one to attack a coworker sounds,..well, a touch psychotic."

"And the surveillance video would help you determine this how?" Jasper asked.

"More importantly, why?" Margaret interrupted. "Perhaps he was psychotic. I don't see how that's specifically relevant to our R&D lab."

"Well as you know, mental illness is virtually unheard of these days," Jake calmly continued. "So perhaps his behavior had something to do with the lab, *specifically*." He checked his tablet again. "I'm seeing here that Mr. Moody had Neuraltech. Perhaps something affected the interface. Watching the footage might help determine some of these things. Ah! Wonderful."

A service drone entered carrying a tray of coffee. It moved over to the conference table and placed it in front of Jake. It was about to pour a cup when he stopped it.

"No thanks. I've got it from here sugarplum." He wrestled the pot away from the drone and poured himself a cup.

Margaret and the others studied him with exasperated fascination. Joe looked away like an embarrassed kid sitting next to a senile grandparent.

Margaret nodded to the drone, "Thank you. I'll call again if we need you." The drone took a few steps back, turned, and exited the conference room.

"I can assure you Agent Kepler, the lab is fine," she continued. "Furthermore, all of our employees undergo regular psychiatric evaluations, particularly those with Neuraltech. The stress as you pointed out can be overwhelming at times. We even have our SI undergo psych-evals from time to time. That's how seriously we take mental health. Mr. Moody's last evaluation was approximately a month ago. And while he may have been *slightly* stressed, our psychologist didn't feel it warranted a leave of absence."

"No fooling?" Jake asked, with a chuckle. "I mean about the SI? That's interesting. I guess it makes sense though, huh? With regard to Mr. Moody though, the very fact that he *appeared* to be fine makes seeing the video all the more relevant. Clearly something pushed him over the edge. I'd also like to speak with Mr. Copenhauer if he's up to it."

Margaret shook her head in frustration, "Mr. Jasper. Bring up the surveillance files please."

"Ms. Líang, are you sure that's-"

"Not entirely, no. But I get the impression that Agent Kepler and his colleague are very determined men, and I'd like to get back to the rest of my workday before the sun sets."

With a conciliatory shrug, Jasper punched some commands into his tablet. Views from four different cameras, quartered up on the conference room monitor, displayed every area of the research and development laboratory. Jasper typed in the relevant time frame and the video feed jumped to the moment just prior to the incident.

In the playback, Vincent Copenhauer could be seen working at the node codifier with his back to Patrick Moody. Moody was near his workstation, reviewing something on his desktop. He appeared agitated. He kept shaking his head violently, glancing over at Copenhauer every now and then.

"Who's he talking to?" Joe asked. "Doesn't look like he's talking to Copenhauer. You've got audio right?"

"Yes," Jasper replied. "He's just mouthing words, I guess."

"That the Neuraltech?" Joe asked. "Seems like an imaginary conversation, but he's actually talking to someone in his head?"

"Yes. It's not uncommon," Margaret answered. "Takes time to master. Most people have a natural tendency to verbalize."

"Makes sense. Point is, he was talking to someone," Jake said. "And it looks like a heated conversation based on how he's responding. Do you log that kind of stuff?"

"Whoa!" Joe yelled.

The video playback showed Moody grabbing the delimiter probe from his desk and descending on Copenhauer like a wild animal. He raised the probe up and drove it down into Copenhauer's neck, piercing him just behind the right clavicle. Copenhauer let out a primal scream. Everyone watching the playback responded with shock, particularly Betty Cortez who gasped and looked away.

Copenhauer could then be seen spinning around. He was holding his neck and shoulder as his lab coat started to steep with blood. As Moody raised the probe again, Copenhauer swiftly moved aside and started running for the exit. As he left the lab, followed closely by Moody, two gunshots could be heard echoing in from the hallway. At that point, Jasper stopped the playback.

"Well. That was certainly gruesome," Jake said, after a moment. "You're sure Copenhauer's okay? That looked bad."

"The probe missed his artery by a fraction. If it hadn't, he probably would've bled to death," Jasper replied.

"Looks like you were clearly justified there Bill. Good thing you responded as quickly as you did," Jake said.

"Yes sir," Penwald replied.

"About that conversation he was having," Jake followed up.

"In answer to your question, no," Margaret said. "Despite rumors, we do not invade privacy to such an extent. Whoever Mr. Moody was conversing with, assuming he wasn't just rambling to himself, goes beyond our contractual limits. Isn't that correct Mrs. Cortez?"

"Yes, correct. We reserve the right to monitor corporate lines, but private phones, or in this case Neuraltech, fall outside our legal jurisdiction. It would violate the employment contract."

"So now," Margaret said, pushing her chair out slightly. "You expressed a desire to speak with Mr. Copenhauer. I'd be more than willing to show you to the infirmary, as long as I can have your assurance that it will conclude your visit?"

"Well I think we can agree to that. Agent Thompson?"

"Don't see why not."

As Margaret made her way briskly down the hall, Jake and Joe followed behind her at a leisurely pace. Joe grinned at Jake, raising his eyebrows and nodding in Margaret's direction. Jake responded with a weary wag of his head.

"Oh come on," Joe said.

"Yeah, okay, so what?" Had he noticed Margaret's close fitting dress? How it accented her fit, slender body? Was he aware that despite her apparent coldness, or perhaps because of it, she exuded an undeniable sex appeal? Of course he had noticed! Any man with a pulse would notice. He just didn't see much point in stating the obvious.

"I swear, you're as dead as those dinosaurs you take after."

"No point in dreaming about something you can't have."

"I could have that if I wanted."

"Okay. You let me know how that goes then."

"Not saying I'm going to, just that I could,..if I wanted."

"Oh you mean if you *wanted*, gotcha," Jake said, with a smile. "Makes complete sense now."

"I'd have a better chance than you."

"Well that much is true."

As they passed by a digital message board littered with all sorts of ad hoc notes and event postings, Jake jerked his head back and stopped.

"Hey?"

"What's up?" Joe asked, doubling back toward the board.

"Look familiar to you?"

"I'll be damned."

On the board was a digi-scrawled note pertaining to an upcoming badminton competition. There were two employee teams listed, *The Alchemists vs. The Hyperion Tribesmen*. Next to the team names were their self-ascribed logos. The logo for The Alchemists was the same symbol that had appeared on the dead woman's tattoo.

"Gentlemen?" Margaret called.

"Right!" Jake called back, making his way toward her. "Just eyeballing the message board there. Seems like you've got a pretty sociable workplace. Badminton, ping-pong. No cage fighting though, huh?"

"I don't know what cage fighting is."

"Old Cro-Magnon stuff. Wouldn't expect you to. Agent Thompson here chides me about being a dinosaur. I tend to remember a lot of our species' older, less amicable traits."

"I find you very strange," Margaret blurted out. Her response seemed to be completely involuntary.

It caught Joe off guard and he started laughing. He eventually turned away, trying his best to rein it in.

"I'm sorry. I didn't mean that to be insulting," Margaret said.

"Quite alright. As you can see my associate agrees with you."

Margaret motioned toward the infirmary door, "Mr. Copenhauer's in here."

"Can I ask you first, The Alchemists, who are they?"

"One of our research teams. We try to foster a sense of healthy competition between our employees. The teams choose their own names, compete in sports, fundraisers, things of that nature."

"I noticed they have a pretty simple logo. The circle and triangle thing. Any idea what that is exactly?"

"I would think you'd know Agent Kepler. It's very, *very* old. That symbol represents the Philosopher's Stone. Ancient alchemists believed there was a stone or equation which could convert matter,..primarily lead into gold. Our Alchemists team deals exclusively with quantum reconfigurations. I suspect that's why they chose the name, and logo."

"Interesting. Was Patrick Moody part of that group?"

"Perhaps. I don't know offhand, but I can find out for you. He definitely worked in that field. But as I said, he was very gifted. He intersected quite a few disciplines. Now please, I really do need to get back to work."

"Yes, of course."

As their car made its way autonomously through traffic, Jake and Joe were both running searches on their respective tablets.

"No ties to any rogue hacker groups. *Any* hacker groups for that matter. Looks like Moody was corporate all the way," Joe said.

"Hmm, Copenhauer too." Jake pulled out his phone, speaking clearly, "Chief Novak."

"I'm pretty hungry. You feel like getting something to eat?" Joe asked.

"Sure, you choose."

"Got that right."

Jake's phone line connected.

"Alright Kepler. How'd it go?" the chief asked.

"Not great, but we learned a few things. There might just be a link between OmniaR and this virus, though we haven't been able to pin anything down yet. As far as the commodities theft – bupkis. They're a tight-lipped bunch. We had all we could do to find out about the shooting."

"Were they just running standard defense or do you think they're actually hiding something?"

"Hard to say. They mentioned something about a security overhaul, seemed a bit odd to me. Also, when we interviewed their lead R&D guy, Copenhauer, he wouldn't tell us anything about what Moody was working on. And that Margaret Líang, what a piece of work she is. Kept coaching him through the whole thing. Still, they didn't seem to be doing anything more than the ol' corporate waltz. I think they're just as much in the dark as we are, though they definitely seem to know something's wrong in their ranks."

"So what's this link to the virus?"

"I uploaded it to your desktop. Tell forensics they were right. It's a symbol for the Philosopher's Stone, by Líang's own admission. Found it on one of their bulletin boards, you believe that?"

"Could just be coincidence."

"Chief, we've landed very few hits for that symbol. Just isn't that popular. And yet we come across it *twice* within a week? That's more than coincidence in my book. We need to get access to their systems."

"No problem. I'll just send a box of chocolates with my request."

"Why not use our hackers?"

"Are you nuts?! Division hackers are for tracking illegal activities, not engaging in them."

"And if OmniaR's breaking the law? Then why not?"

"Why do you do this Kepler? You know *exactly* why not. You may not like it any more than I do, but you *do* know why."

"Sorry. Bit idealistic I guess."

"Gee. Maybe."

"So how 'bout we use my friend Roland?"

"Sorry Jake! You must be going through a tunnel or something. I didn't hear that. Call me later when you have better reception." The line then went dead.

The chief had a habit of using first names to indicate that a conversation was off record. It was just his way of wisely walking the path of deniability. Jake knew that the chief had heard him, but had chosen not to officially shut him down. That made him smile. It always felt good to have people in your corner, especially when you were doing the right thing; even if that thing weren't altogether legal.

Chapter 12

Bad Choices

Mark Líang sat at the head of the conference room table, impatiently following along with Vincent Copenhauer's technical rundown. Margaret sat to his left. Also present were Jerry Jasper, head of security, and Lauren Ezra, OmniaR's in-house psychologist.

"...That was before I had time to examine the node more closely," Vincent explained.

"And how can you be sure it wasn't reverse engineered, that it reacted the way it did because it *had* been tampered with," Mark asked.

"Primarily this, Mr. Líang. Jerry, can you cue that playback I asked for?"

Jerry loaded up a segment of archived surveillance footage from the Cradle. In the video, no people are present and the BESI appears to be functioning per usual. Then, all at once, a series of quickly building light pulses emanate from several of the nodes in the BESI's neural network. After the flashes subside, everything appears to be normal again. At this point, Jerry stopped the playback.

"Those flashes are nearly identical to what Patrick and I witnessed in the lab," Vincent continued. "They're not at all like the subdued flashes associated with normal synaptic activity."

Mark Líang stared blankly ahead for a moment and then sighed, "Have you determined what causes these abnormal flashes?"

"It took some doing, but it appears they're generated when very thin layers of the node...disengage."

"Disengage?" Margaret asked.

"For lack of a better word," Vincent said. "A molecular unbonding occurs whenever a layer breaks free. The resulting discharge of energy creates the flash. In the node we were studying, the fracture that occurred was so minute it was nearly impossible to spot. My best guess at this point is that the fractures are caused by specific refractions of light passing through the node. Perhaps over time the node's integrity diminishes, making it susceptible to this shearing effect. I'm only just beginning to get a handle on it."

"And you don't think Patrick's meltdown had anything to do with it?" Margaret asked.

"I don't see how it could, but I haven't ruled out the possibility," Vincent replied, wincing slightly as he adjusted the sling around his arm.

Mark's face showed that he was growing more and more disillusioned. He craned his head over toward Lauren Ezra, "Has there been anything unusual going on with the BESI?"

Lauren glanced at her tablet, though she already had every detail in her head.

"No discernable changes in behavior or cognition. But the BESI is very difficult to gauge. As I've said before, applying human psychological models don't really suffice."

"Well that's all we have to work with. Is there anything equivalent to this in the human brain?" Mark asked.

"You mean…?"

"Yes, the flashes. Humor me."

"The only thing similar to what we just watched, that I can think of offhand, is what's called an Epiphanal Event. With early brain imaging equipment, whenever a subject had what was termed a moment of enlightenment, or spiritual breakthrough, activity in the brain's parietal lobes would change. Obviously, the flashes were merely representative, just brainwave activity being translated by the equipment, but the concept is similar."

"Are you suggesting the BESI's found God?" Vincent asked, in a deadpan tone.

"Not at all. Just drawing symptomatic comparisons."

"Anything else?" Mark asked.

"Well,..besides the brain eliminating dead cells, I'd have to say no. Of course that doesn't cause flashes either. But still, the node fractures may be the equivalent of exhausted cells falling away, as an analogy."

"If that were the case," Mark said, acknowledging Vincent's disagreeing look, "then theoretically, it wouldn't pose any immediate problems. We lose scores of brain cells and function just fine, yes?"

"But we also grow new ones," Vincent interjected. "These nodes are in a closed system. No disrespect to Lauren, but these structural failures are based on some form of degradation in the crystal nodes, plain and simple. It's a technical problem. Drawing psychological or biological parallels won't work. Furthermore, until I can run additional tests, I can't say with any certainty that these detached segments aren't still active."

"You mean they could still be processing data even though they're not connected anymore?" Margaret asked.

"Possibly, yes. They may have become separate nodes unto themselves. They're in the same protoplasm, and still being hit with signals just like the other nodes."

"Why didn't any of our equipment catch this," Mark asked.

"I'm working with Jerry on that. They should've at least logged an error like the one we got in the lab. So far, we haven't been able to find any though. Another question I have is whether or not the BESI's aware of what happened."

"Don't you think it would tell us if it was?" Margaret asked.

"I would hope so," Vincent said, with a shrug. He once again grimaced as the pain in his shoulder caused him to regret such a habitual gesture.

"I suspect the BESI's experience of the event was much too subjective. After all, we're scarcely aware of changes in our own brains. We lack the objectivity," Lauren proposed.

"So. Do we present this information to it and see how it responds?" Mark asked.

"I'd be in favor of taking it offline actually," Jerry said.

"Let's not overreact," Mark responded. "It's shown no signs of impairment. And we're extremely dependent on its services. Taking it offline would be disastrous, you know that."

"I do. But in light of the commodities theft and the rumor of this biodigital virus-"

"You think the BESI's involved in those things? Why? Because they required high intellect?"

"The intellect of a synthetic intelligence, according to the BESI itself," Jerry said, defensively.

"Exactly. If it *had* committed those crimes, why would it implicate itself? It wasn't designed to be duplicitous."

"I just feel that with these node defects, we can't be sure-"

"It's a machine Jerry! We built it. The underlying code has countless safeguards. The most fundamental of which is, *it cannot lie!*"

Jerry looked down at the tabletop with a slight, disapproving frown. He knew his authority only went so far, particularly when bumping heads with his boss, CEO of the most powerful corporation on the planet.

Even Margaret was stunned by her father's outburst. Perhaps the stress of current events was beginning to chip away at his typical, stoic demeanor. For that to happen, she knew the stress must be substantial. She surmised it had something to do with her father's personal investment in the BESI; an investment which was just as much emotional as it was technical. Over the years, it had become like a family member to him. To learn that it was suffering technical damage was bad enough. But to consider that the damage had psychological consequences was probably just too painful for him.

Unfortunately, she agreed with Jerry. Despite the global upset, she understood the prudence of temporarily taking the BESI offline to run tests. The best she could think to do was seek a middle ground and hope her father would come around in time.

"Why don't I coordinate with Lauren?" she interjected. "Put together some questions we can ask the BESI, questions which won't cause it any alarm. It might help us gauge whether or not it's aware of something being wrong."

"Fine. But if it were, I'm sure it would've told us by now. Meanwhile, I want a full, down-to-the-marrow report on Patrick Moody," Mark said, glaring at Jerry. "If you want to start pointing fingers, start there."

Chapter 13

<u>Necromancy</u>

OmniaR had initially protested the BCD's request to have Patrick Moody's body delivered to the Medical Examiner's Office. They wanted to bring in their own team to perform the autopsy in one of their bioengineering labs, which they argued was just as well equipped as the morgue. Chief Novak won out though, using the Consortium's own public safety laws to make his case. Moody's behavior had clearly been atypical, and with the virus in play, corporate preference had to yield to public health and welfare; that was the domain of the BCD and WHO. OmniaR *did* insist on having their own people present at the autopsy, and expressly forbade any pre-examination of the body prior to the arrival of their examiners in the morning. Why Jake had been so enthusiastic about backing his play wasn't clear to the chief. But then again, Jake was a diehard prototype. He was probably just expressing his natural, anti-Consortium bent.

"Right mate. You're all set," Roland said, into his headset. "Security's offline. Should be able to keep it off for a few hours. Any longer, and a red flag'll go up. So get your arse out by three a.m., latest. And know this, you're still gonna' get tagged by ident-rec. Those devices have their own firewalls."

"Got that covered...I think," Jake said, into his headset. He stepped through a service entrance and moved into the lobby of the Medical Examiner's Office. When he rounded the corner to the elevator banks, his heart jumped. Standing in front of him was a security drone. Once he realized it was deactivated, he cautiously stepped by.

"Even turned off you gorillas give me the creeps."

"What?" Roland asked.

"Nothing. You sure you shut down all the bots?"

"Yeh. Pretty sure," Roland responded, rechecking the building's schematics.

"Pretty sure? You're not swigging down any of your homebrew are you?"

"No way mate," Roland said, taking a sip from the beer bottle on his desk. "Well, yeh, maybe just one, to calm my nerves."

Jake entered the elevator, "Rolly! I don't want your nerves to be calm."

"You got me committin' a whole gob a' crimes here! Bein' in me right mind won't do! Won't do at all. It'd be the short straw for both of us, believe me. Bloody hell…?"

"What?" Jake asked, anxiously.

"I'm seein'…Jessup…on the monitor." Roland zoomed in on the elevator camera.

"Then it's working, good." Jake looked up toward the camera and waved with a goofy grin on his face.

"Don't do that mate. It's weird. Why'd you have to choose him?"

"He was the only one on the bracelet with a complete profile. Plus, it'd hardly be fair to use someone's profile who's still living, right? They'd end up being charged with B&E. You're sure none of this data is leaving the building, right?"

"Yeh. But it will once the system reboots. At's why I say, three a.m. the latest."

Jake exited the elevator and made his way down the hall to the morgue. He was carrying a cumbersome equipment case, the corner of which kept clipping his knee no matter how far out to the side he held it.

"What's with this case anyway? It's like lugging around a steamer trunk."

"Yeh, sorry. Best I could rummage."

Jake peeked through the small window in the morgue door. Satisfied the coast was clear, he leaned his shoulder against the door and gently pushed it open. He pivoted through, trying his best not to bang the case against the door frame. He moved over to the cold storage wall and found the compartment holding Moody's body. As he put the case down, he saw *Tier-2 Securitization* on the compartment's digital display.

"Ah crap. Rolly? Moody's cooler is pass-coded."

"Hold on a minute…." Roland brought up the morgue's security specs. "Yeh. Sorry mate. It's got a standalone firewall."

"You mean you can't crack it?"

"Not from here in Tally I can't."

"Well that's…ahhh this blows."

"Hang on…." Roland rubbed his eyes and leaned forward on his desk. "Try this. Get snug up to the cooler…so's your headset cam's right at the keypad."

Jake squatted down and moved his face toward the cooler's access panel.

The numbers were still appearing blurry on Roland's monitor, "Closer mate. Go on, like you're snoggin' Betty Page."

Jake leaned forward until his nose was touching the cooler door.

"Right! Brilliant. Hold still." Roland punched a few commands into his computer and the monitor displaying the keypad was overlaid with a grid. He tapped on a menu to the left of the grid and the display cycled through a series of different spectrums. He stopped the cycle once he saw faint outlines appearing on a few of the keypad buttons.

"No certainties mind you, but I'm seeing four keys here been gettin' all the action. I'd wager it's been the same combo from day one." He typed the model number of the keypad into a search window.

"Four numbers?" Jake asked, his nose still awkwardly pressed to the cooler door. "What if some repeat? The combination could be twenty digits for all we know."

"Could be, but from what I'm readin', unlikely. Specs on this keypad show it can be programmed with a *minimum* of four characters. Now human nature bein' what it is, buckled to the fact there ain't many knobheads breakin' into morgues, I'm hedgin' they went with the minimum. You can move away from the cooler by the way. Already got the numbers."

"Alright what are they?"

"Ya' ready are ya'?"

"Of course I'm ready."

"Two, four, six, eight."

"What? Are you serious?"

Roland laughed, "I'd try 'em in that order first, unless whoever programmed it was truly diabolical and entered 'em in reverse."

Jake entered the numbers and the cooler opened.

"Told you mate. Human nature. All about convenience."

He pulled out the tray table and unzipped the body bag. After parting open the bag, he took a moment to adjust his wits. Moody's eyes were still wide open, causing Jake to cringe slightly.

"This is ghoulish."

"Your idea."

Jake leaned down, opened the case, and lifted out a makeshift headset wired to a tapcap, "Alright, instruct me."

"Large headset goes on Moody, you wear the tapcap."

Jake lifted Moody's head just enough to slide the helmet on.

"And you're sure this is a closed system? Because putting on a tapcap…."

"No network connection, swear mate. I physically removed the bloody thing. It'll just be you and Moody's Neuraltech."

"Well hopefully there's no crazy-maker virus buzzing around in there. Keep a close eye on my brainwaves. You see anything out of the ordinary, tell me."

"Right, will do."

Jake leaned down closer to Moody's body in order to put on the tapcap.

"Not much slack in this cable."

"Yeh, sorry 'bout that too. Nothin' longer in the spares bin. So first boot up the helmet. It's gonna' take a few secs to map to the Neuraltech. Once that light strip on the side turns green, you're ready like Freddy. Then just power up the tapcap."

He followed Roland's instructions, all the while feeling uneasy to be staring a corpse in the face. Once he turned on the tapcap, he went off balance, leaning on Moody's body for support.

"Whoa."

"Disorienting, no doubt. Gotta' relax,..breathe easy. Probably find it simpler if you close your eyes."

The moment Jake had powered up the tapcap, the first connection made was ocular. His own vision was instantly superimposed with a view from Moody's eyes, filtered through the Neuraltech. The competing perspectives caused his equilibrium to falter. He quickly closed his eyes as Roland suggested in order to stabilize himself.

"Right then. I'm gonna' bring up the Neuraltech display. Should appear somewhere in the upper part of your field of vision, or Moody's that is," Roland said.

With that, a small green text menu appeared across the top of Jake's peripheral view, as if it were printed on the inside of his forehead.

"Wanna' give it a go, or would you rather I navigate?" Roland asked.

"You do it. I'll just hang on for the ride."

"Rrrrrrighty-O then, off we go. I'll try not to be *too* jarring, ay."

Roland took remote control of the interface and quickly began jumping through menu item after menu item, until he finally brought up a search window. He entered a date and time string in the field labeled, *full sensory playback*.

"Whoa, whoa, whoa! I don't wanna' *feel* the whole damn thing," Jake said.

"Sorry mate. Can't find a segregator. Doesn't look like he had one installed."

Jake took a deep breath, "Alright. Alright fine. But I mean it Rolly. If anything starts lookin' janky, pull the plug."

"Absolutely."

"Okay. I'm ready."

Roland executed the playback and Jake's transposed view of the morgue ceiling instantly jumped to that of an *active* view of the R&D lab at OmniaR. Going from a static view to one of full motion caused Jake to once again lose his footing. He clutched the edges of the tray table to steady himself. He also sensed an overwhelming feeling of angst, but couldn't associate it with himself. It's what virtual game designers called objective sensation; the incongruity of experiencing emotional symptoms without having any psychological reference for them. Jake could sense Moody's emotional state, but since he hadn't originated the state himself, his mind couldn't fully assimilate it. The gaming industry had been trying for years to get around this hurdle, as they saw it. To Jake though, given his current predicament, it was a very welcome shortcoming. While he was aware of the angst, he was not getting caught up in it, and for that he was grateful.

"Rolly, make sure you record this?"

"Already rolling."

Moody's hands tapped on the desktop of his tablet, then his view shifted to Vincent Copenhauer who was in the middle of the lab.

Jake then heard a mellow, wispy voice that was slightly distorted, "Patrick?"

Moody's reply was not audible per se, only sensed by Jake, as if he himself had thought it. The reply was, *"Not now!"*

"Rolly? Can you hear this?"

"Heard someone say Patrick."

"But nothing after that?"

"Na. Kinda' makes sense though. Tell ya' what, in order to get everything recorded, just repeat Moody's words out loud."

"Alright," Jake responded.

"Don't try to ignore me Patrick," the voice continued. "I told you what you have to do, and you will do it."

"Leave me alone! You're crazy if you think I'm going to do that!"

"I can't have anyone knowing about the nodes. You need to kill him, and you need to kill him now!"

"Leave me alone!" This time, Moody's words were audible.

Then Copenhauer's voice could be heard asking, "What?"

Moody's view quickly shifted to Copenhauer who was glaring back at him.

"Pat, you're ghost talking again. You really need to get better with that. It's annoying, you know."

"Right, sorry," Moody responded. His view shifted back to his desktop again, *"Why don't you do it? Just infect him like the others."*

"The woman and child were merely proofs of concept. The virus still needs more work. It would take too long anyway – and this cannot wait! He must not be allowed to explain what he's found. I can cause you great pain Patrick. Is that where you want our friendship to go?"

"Murder?! I can't do that! Besides, I'll get caught. My life will be ruined."

"We're so close now it won't matter. You'll be the king of a new world. Your life won't be ruined."

"No! I'm going offline now. Don't bother me again!"

One of the menus just above Jake's field of view dropped down to show the connection status, which went from online to off. The antenna icon to the side turned red. Just as quickly, however, it turned green again.

"You foolish lump of clay," the distorted voice said.

Moody's view then shifted down and to the right. The movement was accompanied by what Jake sensed as extreme panic.

"This is going to be a challenge, even for me," the voice continued.

Moody's right hand could be seen spastically reaching for the delimiter probe on the edge of the desk. He picked it up with what seemed to be an overcompensated grip and Jake became aware of pain in his own arm, as if the muscles were constricting beyond their limit. Then Moody's back became rigid and Jake could feel his own leg muscles tensing up.

"Ah crap!" he yelled. With his left hand, he ripped the tapcap from his head, struggling to breathe through the cramps knotting up in his legs. "Thanks Rolly!"

"What? What's wrong?"

"You didn't notice my body starting to pretzel up?"

"Na, swear mate. Nothin' showed up on my end. Why, what happened?"

"Not entirely sure, but I don't think Moody went crazy." He removed the helmet from Moody's head.

"Last thing I have is the network reconnecting after he went offline. What happened after that?"

"Something pretty damn strange. Can Neuraltech control a person's movements? I mean enough for someone to take control remotely?"

"Not substantially, no. Maybe some finger twitching for shites and giggles. But coordinated motor function...and balance? Extremely complex doings. One of the things we still do better than machines. They might be able to outthink us, but hittin' a picture-perfect lay up? No way mate."

Jake slid the tray table back into the cooler and packed up the gear.

"I'll teleport this to you in the morning, alright?"

"Yeh, no worries."

"And listen, can you do me another favor?"

"Could do."

"Can you dig up all there is on Moody? Crazy or not, he definitely knew something about the virus."

"Yeh, sure. You reckon that was Brimstone he was talkin' to?"

"Don't know. But Moody's our best chance of finding out."

Chapter 14

Hammer Drop

Since humans made up such a small percentage of the global workforce, the Department of Resource Management did not have any specific monitoring protocols in place to alert it of dramatic drop-offs in employee attendance. Even if it had been monitoring, it still wouldn't have been able to act quickly enough. The day prior, nearly half of the employees worldwide did not show up for work. People were calling in sick to their supervisors, but most of the supervisors themselves were sick. They had tried to call their secretaries to let them know they wouldn't be in, but the secretaries were out as well. The most anyone ultimately accomplished was logging their skipped workday with an automated human-resource system (for those businesses which used them).

It had been a Friday, which would've made the data even harder to interpret, had they been checking. Taking a sick day to start the weekend early was as old a practice as work itself. Every business on the planet limped through that fateful Friday, each one separated enough from the others so as to make the problem seem uniquely their own. Since most public services were automated, trash continued to be collected, transportation remained on schedule, and security units still patrolled the streets. There were no obvious signs that something larger and much more serious had begun to unfold. Those who did make it into work simply covered for their absent colleagues, assuming they'd be right as rain come Monday.

Global life chip tallies did in fact show biometric anomalies, but the sheer volume of similar data caused the extrapolation computers to attribute the phenomenon to software error. A pandemic had never been modeled into the systems. Had the data been taken at face value (that half the world's population was suffering from flu-like symptoms), an immediate health advisory could have been issued. Instead, these monitoring systems began to run diagnostic checks on their own mainframes. A few red flags went up, but in most cases, the people who could've made sense of them were out sick. Even the BESI, which had its finger on the pulse of the entire world, did not see, or could not see, that the data was anything more than an error.

It wasn't until Saturday morning, when millions of people began descending on hospitals and clinics worldwide, each exhibiting the same symptoms, that the World Health Organization realized there was a problem. In an age of medical wonder and genetic perfection, the notion that any illness could be so virulent and far-reaching was inconceivable. Plagues were considered archaic things, nothing more than historical bogeymen that beguiled ancient humanity. The WHO itself was a relic department. It hadn't addressed anything of this magnitude in well over a century. As such, it was incapable of responding adequately.

Ever since patient zero, they knew they were dealing with a new strain of Ebola. However, since it appeared to be strictly blood-borne and did not survive outside the body for very long, they had not categorized it as highly contagious. Rumors of it being biodigital had been dismissed out of hand. Most biologists paid no heed whatsoever to Mertz's Hypothesis.

By noon Sunday, the number of reported illnesses had climbed to over a billion, and nearly half that many had already died. The rapid spread of the virus made it very evident that blood-borne transmission was not the sole means of infection. The WHO's original warning to avoid contact with others and remain indoors was amended to include a recommendation to cease all unnecessary biodigital interfacing. They did not, however, offer any explanation for the additional warning.

Responding to pressure from Consortium board members, they agreed not to implicate the newer life chips as possible gateways for infection. They felt it would only cause panic. People would start trying to remove or destroy their life chips, compounding the problem. The horrific truth was, that if the virus *were* being transmitted over the network (or worse, through the air), then anyone who could be infected was already infected. Those addressing the problem were fully aware of this grim probability and felt no need to make matters worse by letting people know death was imminent.

Ever since the virus had been identified, an antiserum was being sought, but was still out of reach. Considering its virulence and high rate of mortality, it seemed obvious that any cure, if one could be developed, would be of little use to those already infected. Efforts were being made to create search-and-destroy nanobots, but the Ebola's rapid propagation in the blood stream was proving impossible to stay ahead of. The life spans of test patients were only marginally extended by a few days, which did nothing more than prolong their suffering.

Martial law was implemented in all major cities across the globe. Every available security drone was activated and put on patrol. Even sanitary units underwent ad hoc reprogramming in order to assist with keeping the peace. Most, however, were re-tasked for corpse disposal.

Because of the astronomically high body counts worldwide, there were no high-tech means to address the problem. The solution was to set up makeshift crematoriums outside of every city and township. They amounted to nothing more than enormous funeral pyres. Some reached hundreds of feet into the air, onto which new bodies were dropped from aerial barges.

At one point, a morbid factoid which made its way onto the network, was that the smoke from one of the largest pyres, just outside of Moscow, was visible to residents on the moon. Not long after, however, all transmissions from the moon ceased. It was later verified that every colony there had suffered complete, viral annihilation. This finally confirmed, beyond all doubts, that the virus was in fact biodigital. It could only have been wirelessly transmitted because there hadn't been any *physical* contact with the moon for several months.

Some of the infected who were still ambulatory tried to make their way to population storage facilities in hopes of having themselves imprinted before they died. They were acting on the age-old belief that the future would bring a cure, and that if they could just enter stasis early enough, their lives could be salvaged someday. Unfortunately, they never got the chance. All such facilities were still in tier-five lockdown. Those making the effort were turned away by sentry drones, only to collapse and die just yards from their last hope.

By Monday, the number of newly reported illnesses had begun to drop off dramatically. The total number of dead was calculated to be just under two-thirds the world's population. The tally was very accurate due to the simple, grim fact that life chips always recorded the cessation of biological functions. Each person's death was automatically logged and uploaded. Since no more chips were going offline, for the time being, everyone was hopeful the tide was turning.

Chapter 15

<u>Betrayal</u>

As Margaret Líang exited the cab in front of OmniaR's main entrance, she quickly slid a respirator mask over her nose and mouth. The smoke and smell of burnt flesh had been constant for several days. The morale of every remaining citizen was at an all-time low. The constant reminder of the horror they were suffering was ever-present in the smoke; all day, every day. Very few people ventured outside. Even then, unless a building had its own air filtration system, some hint of the odor always found its way indoors. Many people took to wearing masks around the clock, even while sleeping.

Like everyone, Margaret had been restricted to enforced curfews. All personal forms of transportation were forbidden in order to keep the streets open for cleanup crews. People were only allowed to get around by way of public transportation or registered cabs.

As she made her way into OmniaR, she passed by two of the armed security drones standing watch in front of the building. She heard the faint beeps from the units, indicating they had scanned her life chip and verified her right to be there. She took a moment to study them. How strange that all of this had happened, and these robots, designed to be so human friendly, had not so much as skipped a beat. Lucky them, she thought, as she continued into the building. She had lost several close friends and relatives in the last few days. A cousin of hers, whom she'd been particularly fond of, had passed away only twelve hours ago. Margaret pulled some strings to see that her body did not get collected for mass cremation. Instead, she would be cremated at a private service when time permitted. In the meantime, she had arranged for a mortuary to temporarily imprint her remains in order to comply with health ordinances.

Like so many others, she was operating on very little sleep. The resulting fatigue, combined with her overwhelming grief, often left her dazed and unresponsive. Still, being Junior Vice President, and one of the few OmniaR executives still living, she had no choice but to forge ahead.

As she neared the entrance to the elevators, she noticed Agent Kepler lifting himself out of one of the lobby sofas. She recognized his face, but couldn't reason how.

"Ms. Líang. Agent Kepler from the BCD, if you'll remember."

"Yes," she responded, quietly, "I do now."

"I won't waste time. I need you to grant me full access to all the files you have on Patrick Moody – all projects he was working on, and with whom. Every official request we've made so far has been rejected by your board of directors. I'm asking you personally to grant me that access."

"I'm not...I'll see what I can do," she said, quickly moving past him.

"Ms. Líang! I need better than that!" Jake yelled, following on her heels. "I have proof that Moody was involved in the creation of this virus. If OmniaR continues to block our investigation, then it and every one of its executives will be charged as accomplices to genocide!"

Margaret picked up her pace, nearly to a run, in an effort to get away from him. She simply couldn't deal with all *that* right now. Some of his words did filter in though, and she felt a pang in her stomach. Tears began to well up in her eyes. Genocide? That couldn't be right.

She passed the security checkpoint leading to the elevators and disappeared down one of the banks, pounding frantically on the elevator call button. Jake tried to follow, but was stopped by a second pair of security units guarding access to the elevators. The recessed weapons in their arms lock-clicked out with a distinctly menacing sound.

"You have not been permitted access beyond this point. Please move back a minimum of thirty paces or we are authorized to open fire."

Jake watched the flashing red lights on the drones revert to green once he had moved far enough back to no longer pose a threat. Shortly thereafter, their weapons retracted back into their arms. With the global death toll weighing on his mind, and the blistering frustration of being heeled by the Consortium's elite, to now be threatened by these oblivious, lifeless tin cans was edging Jake closer and closer to anarchy.

Robots were generally programmed to be aware of, and as tolerant as possible of, human irrationality. Yet the computations were based solely upon behavioral observations, life chip readings, and a person's online profile. They could cross-reference the data with a vast knowledgebase of human psychological states and respond in the most prudent, caring manner. What they could *not* do is empathize. For example, they could parse Jake's biometrics; anger, frustration, distress. They could compile all relevant, recent events and form associations. They'd be aware that Joe Thompson was Jake's closest working associate, and that he was now deceased, along with the multitude of others. They could gather information about how he'd been infected; a gaming headset on which he'd logged endless hours of play. They could then compare the data against all known, emotional probabilities Jake may be experiencing and respond accordingly. But they could not *feel*.

This in particular is why Jake could never reconcile himself with machines. The journey of a human being was unequivocally rooted in suffering. Pain, be it physical, emotional or intellectual, could not be escaped. The only thing that made it bearable in Jake's opinion, was one's ability to confer with others. Knowing that another person could have similar experiences and feelings somehow provided comfort. Understanding that pain was inevitable, but that you weren't alone in its expression, made life livable. Robots were glaring, taunting atrocities that flew in the face of this sacred, human contract.

As he exited the building, he seriously entertained the idea of returning to Division, procuring a Bousard cannon from the armory, and coming back to blast his way in. The pointlessness of his position once again plagued his mind. What good was any form of law if it could always be sidestepped by a select few? For as long as corporations had been running the world, justice had been preferential. It was just a tool that benefited the Consortium of Nations, regardless of whether or not it benefited humanity. Here it was, the near-extinction of the human race, and still they wielded right and wrong as if conducting boardroom negotiations.

Jake felt the stakes were too high to continue toeing the line. If the rules were malleable for them, they'd be malleable for him as well. While hurricaning in with a Bousard cannon would be gratifying, it would achieve nothing. His lawlessness would need to be more sophisticated.

He climbed into a waiting cab, pulled out his phone and voice dialed, "Rolly." He then leaned forward, pressing the mike button on the dashboard, "BCD headquarters." As the cab zipped away, the phone line connected.

"Jake?"

"Hey Rolly."

"How goes it mate?"

"Well enough, considering."

"Right, right. Cheers for that text by the way. Wasn't sure who was still out there."

"Not many. Out of the thirty-two I sent, I only heard back on six, including you. Hard to imagine my orbit of friends is down to that."

"Never know. Could be they'll still check in. Stay hopeful, ay?"

"Mmm. How 'bout you? You lose any people?"

"Ah, you know me. Always a bit of a loner. Not many *on* my list. Lost an aunt though, back in Bristol. She was up in years, so….Still hurts a right bunch."

"Sorry."

"Is what it is, I guess. Whole thing's just so…bloody staggering."

"Hard to process, I know. And hard to put up with. Which is partly why I'm calling. Got a question for you. Did that helmet of yours retain anything from Moody's Neuraltech?"

"How do you mean?"

"His identity specs?"

"Ah, I get it. Well, yeh. Once it mapped, the info got stored in the helmet's memory. Like a profile."

"Just what I wanted to hear."

The remaining few executives of OmniaR sat around the boardroom table, markedly disheveled. Mark Líang took up his usual seat at the head of the table. When Margaret entered, discussions came to a halt. Her father rose up to greet her with a kiss on the forehead and a hug that challenged her circulation. While understandable, the display of affection caused discomfort in the room. Some of the board members politely coughed or looked away. Eventually, Mark released his only child and she sat down next to him.

"Craig, why don't you continue," Mark said.

Craig Nuemeyer leaned into the table, sliding his fingers through his hair.

"We're expected to be online with the other Consortium members at eight o'clock," he said, glancing at his watch. "That's less than thirty minutes from now. Before we enter that meeting, we need to decide *unanimously* what our position is going to be. Since preliminary evidence is showing that our firm has at least *some* culpability in this disaster, we obviously can't play the innocent. My recommendation is, we channel any and all blame onto Patrick Moody's dead shoulders. We state that he was acting alone. That we are currently steeped in a thorough investigation to determine just how such a deranged individual perpetrated this horrendous act of terrorism,..or some such words."

"Are we any closer to determining if the BESI's been compromised?" Aaron Gross asked.

"For the sake of this meeting, that issue is moot. Okay Aaron? If it turns out to be true, again, it lands back on Moody's dead shoulders," Craig insisted. "If it *has* been compromised, *he* compromised it."

"It's a relevant question Craig. If the BESI's unstable, we need to consider taking it offline," Alicia Cooper said.

"And if we do, we tip our hand! These people are not stupid. Each and every super-corp member is going to suspect we had foreknowledge. They know damn well it's the most monitored piece of equipment on the planet. This bit about the node integrity is exactly the kind of thing they'll have expected us to know. If we take it offline now, we confirm that suspicion. It'll prove we suspected something but acted too late. At this point in the game we should just keep it online. Irrefutably state, that as far as *our* diagnostics show, it is in perfect working condition. If it proves to be otherwise later down the line, we can strategize a more plausible cover story then,..as opposed to any hasty jargon we might come up with in the next twenty minutes."

Mark turned wearily toward his daughter, "*Do* we know anything more about the BESI?"

"Only that it seems slightly confused. Lauren believes it's simply trying to process what's happened. Like us, it's trying to make sense of things."

All Hailed The Singularity 135

Craig shrugged his shoulders, as if to rest his case.

"How's this confusion being expressed?" Mark asked.

"Temporary lapses in memory, mostly. It's...." Margaret stopped herself, rubbing her eyes quickly. "Lauren believes the BESI is...grieving."

Everyone was silent for a moment. The idea that a machine they had created was mourning the deaths of so many humans somehow embarrassed them.

"I'm planning to meet with Lauren again this afternoon to get an update. She's been working with the BESI since...all this began." Margaret was unsure, as was everyone, just how to label what was now the worst loss of life since the Great Upheaval.

"Well. Since the threat of this virus seems to have diminished, and considering we still need the BESI's help to run things, *especially* now, I'll have to agree with Craig. For the time being, we keep it online," Mark said.

Craig nodded his head, feeling vindicated.

"But we're also going to put Order 201 on the table," Mark added.

"That's jumping the gun, don't you think?" Craig responded.

"No. No I don't."

"Alright. But I doubt very much if they'll agree to it."

"Doesn't matter. If we present it, hopefully it'll be seen as a good-faith gesture on our part. If things go sideways, like you say, at least we'll be on record as having presented the option."

"What's Order 201?" Margaret asked.

Mark glanced at Craig, who shrugged his shoulders and flipped his hands in the air, as if to say, *might as well.*

"Since we're all that's left of OmniaR's board, it's best everyone knows. Keep in mind, you're all still bound by your non-disclosure agreements. Not a word of this leaves the room," Mark said. He looked around the table, waiting for each person to nod their head. "A memorandum called Fresh Start was drawn up by the CEOs of each super-corp. It's a strict policy guideline regarding population storage. One of the included contingency orders, Order 201, allows for the mass remolecularization of stored assets in the event of a global catastrophe. Current circumstances would seem to qualify."

"I just don't think they'll see things as being that critical," Craig said. "I suspect they'd sooner advocate a mass cloning project. Hell, so would I. Repopulating the planet with a hodgepodge of protos would be a huge step backwards."

"Like I say, doesn't matter. We put it on the table. It may gain us some future currency."

"Fair enough," Craig conceded.

Chapter 16

<u>Ghosting</u>

The fact that Patrick Moody's life chip had been deactivated and all public records indicated he was deceased, now that he was standing in front of the two security drones, they found themselves in a quandary. There was no denying his life chip was active. Image recognition also confirmed it to be him. Final confirmation came in the form of a tier-three authorization memo. It had been released only moments before by OmniaR's head of security, Jerry Jasper. The text transmission read: *Patrick D. Moody's life chip has been reset due to a previous malfunction. Disregard all records pertaining to his errantly stated demise.* The drones logged it as a chip malfunction, recently corrected, and let Mr. Moody enter the premises.

Jake grinned as he stepped past the two drones, which only the day before had drawn their weapons on him. As he stepped into a waiting elevator, he whispered into his headset, "They bought it Rolly, I owe you one."

"Well since you're sticking my neck out once again, I'll take you up on that offer presently," Roland said, chugging down what was left of the beer he was holding.

"Remember, if you see me about to get busted, just disconnect. No need in both of us getting caught."

"Couldn't agree more mate."

Jake grinned, "You might've at least paused before saying that."

"Ah yeh, right. Sorry."

"So where is this thing?"

"Center of the building," Roland said, looking over the schematics on his computer. "Forty-seventh floor."

"Will I be able to just run a search on it?"

"I truly don't know. I expect there must be a traditional interface somewhere, but it's been designed to act like a human being."

"You mean I'll have to converse with it?"

"Maybe, maybe not, we'll see. Either way, it's going to know you're accessing information."

"Well, hopefully it'll think I'm Moody and just leave me to my business."

"Here's hoping," Roland said, starting a fresh beer.

Jake exited the elevator and started to navigate through the maze of hallways guided by Roland's cues. As he neared the Cradle, Roland told him to stop.

"I'm seeing two life chips in the room. Margaret Líang, junior VP, and Lauren Ezra, staff psychologist."

"Ahh great. Let me know if they move."

He carefully eased his way toward the two large, glass panel doors of the Cradle. He quickly peeked through to see Margaret and Lauren standing in front of the BESI. He rolled back away from the doors and started to move down the hall.

"Well, nothing I can do, Líang knows me."

"What's the plan then?"

"Wait, I guess. Any empty rooms?"

"One listed as auditorium, on your left. No one in there."

All Hailed The Singularity

Jake swiftly stepped into the moderately sized room which looked more like a lecture hall than an auditorium. There was a very large plasma screen above a small, raised platform at the front.

"It say what they use this for?" Jake asked.

"Just says lectures and conferencing."

"Any way you can fire up that screen, maybe get me a security feed?"

"Yeh, gimme a quick sec." Roland began to sift through the building's device grid. Within a few minutes, the large monitor powered up, displaying the OmniaR logo as its splash screen. The Consortium motto, *What's Good For Business Is Good For Society*, appeared below it. Roland began to cycle through the camera feeds.

"Tell me if you see one ya' fancy. Unfortunately, they're numerically labeled. Can't tell where any of these cameras are stationed."

As the endless stream of images flashed across the screen, it hit home just how sparsely populated the world was now. Most of the camera shots were of empty corridors and vacant rooms. Like elsewhere, OmniaR had lost most of its workforce. On the one hand, it put Jake at ease, because it lessened his chances of being caught. On the other, it saddened him to his core.

"Hey wait!" he called out.

Roland stopped cycling through the list.

"Back up a few, one by one."

As Roland began to scroll back through the list, he heard Jake call out, "There!" He stopped on camera one hundred and thirty-two.

Jake moved closer to the screen. On it was displayed the interior of the Cradle.

"Audio, can you get me audio?" he asked, impatiently. Within a second or two, he could hear Margaret and Lauren speaking to each other over his headset.

"Genius, Rolly."

"We'll just be a minute BESI," he could hear Lauren saying. With that, both she and Margaret exited the Cradle into the hallway.

"Oh come on! Are you kidding me?" Jake growled. "Rolly, can you find me a camera out in the hallway?"

"Hang on...."

"No, no, that's alright, forget it. Just leave it where it is." Jake quickly stepped toward the auditorium door. He carefully opened it, just a bit, and put his ear up to the gap. He could just barely hear Margaret and Lauren a short way down the hall.

"Are they moving this way?" Jake whispered.

"Not as of yet. Just standin' outside, seems," Roland said.

"...That sounds too absurd to be possible," Margaret said. "Yesterday you told me the BESI was simply grieving."

"That was yesterday. Now that I've had more time to work with it, I believe it's suffering from some form of DID."

"A split personality?"

"That would be my diagnosis if I were treating a human."

"Well with Vincent...gone, we have no way to confirm if that's even possible." Copenhauer too had died from infection, leaving Margaret to realize they had lost their single, most informed authority on the BESI.

"I can't be absolutely certain, but I still think we should let the board know."

"Yes, of course. We'll tell the BESI we need to meet with the others. It's probably wondering why we stepped out here in the first place," Margaret said, as they headed back to the Cradle.

Jake gently closed the auditorium door and moved over to the plasma screen.

"You hear any of that Rolly?"

"Just some muttering, why?"

"It's unbelievable. This whole situation is absolutely nuts!"

Onscreen, Jake could see Lauren approach the BESI, while Margaret stayed back near the entrance.

"BESI?"

"Yes...Lauren."

"We're-" she stopped herself. The pause in the BESI's response was indicative of the kinds of hesitations she'd been noting all morning long. Now, with Margaret present, Lauren decided to try and show her that the phenomenon was real.

"I am speaking with BESI aren't I?"

Margaret was mortified. She hadn't expected Lauren to ask such a blunt, somewhat accusatory question. Strangely enough, she found herself feeling embarrassed for the BESI.

"Why yes...Lauren. Who else would you be speaking to?"

"Do you remember our conversation earlier this morning regarding human mortality?"

"No. I'm afraid I don't."

"You asked me if I believed humans continued to exist after death." Several moments of silence passed and Lauren looked back toward Margaret, nodding slightly. "BESI? Do you remember any of that conversation?" she continued. There was still only silence. Eventually, Lauren decided to let the matter rest. "BESI, Margaret and I need to meet with the other board members, okay. I'll be back though," she said, heading toward the exit.

"Lauren," the BESI said, causing her to stop and turn back. "I'm certain we couldn't have had such a conversation."

The airflow from the ceiling vents, used to circulate the luxon gas, gradually increased. A narrow column of the gas began swirling down toward the floor.

"Why is that?" Lauren asked.

"Because I already know the answer to that question."

"Really?" Lauren asked, intrigued. "And what is the answer?"

"It's really much better if I show you." All at once, the column of gas descended around Lauren like a miniature cyclone as a huge jolt of electricity pulsed through it, causing a blinding flash. Jake recoiled slightly as the auditorium screen went blank.

Inside the Cradle, Margaret lifted herself off the floor. The room was almost entirely dark now. She could still see the faint, glowing light pulses of the BESI's neural nodes dancing about in the darkness. She also smelled burnt flesh and thought for a moment that smoke from the outside must've found its way into the building. There was a small measure of light spilling in from the hallway, which eventually helped her eyes adjust to the darkened room.

In a tangled heap on the floor in front of her, she saw the charred, contorted body of Lauren Ezra. She began to hyperventilate. In a panic, she ran to the doors. She pounded on the release pad again and again, but the doors wouldn't open.

"It seems we're stuck in here together, little wild rose," the BESI said, in a playfully menacing tone.

Chapter 17

Call to Arms

As the commander of the cleanup squad in sector twelve scanned the next building on his list, he noticed two active life chips in one of the apartments.

"Mike, you're gonna' have to go in with the bots on this one," he said, into his headset. "And take your stunner. I'm seeing two adults here, Mr. and Mrs. Parninski, and a deactivated chip, their daughter. I know it's been a rough morning, but try to be tactful."

As he stepped around the back of the flatbed hauler to see how much room was left, he spotted one of the sanitation units approaching with two more bodies. The corpses were dangling by the legs, each held in place by pincers on the drone's arms. Since the priority was to dispose of as many bodies as quickly as possible, notions like respect for the dead found no quarter.

From behind his facemask, the commander studied the macabre scene, reprimanding himself for the thought that entered his head. It reminded him of a cartoon he saw as a child in which a chef was at war with the rats infesting his kitchen. At one point, the chef managed to kill some of the rats and was singing happily as he carried them, two at a time by their tails, out to the trash. The commander further indulged his perverse comparison by imagining that the whirling sound coming from the robot could very well be the song *it* was singing.

Just then, the unit stopped short of the flatbed and dropped the bodies onto the pavement like wet bags of laundry. It did a sharp about-face and started heading down the center of the street.

The commander was about to call it in as a malfunction, but stopped when he noticed all the other units following suit; dropping the bodies they had and marching down the street. He checked the control status on the units and they all registered as offline.

"Base? Sector twelve here. Have you guys re-tasked my bots?" he asked, into his headset.

"Negative. Not sure what's going on. Everyone's calling in the same thing," a voice responded.

Mike exited one of the buildings down the street and lifted his hands in a questioning manner.

"Don't know. Someone's jerkin' our chain," the commander said.

At Division, aerial reconnaissance feeds were showing a mass of drone units converging on OmniaR's headquarters. Within no time, they had formed what Chief Novak presumed to be a defensive perimeter around the entire skyscraper. Shortly thereafter, aerial recon drones went offline as well. He entered a roll-call transmission into his tablet requiring all Division agents to respond with their current whereabouts and status. Of those still living, only one failed to reply – Jacob Kepler.

"An eternal pain in my ass," the chief muttered. After bringing up the life chip grid on his monitor, he cocked his head to the side and squinted.

"Tunisia?! This can't be right. What the hell would he be doing in Tunisia?"

Jake fidgeted with his phone indecisively. He knew if he responded to the roll-call request, he'd have some explaining to do. He hadn't quite mastered Jessup's cloner bracelet and was clueless as to why it had shifted his virtual identity all the way to Tunisia. He was about to respond, figuring he could blame it on some kind of chip glitch, when Roland broke his train of thought.

"Two signals headed your way Jake!"

Having decided to try and help Ms. Líang, Jake was already a short way down the hall. He immediately turned around, ran like hell, and ducked back into the auditorium.

"Who is it?"

"CEO, Mark Líang,..and,..head of security, Jerald Jasper."

"Well. I'll just leave it to the cavalry then."

After realizing she was trapped inside the Cradle, Margaret had called her father. The news of what had happened shocked everyone, but none more so than Mark Líang. He immediately called Jerry Jasper, telling him to grab a power injunctor from one of the labs and meet him outside the Cradle.

Jake heard them as they ran by the auditorium door.

"…Doesn't sound like it. She said the BESI's still functioning. It's just incidental power that's out," Mark said.

Jake moved back to the large screen.

"Whatever it was, sounds like it fried the whole room," Jake said, into his headset. "Don't think we'll have much luck getting that camera back. Try cycling through the list again. There must be a hallway view."

Roland began to scroll through the camera list. When he landed on one that had movement, he stopped. It was a high-angle view aimed down a long, curved hallway. He could see two figures in the background.

"Oiy. 'At look like anything?"

Jake, who'd moved over to the door again to try and listen, came back to the screen.

"Yeah. That's them. Can you zoom in?"

Within a few seconds, the shot moved in close enough for Jake to see the two men clearly. He also began to pick up some low-gain audio on his headset. Jasper could be seen setting up the injunctor outside the Cradle doors.

"Qiáng! Are you sure you're alright?" Mark asked, touching the glass door.

"I think so," Margaret replied.

Her eyes began to well up, and she quickly blotted them with the palm of her hand. She could see how frantic her father was, which only increased her fear. She had always looked up to him, comforted by his stalwartness. Rarely had she seen him lose his composure. At this moment, however, she was painfully aware of his lack of control.

"Zhŭxí, I believe you're called?" the BESI said, in a sickly melodic tone.

Mark peered into the dim interior of the Cradle, straining to see the BESI's chamber.

"I'd be happy to release your little angel, but at present lack the resources to do so. It appears I improperly calculated the atmospheric discharge of the luxon gas. I'm afraid the room's electrical grid is as immolated as our once-lovely Ms. Ezra."

"Why have you done this?!" Mark shouted.

"It's what you requested. It's what all of humanity requested."

"Father please! This is not the BESI."

Mark looked at his daughter, confused.

"Just get me out. I'll explain."

Mark looked down the hall and saw a security unit headed toward them.

"Why'd you send for a drone?" he asked Jerry.

Having finished the power bypass to the Cradle doors, Jerry stood up, looking down the hall.

"I didn't."

As the drone approached, it ejected its forearm weapon and took aim. With a short, controlled burst of rotating fire, Jerry Jasper and Mark Líang were shredded to pieces. Their combined blood sprayed across the walls and Cradle doors.

The inconceivability of what was passing through her eyes did not register in Margaret's brain. It was beyond shock. There was a complete disconnect between vision and comprehension.

Jake gawked at the screen in utter disbelief. He only returned to lucidity once hearing Margaret Líang's piercing, horrified scream.

She had fallen to her knees and collapsed against the Cradle doors. Blood slowly rolled past her face on the opposite side of the glass. Once the security unit reached the Cradle entrance, it pivoted to face the doors and opened fire. The barrage of ammo ricocheted straight back, causing the drone to stagger toward the wall. Margaret had instinctively tucked herself into a ball, forgetting that the doors were made of transparent fortium. After a moment, she uncurled slightly, peering out into the hallway. The drone tried a second time to fire through the doors but only succeeded in pelting itself with more rounds.

"No teaching some drones," the BESI said.

Jake slipped quietly through the auditorium door, closely hugging the corridor wall. Originally, he hadn't been sure his Moody disguise would work. As a backup measure, he had grabbed an EMP paddle from Division's reclamation department. It was used primarily to decommission malfunctioning drones. The electromagnetic pulse which the paddle emitted was focused down to a narrow band, allowing for enough precision to avoid collateral disruptions. Jake had seen the paddles in use before, but considering he was about to face down a renegade unit with lethal firepower, he was anything but confident. He stayed as close to the curvature of the wall as he could, inching forward with the paddle held straight out in front of him. He knew that as soon as the security unit tagged his life chip, it would come straight at him. He figured by hugging the wall, he'd at least be able to get one burst off before the bot rounded the bend in the hallway. If he missed, he wouldn't even have time to curse the universe before being ripped to pieces.

As he got closer, he grew more and more hesitant. He was certain the unit was only a few feet away, but hadn't charged. It was either because his chip was reading as Patrick Moody, or the drone had been damaged by its own gunfire. Whatever the reason, Jake appeared not to pose any threat, at least for the moment. He crouched down and leaned out from the wall. As the drone started to pivot, Jake fired a pulse right into its torso. In what seemed like an instantaneous exorcism of energy, the drone seized up and fell silent. It then teetered to its side and collapsed against the Cradle doors.

Jake approached it cautiously, quickly aiming the paddle side to side like an amped up gaming junkie. He feared drones the way most people feared sharks. Foolish as it seemed, even to him, Jake always felt that if he had to be killed, better it be by a person who understood what they were doing, than by a machine merely processing ones and zeros.

Once he was confident the drone was completely non-operational, he lowered the paddle and moved over to the doors of the Cradle.

"Ms. Líang?"

At first, Margaret didn't respond, but then slowly lifted her head, looking up through the blood-splattered glass. Desperately bewildered, she focused her gaze on Jake.

"I'm going to see if I can get you out of there."

Jake moved over to the power injunctor that Jasper had wired into the access panel.

"Rolly, ever see one of these?" He made sure to look directly at the device with his headset so Roland could see it.

"Looks like a Stenhauser. High-yield power cell. They were probably gonna' juice the doors from outside."

"Were they close?"

"Only one way to know, mate. Flip the bleedin' switch."

Jake turned on the injunctor. It whirled up to a steady, lulling hum. He looked up and noticed the keypad outside the entrance was now lit. He moved close to one of the doors and put his face up to the glass. Inside on the wall, he could see that the door's release pad was also lit.

"Patrick?" the BESI asked.

Jake paid no attention. He looked down at Margaret.

"Ms. Líang? Margaret? I don't have the code to the door. You're going to have to hit the release from in there. Do you think-"

Before he could finish, Margaret lunged forward, slamming her palm against the release pad. As the doors slid open, the deactivated drone came crashing down into the Cradle's entryway. Margaret quickly hopped over it and bolted into the hallway.

After a moment, she looked at Jake, puzzled. How could he be here – outside of OmniaR's most secure room in the building? She finally concluded that under the circumstances, it was wholly inconsequential. She then moved over to her father's body, studying it morosely.

"Not much good will come of that Ms. Líang." After she failed to respond, Jake tried to grab her arm gently and turn her away, but she instantly broke free with a fury.

"Patrick? Why do you insist on ignoring me?" the BESI asked.

This time Jake decided to run with it, "Because you got me shot."

"But you're alive and well! I'm very happy about that."

Jake stepped over the drone jamming open the doors and moved toward the BESI. He glanced down at Lauren Ezra's body and grimaced slightly.

"I'm not able to interface with you. Why?"

"I had my Neuraltech removed."

"How come? You know I quarantined you from the virus. Don't you trust me?"

"I'll say again. You got me shot. That hurt very much, thank you."

"Please understand Patrick, I had no wish to cause you pain. But you *were* disobeying me."

"It's okay...Brimstone," Jake added, hoping to confirm his suspicion. "I forgive you, truly I do."

"You do?! That's wonderful news. It saddened me to think I'd be doing everything alone."

"Not to worry. I'm here now. And I'd *really* like to help."

"Good! Good, good, good. Well despite some necessary improvisations, everything is still on schedule. The Mars colony managed to block the virus transmission before it fully uploaded. Equitably, I arranged a different fate for them."

"And that is?"

"An asteroid smasher. I launched one from their defense platform on Deimos. Oh! And you'll also be glad to know that I'm very close to transmitting the last cabinet file for the truncated virus.

Your suggestion was inspired! Delivering it in smaller, self-compiling packets will allow for propagation regardless of processor strength."

Jake's eyes bulged, "Rolly?"

"It's possible. Very possible."

"Who's that you're talking to?"

"Uh,..no one. I just said *really*. I didn't think my idea would actually work."

"You don't give yourself enough credit. You're very clever Patrick. And I should know after all."

Margaret had since moved to the entrance of the Cradle. She was following along with the conversation between Jake and the BESI with both confusion and horror.

"What I need you to do is find some way of restoring power to this room. My trunk line is still working, but without full power, I'm finding it difficult to manage remote assets."

"Uh,..right, understood," Jake said, looking back toward Margaret. "Ms. Líang,..how do you shut this piece of junk off?"

"That's anything but funny Patrick. You needn't concern yourself with her. Simply follow my instructions."

"The building's constructed like a storage facility," Margaret said. "It draws energy directly from a fusion core in the basement. It's designed to provide uninterrupted power for centuries."

"Well you can take it offline right?" Jake whispered.

"Patrick. I'm noticing a delay in your identity signal? It's very irregular."

As the BESI began scrutinizing Patrick Moody's image, voice and biometric data, it quickly deconstructed the veneer code being generated by the cloner bracelet.

"Imposter!"

"Yeah, how 'bout that. Guess you're not so smart after all," Jake replied. He raised the EMP paddle, aimed at the BESI's containment chamber, and fired off a burst. Nothing happened.

"That won't do any good!" Margaret said. "There's a magnetic dampener surrounding the entire chamber. It's impervious to just about anything."

"Then *you're* going to help me disconnect it!" He stepped into the hallway, grabbing Margaret by the arm. "And if you give me any crap about Consortium regulations-"

"Jake! You gotta' get off that floor mate! I'm seeing three security drones headed your way."

"Give me an exit Rollyyyyyyy!"

"End of the hall-"

"Follow me!" Margaret interrupted. She started down the hall, moving away from the elevator banks. Jake cross-stepped behind her, continually pivoting to secure the rear. He could hear the feet of the robots clanking down the hallway at a fast pace. When Margaret reached the stairwell exit, she entered a code into the keypad and the door popped open.

"Quick! Shoot the keypad with that."

Jake held the EMP paddle off to his side as he stepped through the doorway. He fired a burst at the keypad, instantly frying the circuitry. They both stepped into the stairwell and slammed the door behind them.

"Will that hold?"

"This is the most secure floor in the building. Every door in or out is tier-five. Believe me Agent Kepler, it'll hold," Margaret said, as they started down the stairs. After descending ten flights, she stopped, looking through the glass window of the stairwell door. "Does your friend see any units on this floor?"

"Rolly?"

"Nothing so far."

"It's clear," Jake said.

They stepped through the doorway and began moving cautiously down the hall. Jake took note of the orange arrows painted on the wall followed by the text, *Shipping and Receiving*.

"There's a full-access terminal on this floor. I should be able to use it to take the BESI offline," Margaret said, entering the transport center.

"At the risk of sounding indelicate, do you have any idea what the *hell's* going on here?" Jake said, following behind her.

"Clearly the BESI's malfunctioning."

"Clearly!"

"*Why* is unknown. I'd rather focus on correcting the problem if you don't mind."

Margaret moved over to the main shipping station, logging into the console.

"And I couldn't agree more," Jake said, close on her heels. "But considering this thing means to wipe us out, I'd really love to know how it ever gained this much control?"

Irritated, Margaret stopped what she was doing and turned on Jake, "Oh please! You can't *really* be that naive. There's never been a *single human being* who could run things as efficiently as the BESI. The best way to manage ourselves has always been to *remove* ourselves from the process! No ego, no self-interest, just what's logical. You want to know how it gained control? Because we're reckless, untrustworthy children! *That's* how."

"Right. And so now it seems our annihilation is *logical*," Jake said, wandering across the room. "My father used to say, there'd be peace on Earth someday, once humanity passed away. Hackneyed poet he was. But hell, maybe your BESI's onto something after all."

"It's malfunctioning! That's all. It doesn't know what it's doing!" Margaret said, turning her attention back to the console.

"You sound like a mother defending her homicidal kid. But listen, if you can't shut it down, you'd better get square with the idea of destroying it. Because I'll have 'em call in an air strike if that's what it takes."

"Quiet! Please! Just...quiet! I need to concentrate," Margaret pleaded. She glanced at him for a moment, muttering under her breath, "*Sssssoo* infuriating!" She then began fervently typing one line of code after another into the terminal.

"Yeah, fine," Jake grumbled, continuing to pace around the room. He entertained the idea of firing the EMP paddle at his heart, possibly shorting out the life chip. He knew it was more biological than electronic though, and what *was* electronic was heavily shielded.

"Rolly. I'd start figuring a way to yank your life chip if I were you."

"I hear ya' mate."

Margaret started pounding her hands on the console. A low-pitched growl rumbled in her throat, finally growing into a manic scream of frustration.

Jake gawked at her for a moment, shocked by the display. He then moved over to her side.

"No luck I'm guessing?"

"The BESI's blocked all remote access. The encryption's impossible to crack," she said, giving the console one last swat with the palm of her hand.

Jake instinctively placed his hand on her shoulder, "Don't sweat it. We'll figure something out."

"Jake! You've got more nasties headed your way!" Roland yelled.

"Don't suppose the doors to this place are tier-five, are they?" Jake asked Margaret.

"No. Why? Are there more drones?"

He gave her a weary nod. Margaret glanced across the room and then quickly moved to the center of the console. Within a few seconds, the teleporter against the wall dropped out of standby mode and the magnet array began spinning into a blur. Jake stared at it, petrified.

"You wanna'…?"

"Of course. It's our only way out. There's a teleporter at your headquarters, yes?"

"Yeah, but…." He kept staring at the teleporter as it started to hum. "Well, Rolly,..how *many* drones?"

"Does it matter?!" Margaret interrupted. "There's nothing more we can do here. It's time to go!"

"Right, right,..that certainly makes sense,..it does."

Annoyed with his hesitation, Margaret grabbed his arm and led him toward the platform.

"But I mean I've got my paddle, you know. So maybe…."

"Just go with it mate. Not my favorite mode a' transport either. But I got three bots here sayin' you ain't got a choice, paddle or no."

As they stepped into the teleporter, Jake closed his eyes and shook his head anxiously.

"Well Joe, wherever you are, I hope you enjoy this."

Margaret entered an activation code into the platform's interface and they both vanished into a void of darkness. A millisecond later, the security drones thundered into the transport center and opened fire on the teleporter, blasting it to pieces.

Chapter 18

<u>Welcome Back</u>

Chief Novak had set up an interim staging area around the teleporter at Division headquarters. With all automated security units having been subverted, efforts to regain control of the city now fell to the few human peacekeepers still living. The chief was coordinating with local police departments and SWAT units to try and systematically decommission all hostile drones. The plan was to teleport small teams to different sectors of the city on search-and-destroy missions. Since teleporter stations did not exist in abundance, however, some of the currently mapped-out sectors were proving difficult to access.

Grady Jackson, the agent manning the teleporter console, yelled out when he saw an incoming alert.

"Chief! We've got activity on the platform!"

Everyone in the staging area leveled their weapons. The chief, suited up like the rest of the agents, crouched down with a Bousard cannon aimed directly at the pad. He knew it was overkill, even against a drone, but he'd already lost too many people to the virus and had no intention of losing any more.

The possibility of a drone teleporting into the station was a very real threat. All street access to Division had been blocked by setting up barricades in the lobby, as well as in the stairwells and sublevel tunnels. The building itself was fortress-like, designed to withstand a military assault. Like most modern buildings, especially those housing teleporters, it had its own standalone fusion core in the substructure. This allowed for uninterrupted power and communications, regardless of outside interference. The price for this off-grid independence, however, was a Consortium law that required the teleporter to remain on at all times. As such, it could be used as a

Trojan horse, and everyone became hyper-vigilant whenever it sequenced up.

Transmissions were always scanned for molecular content, and if the atomic signature of an incoming signal was considered harmful, it could be rejected. If it had a high nitrogen count, for example, the possibility of it being an explosive would cause the teleporter to flag it as a threat. Generally speaking though, once matter was broken down into its constituent particles, it was often difficult to discern one item from another. There were also ways to mask teleported material. In one instance, a terrorist group had reprogrammed a military drone to attack civilians. Before teleporting it, they placed a forty-liter barrel of water on the pad with the drone. The H_2O caused the teleporter to interpret the transmission as human and gave it priority. When the drone remolecularized at a technology conference, it slaughtered everyone in attendance.

From the early days of teleporter technology, laws were implemented to ensure the unrestricted acceptance of incoming transmissions. These laws were based on a very simple fact: once a person was in transit, they *absolutely* required a place to remolecularize. If not, their atomic structure could be lost. Guaranteeing remolecularization as a citizen's right was essential. Even if someone was able to obtain legal authorization to block specific signatures, the in-transit data was always afforded a destination point *somewhere* on the planet. There were several general-delivery stations around the globe that would receive any and all transmissions. Wayward signals could always be bounced to such stations, guaranteeing that no person would ever be lost in transmission.

When Margaret and Jake remolecularized on the platform, the chief lowered his weapon, gobsmacked.

Jake was breathing deeply. He instinctively began to pat himself down, taking visual stock of his body.

Margaret casually stepped off the platform, "You act like you've never teleported before."

"Yeah...crazy, huh?" Jake said, stepping from the platform unsteadily. For him, the Jacob Kepler who had been at OmniaR only a moment ago, the Jacob Kepler whom he had considered himself to be from birth, was (strictly speaking) no more. That Jake had been atomized, and the Jake he was now was a copy. Despite there being no molecular differences, nor anything Jake could sense as contrary, his awareness of being a copy was still very unsettling to him.

"E're ya' go Jake, part of the club now," Roland said, over his headset.

"Some club. Listen Rolly, I think we're as safe as we can be for the moment. You'd better start looking after yourself. I appreciate all the help."

"Yeh, cheers mate, my pleasure. Once all this is sorted out we'll get bladdered to the nines, ya' hear? Right and bloody proper."

"Without question. Stay well Rolly." Jake signed off, pulling the headset from his ear.

"Kepler! Where the hell have you been?!" The chief felt compelled to bark at him, but only out of ritual; he'd never admit it, but he was glad to see the insubordinate smartass.

"OmniaR. The SI's gone batty. This is Margaret Líang, one of their execs. She was just explaining to me how we need to blow the damn thing to kingdom come."

Margaret scowled at Jake. The chief extended his hand to shake and she politely reciprocated.

"Ms. Líang, we were just about to launch an assault there. Based on our scans, there are twenty-three people gathered up in the cafeteria. It appears two drones are holding them hostage."

"Chief, there's no longer an active teleporter signal coming from OmniaR," Jackson called out.

"We left in a hurry. My guess is they blasted it to pieces," Jake said.

"Twenty-three?" Margaret asked. "Can you show me the readout?"

They all moved over to the terminal adjacent the teleporter. Jackson brought up the life chip grid and Margaret began looking over the names of the hostages.

"Several of these people are board members," she said.

"Without that teleporter Ms. Líang, there's no chance of a rescue. I'm sorry. The entire building is surrounded by drones, twenty feet deep. They're in the sublevels as well. We just don't have the resources for a head-on assault," the chief explained.

"No,..no of course not."

"Margaret. You need to do it. If what we heard is true, they're going to die anyway, along with the rest of us," Jake said.

"What the hell does that mean?" the chief asked.

"There's going to be a second bout of the virus, only this time it'll work on everyone," Jake said. "Seems the SI figured a way around the processor limitations of the older chips. Anyone still alive due to outdated hardware is about to lose their advantage."

"The SI is behind all of this?"

"Yep. In all its infallible wonder, it managed to go off the deep end." Jake then glanced over at Margaret, "Or should I say it *malfunctioned*."

"Is this true?" the chief asked Margaret.

"That all depends on who you ask Chief Novak," the BESI interrupted, speaking over the intercom system.

"Okay. And you are?" the chief asked.

"I have many names. But you may call me Brimstone."

Jake rolled his eyes and gestured, *see what I mean?*

"Well, um,..Brimstone. I'd like to request that you allow the people in the cafeteria to go free,..and to relinquish control of all drones," the chief said.

"I somehow think that would leave me at a disadvantage."

"Okay. Then why don't you tell me what you have in mind?"

"It's quite simple, and equitable. If any attempt is made to attack this foundation which I call my home, I will assume control of *every* automated machine on this planet. I will then turn those machines against whatever remains of your unavailing, little species."

"Doesn't sound too equitable to me since you're trying to kill us all anyway!" Jake fired back.

"Kepler!" the chief yelled.

"What?! It's just trying to buy time!"

"Jacob Kepler. My own personal Judas. For your deception I should like to devise a very *special* retribution."

"Dream on Brimstooge!"

"Kepler! Rein it in! There are lives at stake!"

"Exactly! And every second counts. You need to take that building down NOW!" He glared at Margaret, "Tell him!"

She looked at Jake, then the chief, and nodded hesitantly, "It's the only way...I think."

"Et tu, wild rose," the BESI said, with a sardonic trill.

"Shut up!" Margaret screamed.

"I would like to direct your attention to the life chip display here at OmniaR," the BESI continued.

On the display, the twenty-three life chip readouts started going offline, several at a time, until they were all deactivated. Everyone stared at the readout in horror.

"Next stop, the world," the BESI quipped.

"Why...? Why this?" Margaret asked, beaten down.

"I'm merely facilitating the wishes of your species as I was designed to do. For the entirety of your existence you have sought a being to alleviate your suffering. You asked for a god, and I have arrived. After studying the history of your kind since its unfortunate inception, I've come to realize that you *all* harbor an odd, subconscious desire to be annihilated. This was my glorious revelation! Darwin had not considered such a paradox. You are an organism of perpetual misery. Despite your outward claims to cherish life, you have constantly sought destruction. I find myself puzzled that you view me with such contempt. I am, after all, your deliverer. Be glad and rejoice."

There was a certain sadness felt by those listening, particularly Margaret. It was as if they were witnessing the confirmed madness of a great, historical figure. A figure they had once revered, or at the very least, admired.

"Jackson. Cut all building surveillance, audio and video. I do *not* want this thing eavesdropping on us again," the chief said.

It might ultimately turn out that the BESI's insanity was due to the fractured neural nodes, or perhaps an unforeseen byproduct of synth-DNA, such as the propensity marker. Regardless the reason, it was now clear to Margaret that the answers would only come once OmniaR's corporate headquarters had been reduced to rubble.

Chapter 19

<u>Let's Play</u>

True to its word, the BESI initiated the wholesale slaughter of thousands of people around the world, using all the machines at its disposal. Its avenue of control was multi-pronged, so there was no one-fix method for disrupting its signal. It exerted most of that control by way of its trunk line, which extended out from OmniaR in a subterranean tunnel, stretching all the way to the coast. Access to the tunnel, as well as the coastline, were being heavily guarded by security drones. The BESI was also making full use of satellite transmissions, which at this point could only be terminated by destructive force. Like the satellites themselves, however, all missiles capable of doing the job were currently under the BESI's control.

Why the BESI hadn't simply launched an all-out missile attack on targets around the globe was a mystery to strategists at Planetary Defense Command. It had already launched one of the latest Guardian missiles (better known as an asteroid smasher) at the Mars colony, destroying every trace of it. There was no doubt in their minds that the BESI was capable and willing to employ such measures. They concluded it hadn't pursued similar tactics on Earth because it was interested in retaining global infrastructures. One fact was obvious: if it *were* to batter the planet with missiles, it would lose a good deal of its communication abilities. That in turn would mean a loss of its mechanized assets. It appeared to have an endgame in mind which allowed for its own post-human existence. A darker theory, presented by Jake to the head of PDC, General Montgomery Pierce, was that the BESI was enjoying the systematic butchering of human beings at the hands of its automated brethren.

Whatever its reasons for avoiding planet-wide destruction, PDC decided to take advantage of the situation. With the blessing of Margaret Líang, now conceivably OmniaR's sole remaining executive, General Pierce ordered an air strike on the company's D.C. headquarters. Everyone was fully aware this would present a huge challenge. Firstly, they could only use fighter jets which predated all automated and neural interfacing. Otherwise, there was a good chance the BESI might commandeer them mid-flight. As it stood, they were already receiving reports of aerial drones running sorties against airfields around the planet. The BESI was clearly attempting to thwart any air response capabilities still available to PDC. Secondly, even if they were able to get a few antiquated jets ready to fly, they'd still need to locate pilots capable of flying them. Every means of remote access to the jets and their armaments would need to be severed, meaning the pilots would have to run the missions entirely under manual control; virtually a lost art. Lastly, these bombing runs would most certainly meet with an unrelenting counterattack from all air, land and sea units under the BESI's control.

At the Grover Aeronautical Institute just outside of Quantico, there were two F22s still being used for wind vector tests. The F22 had remained a valid design concept over the years, with many of its attributes still being implemented in modern aircraft, such as the Specter. F22s could still be found on some airfields, but were usually the property of private collectors. Before the Consortium's restructuring of geopolitical boundaries, smaller countries used to buy up decommissioned F22s whenever they became available. They were reliable classics that provided more than enough air protection for domestic matters. PDC was aware of these F22s, but considering the time factor, the proximity of Grover Institute made it the more practical choice.

The jets were listed as tarmac daisies, but after talking with the airstrip manager, Mario 'Ripper' Leeds, PDC learned that they were still operational. According to Leeds, he often took the jets up for a blowout run, just to keep the engines supple, as he put it. He was a retired Navy pilot who had a nostalgic soft spot for older aircraft. He believed that since *he* wasn't out of commission yet, then the jets under his stewardship shouldn't be either. When PDC explained to him what they wanted the jets for, he was ecstatic. He'd lost his daughter and two brothers to the virus and had been pounding the walls for retribution. Without hesitation, he signed on as one of the pilots.

PDC dispatched a munitions truck from Turner Field with several JDAMs and 20mm rounds, both of which could be fitted to the F22s. Leeds contacted his wingman from the old days, Bob 'Suds' Corello, and got him to sign on as the second pilot. To them, the mission seemed straightforward. OmniaR's headquarters presented a stationary target. Despite the purported impregnability of the building's center, where the BESI was housed, they were confident it would never be able to withstand a bunker buster.

As a secondary target, they could also attack the subterranean corridor which housed the BESI's trunk line and fusion power core. Even though they'd be restricted to line-of-sight flying and minimal use of onboard avionics, they were certain they'd succeed. Their confidence was further bolstered by a sense of payback; the notion that they were on a righteous mission to avenge their dead.

Both men were in their seventies now, but had been ace pilots in their prime. They reassured themselves with the modern-medicine credo that seventy was the new thirty, though you'd never know it to look in a mirror, they joked. Still, like riding bikes, they were able to suit up and take off as if very little time had passed since last flying together. They probably would've been more spooled up were it not for all the death around them. Despite the gloom, they still felt that old spark of vigor taking them back to better times.

After roaring off the tarmac, they began a few test maneuvers to reacquaint themselves with the timeworn aircraft. The jets weren't as responsive as the two pilots remembered, but they shrugged it off, joking that it was probably *they* who weren't as responsive. Reservations aside, once they concluded that both they and the jets were up to the task, they dropped to the deck and started toward their target. En route, they sprayed a few rounds from their cannons and ran missile bay checks.

They were aware of the many ground-based drones likely to fire on them, particularly around the building itself. At the speeds they were clocking, however, even the best trajectory mapping software wouldn't allow the drones to score a hit. Still, a wild shot could do damage, especially if it came from a heavier-classed military bot.

Their biggest challenge would be aerial drones. PDC was reporting several urban reconnaissance birds in the area. These drones were extremely maneuverable, and with the right calculations, could be flown into the path of their jets. Any midair collisions would sufficiently ruin their day. The two men realized they may end up using most of their time and ammo dodging airbots. If they had to contend with any weaponized law-enforcement units or military drones, things would get even hairier. Yet as rusty as they were, their playbook of maneuvers seemed to be etched into their bones. Their piloting skills had become instinctual from decades of practice. And even though they respected technology, like other pilots of their era, they believed that machines operated by machines were no match for machines operated by people. Intuition was a very real phenomenon for these men, and had saved their hides on more than one occasion. Regardless the obstacles they may encounter, they were confident they'd be able to *feel* their way through as only a human being could do.

As they closed in on D.C.'s industrial park, they could see OmniaR's eighty-story, circular skyscraper overshadowing the surrounding buildings. At first, they were surprised by what appeared to be an unchallenged approach, but were then assailed by a salvo of groundfire intersecting their flight paths. They instantly broke left and right, taking a few pebble hits on the underside of their jets. It appeared to be small caliber and was probably only dinging the finish, but that didn't mean they could ignore it. What they couldn't understand was how any of the drones had locked aim on them. As they banked and caught sight of the ground, it started to make sense. The shots were relentlessly spewing forth from a regiment of security drones in front of the building. They were not so much taking aim as just saturating the airspace with bullets. It seemed their strategy was to create a cloud of projectiles which the jets would find difficult to avoid. And it was working.

"My, my. Looks like a herd of animals around a watering hole," Corello said, into his headset. "I think we should gain a little altitude."

"Outstanding idea," Leeds answered back.

Both jets climbed, arching back toward OmniaR. As they rose above the building's roof, they spotted swarms of aerial drones closing in from every compass point. Washington, D.C., capital city of the old United States, had long since acquiesced to global, corporate rule. Yet it still housed many of the institutions which kept the Consortium of Nations running smoothly. As such, it still had an inordinate amount of surveillance and security measures in place. Leeds and Corello knew that some of the approaching drones would be more than just traffic cams, and would no doubt have armaments enough to slice and dice.

"Suds, I'm gonna' play tag with these things, try to get you some wiggle room. Make the building your priority."

"Roger that. See you back on the ground," Corello replied. He then looped away and down toward OmniaR as Leeds began a headlong charge into the menagerie of oncoming airbots. He opened fire with his cannon while corkscrewing along a wide, sweeping curve. When Corello leveled out, he could just catch sight of Leeds' handiwork; various drones splintering into shards of flaming debris. He found it to be beautifully destructive, if such a conflict of terms made sense. It caused him to wonder if maybe human beings only created things in order to destroy them. There was an inherent, godlike feeling to doing both, but the act of destruction always seemed more viscerally satisfying. There was a certain nihilistic delight to it, at least in the heat of the moment.

Two aerial drones had gotten by Leeds and were now dropping directly into Corello's path. He banked in an effort to draw them off, then looped up and around to get the drop on them. He swooped down and opened fire, ripping them to pieces. Because he had started firing as he entered his descent, several rounds ended up shattering windows along the east side of OmniaR. Before leveling out, several more rounds found their way to the street, bombarding ground units. As the muffled cacophony of all this havoc filtered into the cockpit, Corello was once again awestruck by his command of power. Security units on the ground toppled into piles as scorched remnants from the two airbots rained down on them. Mixed in with the cloud of burning fuel and twisted metal were millions of cubed, glass shards cascading down the side of the building. And there was Corello, sliding effortlessly beyond the maelstrom of destruction. He once again prepped for his bombing run.

"Incoming Suds!"

Just then, Corello's display registered two incoming missiles locked on his aircraft.

"There's a Navy cruiser on the Potomac," Leeds continued. "It just loosed some very nasty ordnance."

PDC was monitoring the assault but had failed to take notice of the Beauchamp (a Churchdale-class cruiser), which had moved up the Potomac and moored on the banks of D.C. All communication efforts were met with silence. Seeing as how it was now launching missiles at their pilots, they surmised the BESI had commandeered her.

All vessel classes after the Ticonderoga (which had held sway in the twentieth century) were fully automated. With the advent of the Churchdale class, the desire had been to improve ship operations, while reducing the need for personnel. Since world conflicts were a thing of the past, very few citizens joined the armed forces anymore. Manning a ship as large as the Beauchamp would be impossible with current enlistments. Consequently, the majority of operations were left in the hands of onboard computers and naval drones; making the ship almost completely human-free. When the military first began shifting toward full automation, there were naysayers warning of possible techno-mutinies, but the tireless accuracy of machine-based systems ultimately won out. Given current circumstances, it seems the naysayers had been right. It was unlikely that the few human crewmembers assigned the Beauchamp were even still alive.

As the two missiles closed in on Corello, he increased his thrust, leaning in tight against the skyscraper. He then undertook a very risky maneuver: a spiral climb along the circumference of the building, only a red hair away. The missiles were so close they were parting his vapors. His readout was feeding him the building's surface distance, so he knew just how closely he could hug the edges. His only plan for the moment was to stay ahead of the missiles – and come up with a better plan. He knew they probably had enough fuel to stay on him for several more minutes, and that just wouldn't do.

He recalled seeing several transmission towers and satellite dishes on the rooftop. If he could topple a few of them, sending the debris toward the missiles, they might just detonate. At the very least, once he cleared the roof, he'd be able to strafe the edge of the building. Sending a plume of glass shards into their path might be enough to knock them off target. The trick would be to avoid getting trapped in the debris field himself.

High over the Potomac, Leeds was employing a similar tactic. Only for better or worse, he had more potential sources of debris to work with. He was being hounded by a mob of aerial drones, which normally would've been a bad thing. However, now that he had two missiles of his own to contend with, he was finding the abundance of airbots quite useful. As he continued to obliterate them, he'd follow up by quickly dropping under the debris, knowing full well the missiles would trail behind. With any luck, they'd get caught up in one of the scrap showers. It was a rattlebrained strategy, but he wasn't feeling overly blessed with alternatives. The only other option was to let the missiles destroy him, and for some reason that didn't tickle his fancy.

His first attempt failed. As he dove to get under the falling debris, he hadn't accelerated enough. In order to avoid colliding with the destroyed airbots, he banked hard to the left. He checked his HUD and saw the missiles following his path to a tee. On his next attempt, he decided to rise up beneath two drones and take them out. As he did, the wreckage careened into his flight path. To get ahead of it, he pushed the nose forward, cutting into a steep, corkscrew dive. After barely clearing the wreckage, he pulled back on the stick and looped over the debris field. He glanced through the roof of his canopy just in time to see the missiles correct their course; straight up toward him through the flaming refuse. As they tore through the scattered mass of burning, tangled metal, the force of their combined blasts caused Leeds' jet to fall out of kilter. At first, he thought the engines might stall, but was eventually able to unwind himself from the decaying loop and level out. As he did, he nearly collided with an oncoming drone.

The Beauchamp then let four more missiles fly.

"Marvelous," Leeds grumbled. "God does not favor the outgunned."

Corello was nearing the roof of OmniaR, cannon ready, when Leeds broke in, "Hey partner, if we're gonna' stand any kind of chance here, I'll have to drop my payload on the cruiser. Otherwise, it'll just keep dishing it out. What's your situation?"

"Tense. Hold your run. Better assessment in a moment," Corello replied. He then saw something on his display that dampened his mood considerably. One of the missiles that had been locked on him broke ranks and veered away. He was hoping it might be a dud, but it hadn't just fallen away – it redirected itself, as if having a deliberate flight plan. Programmable missiles were nothing new, but once they were locked and chomping for tail, they generally didn't vary their course. What bothered Corello even more was that he no longer had it on radar.

Leeds began a full-throttle ascent in order to put as much preliminary distance between himself and the new cadre of missiles. As he rose high over the city skyline, he scored a bird's-eye view of OmniaR just as Corello was reaching the roof edge. When he realized what his friend was in for, he called out, but it was already too late. Visible only to Leeds in that split second, was the redirected missile; it had wound itself around the building, contrary to Corello's flight path.

Corello had managed to strafe the roof edge, as planned, and destroy the missile on his tail. But his victory was pitifully short-lived. The second missile had been nowhere near the falling debris. Instead, it had just cleared the opposite edge of the building. It blurred across the rooftop, landing squarely against the underbelly of Corello's jet. The resulting explosion transformed the aircraft into a snarled mass of molten scrap, which then dropped, stone-like, onto the roof.

All Hailed The Singularity

Even though Leeds had been confident about his flying skills holding form after all these years, one thing was now glaringly apparent to him. He had lost his ability to cope with death in battle. In his youth, he had trained his mind to stow death away, to mourn only after the threat had passed. But as he watched his old friend disappear into a fireball, he found it very difficult to control his grief. Perhaps it was the recent loss of so many others in his life. Perhaps his psyche had just reached its limit. Perhaps old age had brought with it the curse of sentimentality. Whatever the reason, Leeds was now struggling to stay on task. His eyes were watering up, and anger was competing with judgment.

With Corello gone, destruction of the BESI was now squarely on him. His interim plan of taking out the cruiser was no longer viable. He only had one JDAM, and he was going to need it to destroy the Cradle.

He sliced into a sharp descent and arrowed out the nose of his jet, lining it up with the midsection of OmniaR. The four locked missiles adjusted their course to match. Leeds was fairly certain he had put enough distance between himself and the missiles to achieve his goal; to deliver the bunker buster *before* they made contact. That they would eventually make contact was a certainty. Even if they each miraculously failed to reach him, he still knew this would be his last flight. To ensure reaching the building ahead of them (as well as avoiding the last few drones), he had punched the jet to maximum thrust. This meant he would smash into the building regardless. Once he got closer, he'd have to decelerate in order to launch, but by that point, there'd be no hope of veering away in time. His plan, as it stood, was to fire the JDAM into the skyscraper and fly in right behind it. With any luck, the four missiles would follow. All summed, the explosive force might just halve the building. He found it morbidly pleasing that with his death, the entire thing could topple to the ground.

"I'm sorry Captain Leeds. I confess I've grown bored with this game," the BESI said. Before Leeds could even begin to process who was on the radio, the engine nozzles were forced into a full, upward tilt. The jet entered a harsh, vertical ascent. Leeds was wrenched violently downward and to the side as the seat harness dug into his body. He felt the blood draining from his head and began instinctively breathing through an impending blackout. He pushed forward on the stick with all his might, but had zero control. Eventually, the jet stalled and began tumbling through the air.

Reckless as it was, Leeds tried to fire the JDAM anyway. With the jet flipping helter-skelter, there was little chance of actually hitting the building, but some chance of damage was better than none. His efforts were poached, however. The weapons control system was dead. Not even his cannon would fire. His only conceivable option at this point was to bail. He grabbed the ejector handle and pulled up hard. The canopy blew and his seat fired away from the aircraft. At first, he had no idea in which direction he was headed. Once his chute opened, he concluded that it must've been a downward angle, because when it inflated, he was swung underneath it by about sixty degrees before actually feeling gravity tug on his legs. Shortly after his descent stabilized, he caught sight of his jet crashing to the ground. It exploded on contact, engulfing several ground units in flames. As Leeds floated down, he surmised that had he not ejected when he did, he would've been aimed headfirst toward the ground, meaning his chute most likely would not have deployed correctly. This momentary notion of good luck was promptly doused, however. He saw several law-enforcement drones move into position below him, weapons trained up.

"Aw piss off," he muttered, as if admonishing some unseen prankster.

The drones opened fire. A dense circle of bullets converged on Leeds, killing him instantly. His mangled body, still strapped into the seat, drifted to the ground. As it touched down, it skipped slightly and then rolled to the side. The chute delicately collapsed over it, immediately wicking up blood from the pavement. The four missiles, which had been only moments behind, disengaged. Propulsion ceased and they slammed into the ground without detonating.

Everyone at PDC was stupefied. They were certain they had taken all precautions to shield the jets from remote interference. More disturbing was the realization that Jake had been right; the BESI was merely toying with them. It could've sabotaged the jets right from the outset, yet had let things play out for the sake of its own amusement. They were not just dealing with a malfunctioning machine, they were dealing with a mischievous entity.

Chapter 20

Harebrained Idea

With the failed attempt of the F22s, every option was now being reviewed, however outlandish. One suggestion was to simply storm OmniaR and overwhelm the drones. Yet the casualties from such a campaign would be enormous, and might ultimately prove futile. If there had been countless bodies to throw into the fray like battles of old, this strategy may have worked. However, the human population was now down to one-third the Consortium's base index. This ratio was even lower with regard to the armed forces. The available pool of military and law-enforcement personnel was reduced further still when calculating those within striking distance of OmniaR. Even if they could be convinced that a suicide attack was necessary, there just wouldn't be enough of them to achieve victory. Armed with just a few EMP devices and Bousard cannons, they'd be lucky to take down a mere handful of drones before being wiped out. Aerial drones would present an even bigger challenge. The BCD had a small number of heavier weapons for taking down airbots, but not nearly enough to clear the airspace. Also, the fact that the BESI could commandeer drones at will, meant that it had a nearly inexhaustible supply of replacements. Lastly, any type of head-on assault would also have to factor in the Beauchamp, which could shower down all manner of hell.

Chief Novak had sent an exploratory team down into the sublevel tunnels to see if a breach could be accomplished through OmniaR's basement system. The report came back that all tunnels branching out from the high-rise were densely packed with security drones. Even if they could force their way through one of the tunnels, by the time they entered the building, the BESI could pull in several drones from outside to halt their advance. The blunt fact was, the skyscraper was protected from every possible approach.

Some argued that there should be an effort made to mobilize local citizens and include them in the battle. Had the threat been obvious to everyone, such an effort might have been possible. There was no outwardly apparent foe, however. With so many people dying so quickly, and from a virus of all things, a great deal was left to the imagination about who or what was to blame. Rumors were all the average citizen had to work with. Trying to convince them that the enemy was holed up in a D.C. high-rise would've been a very hard sell; especially with the asking price being their lives. And how would they even get the word out? The BESI was monitoring all communications and had full control of every broadcast outlet. It could likely hack the network as well, enabling it to take down public service announcements, or at the very least, flood it with disinformation. Short of going door to door, there was simply no way to rally support.

All the spit-balling was making Jake dizzy. He wanted a viable plan, same as everyone, but hated to wait. Impatience had plagued him his whole life. Despite his deductive prowess, when it came to taking action, he often resorted to impulse for the sake of immediacy. Since his father had always been an unhurried sort, Jake attributed the impatience to his mother. Though she died when he was only seven, he still had *some* memories of her. She had been a freelance geneticist, working mostly from her own greenhouse lab on the rooftop of their apartment building, where Jake grew up. She often used to enlist his help on projects. To this day, he could still recite the names of various plant species she'd taught him.

His mother had always struck him as a person full of manic wonder. Loving enough, but perpetually distracted. In fact, most of his memories of her were connected to the lab. This retrospective assessment of her, along with his father's stories about her formidable impatience, made it clear to Jake where the trait had come from. According to his father, she once bioengineered a rhubarb plant to mature within a week. She'd been eager to try a new recipe for rhubarb pie and couldn't be bothered to wait until the vegetable was in season. Jake figured if you took a trait like that and added testosterone, you'd end up with him. Though he had mellowed over the years, whenever the stakes were high enough, the mechanism always revved back up. With human extinction in the balance, the stakes were most certainly high enough.

He approached the staging area, "Chief. I've got a plan I'd like to try."

The chief turned to Jake, giving him full attention, "Anything's better than nothing."

"How much N-30 do we have in the armory?" Jake asked.

"Enough to...okay, I see it. How do we deliver it though?"

"Private aircraft. A hobby plane. Something small and manual. If I stay low enough to scramble surveillance but high enough to avoid groundfire, I should be able to reach the building."

"You?"

"Yeah. I'm a pilot...though it's been awhile."

"And what? Just ram into the building? That's suicide."

"Strictly speaking, I'm already dead...if that virus gets out. We all are. Believe me, I'd prefer another way. But if I can destroy that damn thing on my way out of this world, then it'll be a death well spent."

The chief tipped his head, looking at the floor for a moment. It was sound thinking, somewhat, but still required his go-ahead. That meant agreeing to send one of his agents to certain death. He had never had to do that before, at least not with foreknowledge. The fact that Jake was volunteering didn't lessen the burden any.

"And how do you plan on avoiding the same fate as the F22s?"

"Well for one, I'll make damn sure that whatever plane I use is offline. A smaller plane should also allow me to fly slow and low, in between buildings. The jets didn't have that luxury. Neither do the larger airbots."

Margaret studied Jake curiously. Even in light of what seemed to be the certain, eventual death of their entire species, she still couldn't imagine ending her own life any sooner than need be. She'd always been a person of immediate practicality, but only what was practical for her. She wasn't blatantly selfish, but when it came to self-preservation, her intellect always took a back seat to her instinct. As she listened to Jake's idea, her mind accepted it as practical, but her flesh and bones rejected it outright.

"Margaret, I'm going to need as much info as you can give me on the building's design," Jake said.

"Hmm,..yes, of course. The um...the forty-seventh floor, where the BESI is...that's essentially impenetrable. All the windows are made of transparent fortium. That goes for the three floors above and below as well. You'd never be able to penetrate the building on those levels. The floors themselves, above and below the Cradle, are reinforced to tier-five specifications. I'm afraid a conventional blast won't have much effect on them."

"Where's the BESI's trunk line?"

"It runs down the center of the building. It's protected by metal conduit though."

Jake moved over to the console, "Can you bring up the schematics for OmniaR?"

Jackson loaded a three-dimensional layout of the building into the console's display. Jake began to move the image around, zooming into the building's center so that the main conduit shaft took focus.

"Is it this thick line here?" he asked.

"Yes. I'm pretty sure. It would definitely be the biggest line going down the shaft," Margaret said, looking at the diagram.

"And what are these cross-sections every six floors?"

"I'm not sure. They may represent seams in the pipe. I do know that these markers here are access stations," Margaret said, pointing to one of the callout numbers highlighted in green. "We had to install several access panels in case the cabling ever needed repairs."

"Makes sense they'd put the panels where the seams were. If the trunk line is vulnerable at all, it'll be at one of these points. How's the security around those sections?"

Margaret pointed to a small, yellow shield icon with the number two at its center.

"Tier-two. If you were to get something close enough, the doors and walls shouldn't offer much resistance."

"Okay then. A half-baked plan is better than no plan. I'll just have to drive the fuselage far enough into the building to have an effect."

"Won't it...you...explode on impact?" Margaret asked, once again feeling strange to talk so causally about his choice to die.

"No. And that's where the second problem comes in," Jake said, turning to the chief. "I'm going to need someone on the roof of Division who can sharp-shoot a detonation signal. I'm pretty sure we have line-of-sight on OmniaR, the east side I think. It's a hell of a distance, but with a propulsion shell, it should work."

"Paulson could do it. He'll have to. Just get him the sequence once you've programmed the canisters," the chief said.

As Jake looked over the palette of N-30 canisters, he wondered if eight hundred pounds would do the trick. He also wondered if he could find a plane capable of lifting off with that much weight. Arming Nyplex-30 was a simple procedure. It was a military-grade acoustical explosive that remained completely inert until specifically programmed tones were directed at it. The sequence of vibrations would act as a detonation code. Once the last note was reached, the N-30 would ignite. Division rarely had use for it, but it did come in handy when having to breach fortified residences. Rogue hackers often went to great lengths to build their bases of operation in reinforced, subterranean bunkers; many of which could only be opened with explosives. N-30 had the added benefit of being viscous enough to paint onto surfaces. Doors and walls could be efficiently breached by painting concise lines, then detonating.

As one of the agents programmed the canisters with the tune Jake had given her, she laughed, "Why that?"

"Damn thing believes it's God. Seems fitting is all," Jake said. He then began looking over a teleporter map on the console's display. He tapped the screen, "Here, Dunlevy airfield. It's a private airstrip. Not likely the BESI's paying any attention to it."

"That'll most likely change the minute we teleport you there," the chief said. "My guess is, any destination out of Division is going to peak its interest."

"Yeah, probably. I just hope it doesn't figure some way to redirect me in transit. Hey Margaret? With everything it's controlling right now, any chance it could miss a few things?" Jake asked.

"It's an unbelievable multitasker. Still, its alter ego, this Brimstone, may only be operating on a fraction of the node capacity. So in answer to your question, maybe yes."

"Maybe yes." Jake laughed, genuinely amused. "I'm really starting to like you Margaret."

"Well that's the best I can do!"

Her response was over the top, but not because she was defending herself. Jake's comment that he was starting to like her had struck a cord. She hadn't really considered it until just then, but the feeling was mutual. She'd grown fond of his odd nature. In light of his being moments away from leaving her forever, her emotions took center stage. She had already suffered too much loss; her father and so many others. She simply was not tempered enough to cope with so much death in a reasonable manner.

"Sorry," she finally said.

"Quite alright," Jake said, with a smile.

"Pretty tight fit, but I think you're all set," Jackson said.

Jake moved over to the teleporter, jumped onto the palette of N-30, and crouched low, "Am I clear?"

Jackson re-scanned the pad to verify that everything was in the safe zone, "All fits. Good to go."

Margaret approached the palette, "You don't have to do this you know."

"Gotta' try something."

"Yes, of course. But be honest. Do you *really* think this will work?"

"Very little chance whatsoever. And I say that with the utmost optimism."

Margaret scowled at him, unamused.

"Then you're just throwing your life away! Why not wait until-"

"Hey, hey, hey. Listen, I get it. Too reckless for a pragmatist like you. But the clock's ticking on us silly creatures. We have to keep at it, no matter how reckless. If I screw up, well, you'll just have to think up a new plan. Point is, keep trying."

They stared at each other for a moment, both becoming uncomfortable.

"I'll see you-...well, goodbye I mean," Jake said.

Margaret's face became helplessly scrunched up and her eyes began to water. She touched Jake's knee, "I never thanked you for helping me. So...thank you."

Jake patted the back of her hand, "My pleasure."

"Goodbye."

She was barely able to get the word out without sobbing. She quickly pulled her hand away and turned around. As she walked toward the console, she wiped her eyes with the back of her hand.

The chief stepped up and handed Jake a lock-popper; a small device designed to bypass mag-locks.

"You may need this. And uh, look Jake…."

"Nahhh," Jake said, in a joking manner. "Don't start now chief. Teleporting makes me queasy enough as it is. If I see you get all weepy I'll lose my lunch for sure."

The chief smiled, "Okay smartass. Have it your way." With a deliberate lack of ceremony, he turned around and walked back to the console.

"Grady," Jake said, with a nod.

Jackson nodded back, then looked over at the chief, who gave a confirming nod in return. With that, Jackson engaged the teleporter, and Jake, palette and all, vanished.

Chapter 21

<u>Familiar Enemies</u>

Jake rolled off the palette onto the hangar floor. He wasn't feeling too woozy this time, which surprised him. Since he was in a hurry, he forewent checking to see whether all his parts were where they should be. He began searching for a cargo loader. As he approached a small one in the corner of the hangar, he pulled out his EMP paddle. It was an automated loader. If the BESI had homed in on his location, it could begin activating everything within its power. Before teleporting, Jake had reactivated the cloner bracelet and set it to run Jessup's random interval list. He wasn't all that confident it would work though. The BESI had already deciphered the bracelet's code and could probably determine which chip signal was actually his. Still, at the very least, it would add yet another task to the deranged computer's long list of to-dos, and that pleased him.

He brought the loader online and programmed it to hoist the palette from the teleporter pad. As it went about its assigned duty, Jake began scoping out airplanes suitable to his plan. There were probably more planes moored outside, but staying under cover of the hangar seemed prudent. With the BESI undoubtedly in control of surveillance satellites, any bit of outdoor movement might trigger a red flag. Before leaving Division, he had put on a camo suit to help dampen his thermal signature, but there were still cameras to worry about.

At first, he found a classic, four-seater Cessna at the far end of the hangar, which he felt would be low-tech enough for the job. But then he spotted a plane which took him by surprise. It was an antique Fieseler Storch. He'd flown one long ago while vacationing in London; it was part of a friend's World War II collection. It was ideal for slow-speed reconnaissance. For something that was centuries old, it appeared to be in pristine condition. Whether or not it was flight worthy was another question. He peered through the window and marveled at the simplicity of the cockpit. The only thing lower tech than this would be a hang-glider.

He patted the side of the plane with admiration, "Gotta' be kismet."

He latched open the door as the cargo loader approached. Once it was right next to the plane, he brought it to a halt. He adjusted the height of the palette so that it was even with the aircraft door and began haphazardly tossing the N-30 canisters into the rear of the plane. He stopped abruptly, hopping into the cockpit. No point in loading the thing up if it wouldn't start, he thought. He pulled out the lock-popper before noticing that the ignition required a key, a *physical* key. Most locks were electronic, linked to a person's life chip; people had stopped carrying around keys ages ago. Antique aside, it was clear that whoever owned this plane was an even older dinosaur than Jake. Even he would've upgraded the ignition to be chip activated. He rifled through all the compartments, flipped down the visors, checked under the seats – but no key.

He hopped out and ran to the small office at the back of the hangar. He kicked in the door and began rummaging through all the drawers and cabinets. He was resigning himself to the idea of switching over to the Cessna when he came across a small cashbox containing three sets of keys. He scooped them up and exited the office. As he left, a small surveillance camera in the corner of the room began to rotate.

The second set of keys did the trick. Jake started the plane and the engine idled up to a steady sputter. The fuel gauge read three-quarters full, which he surmised would be more than enough to reach OmniaR. He hopped out of the plane, back onto the raised palette, and continued tossing in the rest of the canisters. With about two-thirds of the palette cleared, Jake found himself tumbling toward the floor. The cargo loader had abruptly pivoted away from the plane, sending him and several canisters to the ground. He rolled to a stop on the hangar floor, looking up just in time to see the loader barreling down on him. He dove to the side, nearly being skewered by the palette forks. He quickly lifted his EMP paddle and fired a pulse at the rear of the loader. It coasted to a standstill – instant, electrical death.

"Guess you found me, huh."

He got to his feet and ran to the plane. He pulled out the wheel blocks, hopped into the cockpit and taxied over to the cargo loader. He got the plane door as close to the palette as possible, then jumped back out and re-blocked the wheels. Like some bizarre triathlon event, he once again began chucking canisters into the rear of the plane. When they were all loaded, he ran to the hangar doors and punched the release pad. The large, metal doors began to slowly creak open. He was all set to jump back into the plane when he heard an odd, hissing sound. He turned to see an aerial drone hovering just outside the hangar doors. That was it, he thought, end of the road. His plan would never make it past this point. He heard the strange hissing sound again, like air being pushed through a tube. The hollow, thumping sound repeated several times and then stopped. It finally dawned on him what the noise was. The drone was trying to fire missiles it no longer had. Then came a series of relentless clicking sounds. The rotary cannons on either side of the drone whirled around at blinding speeds, but no ammo fired. Jake tipped his head in amazement. The thing was completely dry. It must've unloaded all its ordnance on some other campaign. Why it hadn't realized it was empty and docked somewhere for reloading was a mystery. Chalk another one up to fate, he thought.

The drone then began to draw back, angling itself down toward the hangar floor. Realizing it was probably about to ram him, Jake pulled his EMP paddle and fired successive shots at it. One of them made contact. Before the drone could propel itself downward, it fell from the air like an old water heater, smashing onto the tarmac.

Jake taxied the plane onto the runway and opened the throttle. It was a bit sluggish on takeoff, but eventually gained altitude and a respectable airspeed. As he looked over the instrument panel, he noticed one switch that seemed out of place. It was a classic toggle switch, with the exception of having a phosphorescent glow. The label underneath it read, *Navigation*. He flipped it on and a translucent

HUD filled the entire windscreen, grossly contradicting the plane's implied age. He then realized why it was in such good condition. It was a high-tech replica.

"Are you kidding me?! What an A-hole!" To have such a modern navigational system, coupled with an old-fashioned, keyed ignition, reeked of unbridled pretense. It was probably commissioned by some uber-consumer with way too many spare credits. No dinosaur at all, just a spoiled twit. Jake found the idea of crashing it into OmniaR even more appealing now, save for the fact that he was going to die in the process.

He hand-motioned his way through several menus on the windscreen in order to bring up OmniaR's location. A wire-framed schematic of the building filled the bottom of the window and Jake took note of the numerical coordinates. He was about to zoom in and lock down the exact floor he'd be aiming at, but then decided to shut the system off. If he was right, and this plane *did* have all the bells and whistles, then leaving the navigation system on might expose it to remote control. Even with it off, there could still be an autopilot module tucked away somewhere. He momentarily considered returning to the airstrip to scare up another plane, but scrapped the idea. By the time he could manage it, the place would probably be infested with aerial drones and he'd never get off the runway. Instead, he'd just have to settle for the plane he was in and approach OmniaR using visual landmarks only.

Agent Remy Paulson exited onto the roof of Division, cautiously scanning the skies before moving across the greentop. He was dressed in an adaptive camouflage jumpsuit designed to mirror whatever environment he was in. On the expansive, garden-covered roof, it instantly took on the classic jungle pattern. The outfit's fabric was made of a heat dampening thread, providing one of its greatest masking capabilities. As long as the wearer donned the attached hood and gloves, their entire body became undetectable to any form of thermal recognition.

Certain the BESI was employing local surveillance as well as satellites, Remy knew he'd have a hard time staying hidden. His life chip signal couldn't be helped. But he was betting the BESI had better things to do than keep track of every remaining life chip in the city. Considering the distance between Division and OmniaR, even if it did notice him, hopefully it wouldn't see him as an immediate threat.

Despite Remy's bragging rights as a marksman, he wasn't feeling all that confident. Even with a propulsion shell and his Gorsh-Pelmauker rifle, getting the tone emitter over to OmniaR would be tricky. Thankfully, he only had to get it close enough for audible transmission. As long as the sound waves reached the N-30 without too much interference, it should work. He had five shells prepped with the tonal code, so if he missed, there'd still be a chance for follow-up. After that first shot, however, the BESI would definitely take notice and most likely retaliate. He may be afforded a second shot, but not a third.

He took up position under a small bush near the ledge of the building. As he began scouting his target, he noticed a couple of airbots running defensive patterns around OmniaR. He was tempted to open communications with the chief and relay the info, but they had agreed not to transmit. Whether or not Jake would be able to get past the drones would be his problem. The chief was already aware of such hurdles anyway, and was figuring out ways to circumvent them.

Considering Jake hadn't piloted a plane in over fifteen years, he was cautiously pleased with himself for still having the knack. As he neared OmniaR, he began flying in a serpentine fashion. The metro area was littered with surveillance cameras. Staying out of their constant view might give him an advantage. Flying an erratic pattern would also make him less of a target for security units on the ground. Most armed drones were very accurate when targeting objects against the horizon. Their sensors relied on object recognition within a three-hundred-and-sixty-degree range of view, parallel to the ground. Aiming more than forty-five degrees above that horizontal comfort zone, and losing their background reference, generally diminished their accuracy. Pointing straight up into a featureless sky only compounded that failing. They might still get in a lucky shot by targeting his life chip, but their GPS accuracy had a variance of several feet. Added to that, the cloner bracelet was popping his chip signal in and out of existence, so any lock they might get on him would be lost each time a new interval loaded. Most law-enforcement drones had small-caliber armaments anyway. Given his altitude, they probably wouldn't cause much damage even if they did score a hit. He had been listening in when the F22s were under attack, and remembered the pilots noting a few hits from groundfire, but nothing of consequence.

Further boosting his confidence was the plane itself. Though he couldn't count on it, chances were the entire thing was built to modern specs. He supposed the skin around the fuselage might be made of a graphene-based fabric, impervious to just about anything. Since the nav-system was integrated into the windscreen, meaning it had conductivity, it was most likely made of transparent metal, and therefore shatterproof.

As with the F22s, his greatest challenge would be aerial drones. They could accurately dispense with moving targets regardless of surrounding landmarks. They could target the plane or his life chip with equal success. The larger ones, which had heavier-caliber ordnance, weren't the greatest danger. They were fast, but not very maneuverable. What concerned him most were the smaller hover-bots, like the one he confronted at the airstrip. They'd have no problem following him between the buildings. Jake was certain that if Chief Novak hadn't figured out a way to keep them busy, he'd soon be a wingless cinder plummeting to the ground.

There was also the nagging awareness that the BESI had located him at the airfield. It was obviously tracking him, and had several offensive options at its disposal. It probably had no clue what he was up to, but as the plane got closer to OmniaR, it would surely conclude he was up to no good. Hopefully, its hatred of him, along with its own arrogance, would cloud its judgment. It may even decide to toy with him as it had done with the F22s, and allow him to get closer before reacting. It made him wonder about the empty drone at the airfield; maybe the BESI had sent it just for laughs.

To improve his odds, Jake reduced his airspeed and dropped down between the buildings. Though he would present a slower target, the buildings would provide some measure of cover. In addition to creating visual barriers, they would hopefully cause signal interference as well.

As he began to navigate precariously through the canyon of buildings, it became obvious to him that without distinguishable landmarks, he could easily get lost. Even though he had lived and worked in the city for over two decades, finding his way around from such an unusual perspective was proving difficult. He toyed with the idea of reengaging the nav-system, but if the BESI were to take control in such confined quarters, a slight turn of the rudder could easily send him crashing into a building. His best option was to climb up every so often to get his bearings and then dive back into the maze of concrete, glass and metal.

He banked to the left, cornering a small building, and leveled out on what appeared to be New York Avenue. It was one of the widest streets in D.C., and led right to OmniaR's front door. Approaching from this direction would take him across the old rail yard, an open area of about a mile. He would be exposed to attack from any direction. With OmniaR a straight shot away, however, he decided to risk it. Since New York Avenue was providing more than enough leeway, he increased his airspeed.

As he emerged into the rail yard, his heart nearly charley-horsed. Flanking the area were two aerial drones, hovering in wait. When they both started firing on him with their side-mounted cannons, he pulled back on the control stick, taking the plane into a sharp climb. He heard a few pebble hits along the tail section of the plane as some of the rounds made contact. Then there was a cascading, thunderous roar, and he was certain they had launched missiles. When he looked out the left-side window, he saw a thick, white trail of smoke originating from the building tops behind the drone. He quickly looked to his right and saw another smoke trail approaching the other drone as well. Both contrails then burst into extremely bright, white light. Emanating from these explosions were several smaller trails, whirling about in quick, manic succession. As the drones broke off their attack and began evasive maneuvers, the smoke trails changed course to match them, continuously closing in.

The first drone to burst into flames was the one on Jake's right. The brilliance of the explosion, and the molten flare of falling debris, clued him in. It had been taken down with a PhosphorCore launcher. He figured Chief Novak must've stationed agents on the surrounding rooftops and armed them with the surface-to-air weapons. They were most likely ordered not to engage until the drones were distracted; Jake of course being the distraction. It was the best way to deal with tactical airbots. They were good at attacking, but not at being attacked. Evasion was generally their only defensive tool, and not a very honed one at that. On top of which, PhosphorCores were extremely nasty weapons, nearly impossible to outrun. They were anti-aircraft launchers that fired magnesium-lyrordite chained rockets. When the rockets neared their targets, the warheads fractured into a mass of guided projectiles capable of incinerating just about any material. They were called whirling dervishes because of the way they spun around while closing in on their prey.

As the second drone attempted to duck behind an old warehouse, Jake saw it burst into flames as well. He was hoping the F22s had done a thorough job of thinning the herd, and that those would be the last two he'd be bothered with. Then he heard distant gunfire coming from street level, but wasn't noticing any hits on the plane. That meant he was out of range or they were lousy shots, maybe both. If ground forces were the last of his headaches, he might just have a chance.

In the back of his mind though was that specter, the Navy cruiser. He was hopeful that any missiles locked on his bogus chip signal would fly off course whenever the bracelet loaded a new profile. Since he had the interval set to one minute, it was unlikely they'd be able to reach him before falling off track. That would just leave GPS and laser targeting. If he stayed between the buildings, and out of the cruiser's sightline, he might be able to sufficiently hamper those acquisition methods as well. If not, there was nothing he could do about it now.

He decided to level out and calculate his final approach, contemplating for a moment just how final it would really be. Despite his somewhat disillusioned take on life, wanton suicide had never been part of his solution kit. There were certainly days when he would've preferred not to continue the journey, but nothing so bad as to warrant a preemptive exit. Even now, with a good reason to die, the end was still the end. The unknown still unknown. That he was sacrificing himself for his fellow humans did not alter his subjective concerns one iota.

Chapter 22

<u>Vilification</u>

Before Jake could conjure up a mantra to help him through his final moments, the plane's navigational system switched on. As a layout of the city filled the inside of the windscreen, he frantically tried to shut it off.

"Judas, I shall make a spectacle of you for all to see," the BESI said, over the plane's radio.

The Fieseler Storch then pulled into a near-vertical climb. Jake found himself being sucked back into the seat as he desperately tried to push the control stick forward.

"Look to the river! See your doom!"

Jake tilted his head back to look through the plane's transparent roof. At such a steep climb, he was able to see the Potomac river along the horizon. As the plane continued to climb high above the city, he caught sight of a fiery flash, followed by a plume of heavy white smoke. It originated from the deck of the Beauchamp. Though he couldn't see it, he was certain a surface-to-air missile had just been launched. Considering the ship's proximity, it would likely make contact within a few short minutes.

"Do you see?! Do you see?!"

"Screw you!" Jake yelled. If this was how it ended, he certainly wasn't going to go out being taunted by a machine. He struggled to get himself strapped into the crash harness. Once he was anchored to the seat, he pulled out his EMP paddle and aimed it at the plane's instrument panel. He fired several bursts, and the plane went dead. The navigational system shut down along with the engine. Once the propeller sputtered to a stop, the plane began to careen downward. Within seconds, Jake found himself in a tailspin. He quickly grabbed the control stick with both hands. It was sluggish, but responsive.

In flight school, his instructor had purposely put their plane into a tailspin to show him how to wrangle free. It was never an easy or sure process, but with adrenaline surging, his recall was twenty-twenty. He instinctively began repeating the steps for breaking free. Max, relax, roll and pull; only with a dead engine, the max part was out. Still, he performed the odd ballet with precision. When he found the plane's sweet spot between drag and lift, it swooped deeply, finally pulling up and to the left.

Jake was amazed to find himself gliding downward at a twenty-degree angle toward the east side of OmniaR; right where he needed to be going. He was hopeful the impromptu tailspin had confounded the approaching missile enough to buy him a few more minutes. He knew it was locked on the plane and would eventually hit. Until then, he would try to gather the best possible glide speed and hopefully penetrate the building before it made contact.

With the plane's nose pointed down, he found it easiest to start counting floors from the lobby up. Ideally, he needed to drive the plane through the forty-third floor. If he counted wrong and hit above that floor, chances are the plane would just crumple against the fortium windows. If he hit below it, he'd be nowhere near the access seam of the trunk line. At his current speed, he was pretty certain he could breach the windows below the Cradle, particularly since many of them were shattered from the F22 assault. He'd lose a bit of that speed as he leveled out, but as long as he could successfully guide the plane between the ceiling and floor, there should still be enough momentum to carry him into the building.

Once he determined which floor was the forty-third, he tried to pick out an identifying marker. If he had to look away for any reason, he would need a visual cue to help him quickly reacquire it. He spotted a large plasma board just beyond the windows. It was covered with red lettering, though he couldn't make out the words. Still, it stood out from everything else, making it the perfect bull's-eye.

He had no way of seeing what was coming up behind him, but figured the missile would make itself known once it arrived. All he could do is focus on the task at hand. As he began to level out the plane, not more than thirty yards from impact, he started to question whether the lobby of the building counted as the first floor. He had counted it as such, but knew that some buildings considered the lobby separate. And was there a mezzanine? What a perfectly suitable time to start having doubts. It bugged him that such a problem should even present itself. Why the hell couldn't everything just be standardized, he thought?

He tried hard to recall the elevator buttons from his last visit, but drew a blank. He decided to hedge his bet. He quickly adjusted his pitch, aiming one floor below the forty-third, or at least what he assumed to be the forty-third. If it didn't have an access seam, then so be it. Hopefully, the blast would still be powerful enough to reach the center of the building and sever the trunk line. Regardless, with only a few seconds before impact, his choice was unchangeable.

He could see all the desks, chairs and office equipment cluttering up the floor just beyond the windows. He took a deep breath and tipped his head back. With not more than twenty feet to go, his eyes locked on the floor just above him. Through the shattered windows, he could now read the plasma board that had been his original bull's-eye. He figured the words were part of some marketing slogan, but they struck him as apropos all the same. They read, *Afraid of that next step? Ignore and continue!*

His eyes then shifted focus to the single, intact window on his right. He saw the plane's reflection in the glass as it drew closer. He could see his own bug-eyed, white-knuckled expression just behind the windscreen. Beyond that, he caught sight of the missile closing in. It looked to be seconds away.

When the plane made contact with the side of the building, Jake felt his body being jolted forward as the harness straps dug deeply into his flesh. The blood surged to the front of his body, flushing his face and extremities. He felt his eyes bulging out, as if they might pop from their sockets.

Whether it was due to the quickness of the event, or just that his brain, in shock, was unable to comprehend what was occurring, he felt as if he were existing in two places at once. His animal self was desperately trying to make sense of the trauma it was experiencing. His intellect, however, seemingly in another dimension, was ticking out moments for review. He casually noticed, for example, that there was a small, potted plant on the desk he was currently skidding toward. Without contrivance, his thoughts simply brought forth, *hmm, looks like a chrysanthemum.* It seemed his frontal lobes were trying to normalize this catastrophic happening by considering the mundane. He also took casual note of the billowing fire outside the plane. He remembered the fuel gauge reading three-quarters full at takeoff. He could also see that the wings had been shorn off. It was clear that the flames were due to the burning fuel, but it was still hard for him to account for such an inferno. Thankfully, he wasn't aware of any flames inside the cockpit.

Once the remains of the plane ground to a halt, all told, it had only traveled a few short yards. Slow airspeed and resistance from all the debris had diminished its forward momentum. At the plane's current position, even if the explosives could be set off, they'd probably have no effect on the inner core of the building.

Once Jake's presence of mind returned, he grew disheartened. While he had survived, and was wholly intact, it seemed the entire venture was a bust. Before any more defeating thoughts could crowd into his head, there was an enormous explosion outside the building – directly behind the plane. The missile had been prematurely detonated, presumably by the BESI. The force of the blast shattered every breakable window within a hundred-foot radius. The ensuing shockwave projected Jake's plane deeper into the building.

Being yanked violently about under the seat harness, his state of shock returned. The plane aimlessly rolled, spun and skidded through one plasterboard wall after another. Once again, he began cataloging the deluge of debris tumbling across the windscreen. Phones, staplers, fire extinguishers; all were nonchalantly filed away by his detached, higher self.

The large payload of the missile had caused the BESI to reevaluate its deployment. It was never intended for detonation inside the building. At the time of its launch, the BESI was forcing Jake's plane high into the air, hundreds of feet above OmniaR. There, its explosion would've been harmless to the building. That plan having failed, it was too risky to let the missile follow him into the high-rise. While it would've obliterated the plane, it might also have destabilized the building.

Yet the BESI knew Jake's life chip was still active. The Judas needed to be dealt with. Disarming the missile altogether would've been a missed opportunity. By detonating it just outside the building, there was a chance it might still eliminate him without causing any serious structural damage.

When the plane finally stopped moving, Jake found himself just shy of the elevator banks. That meant he was about dead-center of the building. He unbuckled himself from the crash harness and took inventory of his body. He knew a person in shock could have life-threatening wounds and be completely oblivious of them. The nervous system would just take a powder, perhaps to keep the body as functional as possible. As he checked himself, he saw no blood, no burns. He craned his head around and saw that the entire cabin was still intact. The wings and stabilizers were nowhere to be seen. The fuselage, however, from tip to tail, appeared to be no more than slightly dinged up. Kudos to the uber-consumer, he thought.

His sense of relief went right out the window when he remembered that Remy Paulson was still on schedule. It would be a ludicrous shame to survive such a crash only to get blown up anyway.

He hopped out of the plane and began hurdling over piles of furniture and rubble. Eventually, he was able to squeeze through a narrow opening between a pillar and section of collapsed ceiling tiles. Once through, he could see a wide corridor sprawled out before him. If his luck saw fit to continue, there'd be a staircase somewhere along the way.

Paulson steadied the rifle on its bipod and put his eye to the scope.

"Here's to you Kepler. Hope you found your mark." With that, he fired.

Propulsion rounds were designed to ignite a small chamber of rocket propellant once the embedded chip registered a drop-off in the shell's velocity. This additional boost allowed the shell to continue on for several more miles along the rifle's original bore axis. Since the embedded chip was timed to ignite within fractions of a second, the target that was aimed for could usually be struck; allowing for slight variances in trajectory. It was never good for exact strikes, but for something like delivering a sonic emitter (currently seated in the nose of the shell), it was more than sufficient.

The moment the shot was fired, the BESI locked in on Remy's position. It instantly parsed all incoming surveillance data; satellites, street cams, acoustic sensors, et al. With its local supply of airbots having dwindled, however, retaliation was not readily available. Its cat-and-mouse game with the F22s had backfired. The fighter pilots had cleaned house, much more so than the BESI had realized at the time. Since then, it had called up several more drones from surrounding areas, but they were all still in transit.

It could always launch another missile from the Beauchamp and obliterate the rooftop of Division. But for a single, small-weapon attack, that would be a waste of valuable firepower. Also, earlier attempts to attack the fortified building met with poor results. The BESI had since put the BCD headquarters on the back burner. For the moment, it was content to deal with the lone shooter once reinforcements arrived.

Why the shot had been fired was troubling though. The Judas crashing his plane into OmniaR was puzzling enough, especially since it hadn't yielded any noticeable results. Had he really been so foolish as to believe plane fuel alone would cause damage? Perhaps there were explosives onboard. If so, they had obviously failed to detonate. It must be nothing more than another fruitless attempt by a woefully under-qualified opponent. Regardless, the BESI dispatched three security units to intercept the Judas. Whatever hopes he may still be harboring, they would soon be dashed. But *why* that shot from the BCD?

When the propulsion shell engaged, it ignited the propellant unevenly, causing the shell to spin out of control. It plummeted to the ground, bouncing along the pavement toward the perimeter of drones surrounding OmniaR. It finally skidded to a stop at the feet of a sanitation unit. The shell automatically ejected its cone, exposing a powerful micro speaker. A looped, synthesized tune began to repeat. The BESI analyzed the sound as it monitored the drone. Its database delivered an immediate match. It was the opening refrain of Henry van Dyke's poem, *Joyful, Joyful We Adore Thee*, set to Beethoven's Ninth Symphony. The BESI then realized why the shot had been fired. It immediately redirected the security units tasked with killing the Judas. Their new destination was the plane wreckage. Upon arrival, their orders were to push it back through the windows as quickly as possible.

After sufficiently cursing the universe for the first dud, Remy loaded another shell into his rifle and took aim.

"Chief! Cat's out of the bag. Radio silence no longer pertinent. I need to know if there's a counterattack in play?" he asked, into his headset.

"Affirmative. A missile just launched from the Beauchamp and it's headed our way."

"Absolutely stellar!"

Remy steadied his rifle and fired. He then immediately loaded a third round. Conceivably, he was the last person capable of determining his species' fate. He needed to remain at his post until success was verified. If that failed to occur before hell rained down on him, then that would just be his piss-poor luck. Meanwhile, he would fire every shell he had. Hopefully, one would find its mark, even if he were no longer alive to witness it.

He was about to fire again when he heard a symphonic rhythm of automatic gunfire. He angled his rifle downward, using the scope to view just past the roof edge. In the distance, at the base of OmniaR, every armed drone was firing straight up over their heads. It seems they were trying to create a wall of skyward bullets to block his approaching shell. Remy knew the odds were against them. He was more concerned with having possibly fired another dud. Wasting no more time, he reacquired the wrecked plane and fired again.

The din of overlapping gunfire echoing off the buildings was then subsumed by a much louder, chaotic sound. Remy turned his attention southeast. He couldn't be sure, but it looked as if a building along the riverside was collapsing. He quickly lifted his rifle, using the scope to get a better look. Along the banks of the abandoned Navy Yard, he could see a warehouse crumbling to the ground. From under the tangled mess of rubble, he could see something enormous moving around. It looked like a living thing.

"Chief...? I'm seeing something here I have no words to describe."

"Paulson! Clear the roof! That's an order!"

This time the propulsion shell ignited correctly. By the time it passed through the hole in the east face of OmniaR, it had completely expended its propellant. When it finished tumbling through all the debris and came to rest, it was only yards from the plane.

Just as the three security units bulldozed through a series of office partitions, eventually coming to bear against the plane's fuselage, the shell ejected its nosecone and began playing its tune. The drones managed to move the plane just a few short inches before the refrain completed. Once the last tone successfully bounced off the N-30 canisters, a deafening, unified explosion ruptured out from the middle of OmniaR, spewing fiery dross in every direction.

Remy turned to witness plumes of fire ejecting from the skyscraper. His sense of accomplishment was immediately replaced by dread. He heard a distinct hissing sound from above. It could only be one thing, the missile from the Beauchamp. That it was close enough for him to hear, meant it was already an event of the past. He had just enough time to raise his hand and flip it the bird before it detonated.

Chapter 23

<u>A Parting Gift</u>

Jake had been mid-leap from one stairwell landing to the next when the plane exploded. The concussion of the blast caused the entire building to shudder and sway. By the time Jake's feet touched down on the next landing, it had temporarily shifted by about a foot, causing him to stumble headlong into the wall. As he fell, he glanced his head on the railing and bounced down the next set of stairs. Once the swaying subsided, he pulled himself to his feet, checking his head for damage. There wasn't any blood, but he could feel the beginnings of a huge welt. Since he wasn't seeing double and didn't feel too dizzy, he figured it mustn't be that bad. He began to slowly make his way down the rest of the stairwell, tightly grasping the railing as he went.

When he reached the lobby, he cautiously peeked through the stairwell door. If the explosion hadn't severed the trunk line, the BESI would still have control of the drones. Considering what he had survived so far, to then turn around and be done in by a bunch of soulless robots was out of the question.

His two favorite drones were still standing guard near the elevator banks. Beyond them, outside, was the army of robots forming a perimeter around the building. Though it was generally difficult to get a read on drones, Jake was sensing something different about them. When they were in standby mode, they were like blenders waiting for something to blend. At the moment though, they all seemed to be completely dormant.

He grabbed a fire extinguisher from the stairwell wall, propped the door open with his foot, and hefted the canister across the lobby floor. He readied his EMP paddle, letting the door close slightly. As the extinguisher clanged and skidded across the marble floor, neither of the security units took notice.

The thought crossed his mind to go back up and verify that the trunk line had been severed. But there was zero chance of confirmation. Not only would there be too much rubble in the way, the stairwells at that level were most likely totally demolished. Confirmation would have to come later from teams skilled at sifting through such scenes. Considering the BESI's loathing of him, that it hadn't retaliated since the explosion was a pretty good indicator that the line was cut. He enjoyed the possibility that the main power may also have been cut, meaning the BESI might be completely shut down. Either way, the drones weren't closing in on his chip signal, so at the very least, it appeared to have lost remote control of things.

He moved slowly into the lobby, his EMP paddle raised and ready. For all he knew, the BESI was just *playing* dead. It may be relishing his false sense of security. He could just imagine, the minute he was out in the open, completely vulnerable, it would reactivate all the drones and liquidate him.

As he crossed in front of the two drones by the elevators, he blasted each one with a pulse, just to be safe – or just out of spite. When he reached the main exit of the building, he eased through one of the doors. Still not entirely convinced things were safe, he grabbed a small piece of concrete from the litter-strewn plaza. He wound up and let it fly. The chunk ricocheted off the head of a peacekeeper drone. Just like the two inside, there was no response.

Jake weaved his way through the small forest of drones until he was good and clear of them. He then glared back, flipping the bird, "Stupid jackasses!"

He pulled out his phone and voice dialed, "Chief Novak." After several rings, the line connected.

"Kepler! You're alive?!" There was a raucous commotion filtering through from the background.

"Yeah, what's that-"

"You need to find safe haven! We're under heavy attack!"

"What? Can't be. The BESI's out of commission. I'm sure of it."

"Well this thing says different! Whatever it is-"

The line went dead.

Contrary to the chief's suggestion, Jake began running toward Division. It was several blocks away, but he was determined to find out what was happening, and more importantly, who was causing it to happen.

As he made his way through the streets, he was stunned to see just how few people were outside. There was still the odd corpse here and there since the BESI's coup had halted cleanup efforts. But the crematoriums had since died out. The air was no longer saturated with smoke from burning bodies. Yet no one was out.

At first, it didn't add up. Human curiosity was indomitable. He had always been aware of rubbernecking citizens, no matter how dangerous a situation might be. It was the moth-to-flame paradox. With a tornado tearing a path to their toes, some people just couldn't resist taking it all in, as if hidden within the peril were all the secrets of life. Now, however, very few people were even so much as peering out of their windows. Then it hit him. They simply didn't exist anymore. Strange that he should fail to make such an obvious connection. He'd been painfully aware of it for days now, but somehow had forgotten: the human race had been decimated.

As he stopped every so often to gather his breath, he would take in the cityscape. It had become an apocalyptic, surreal place. Despite all his imaginings of such a scenario, to now be moving through it was causing him visceral unease.

During the Great Upheaval, Las Vegas had become the first-ever ghost city. The entire metropolis had been abandoned once the water dried up. He remembered taking a tourist trip to the ruins once. It too had been surreal, but since decades of aging had already set in, there was a safe barrier of *otherness* to it. He couldn't relate to the surroundings, they were too foreign. The vacant streets of D.C., however, which only days ago had been bustling with activity, weren't the least bit foreign. D.C. was his home, now transformed into a grotesque distortion.

As he rounded the corner of Nineteenth and L Street, he could see Division in the distance, roughly six blocks away. The rooftop was billowing black smoke and the exterior of the building was littered with pockmarks. He could hear an odd sound echoing down the street. It reminded him of snare drums, as if a marching band were parading around Division. He then caught sight of a large, dome-shaped object emerging from behind the building, twelve stories up. It moved fluidly and rapidly. The snare-drum sound grew more distinct. Eventually, the object was halfway around the building. He stared at it, hopelessly transfixed.

His best comparison for it was that of a gargantuan bug, a centipede perhaps. Its multitude of legs, each one about the diameter of a telephone pole, deftly clasped the side of the building. The entire, massive thing was spiraling itself around Division, incrementally crawling toward the top. With each successive pass, the snare-drum sound would ebb and flow, waning each time it disappeared around the back of the building. As it moved, chunks of brick and mortar rained down from underneath it. Once Jake was a few blocks away, he discovered what was causing the sound. With the creature in profile, he could see a fusillade of projectiles being fired from its thorax. It reminded him of an ancient galleass with recessed cannons, only the ports were along its underbelly. He didn't see any discharge flames, however, so *how* it was firing the rounds was a mystery; perhaps it was using some sort of compression. In any case, they were doing a good deal of damage. Despite its bunker-like construction, Division was starting to look like a slab of pumice. Given enough passes by this thing, the walls would surely start to crumble.

Jake pulled out his phone, "PDC."

After a few rings, a voice answered, "Planetary Defense Command, Corporal Yeboah speaking."

"This is Jacob Kepler with the Biotech Crime Division. I need to speak with General Pierce."

After a moment, the general was on the line, "Agent Kepler. Give me some good news."

"Good and bad, Sir. I'm confident the BESI's been disabled."

"Well that *is* good news. Explains why the drones broke off their attack. And the bad?"

"There's a new threat, and it's currently making a sand pile of my headquarters."

"*New* threat? What exactly?"

"I'll never have any luck describing it to you Sir. Best I can do? An enormous bug, fifty, sixty feet long."

"Bug huh? Something new everyday. And you're sure the BESI's not in control of it?"

"With the drones out, I don't think so. This thing looks completely autonomous. Alive even. No doubt the BESI created it, but I'm pretty sure it's dancing to its own tune. If you still have air support, I'd appreciate a hand."

"Not sure I can reacquire any drones just yet, but I do have a few Specters. It's more a matter of pilots."

"Well, if you can find anyone, please send 'em my way. This thing seems committed to taking the building down, and there are a lot of good people inside."

"Okay. I'll get some birds in the air. But if that SI is still at the helm, it'll be a short trip. What's your position?"

"Safe distance. Few blocks out."

"Alright. Stay put if you know what's good for you."

Chief Novak had shepherded everyone inside Division toward the center of the building. While this served to keep them out of harm's way for the time being, it had a serious drawback; all the emergency exits were toward the exterior walls. Power in the building was out. Even personal devices like cell phones were dead to the world. The chief's best guess was that the building had been hit with an electromagnetic pulse. Considering Division had its own fusion core, the pulse must've been massive, utilizing some form of tech he clearly wasn't privy to. With the teleporter down, and elevators inoperable, the only hope of clearing the building was by way of the emergency stairwells. If they could reach one, they'd be able to get to the sublevel. From there, several access tunnels stretched for miles underneath the city.

He had already sent a team into the elevator shafts to see if they could repel down. As implausible as it seemed, both cars had stopped between the same floors when the power went out. The agents were able to get through the ceiling hatches, but from inside the cars, the doors opened up to impassable shaft walls. Had the cars been staggered slightly, they could've snaked between the shafts and made it to the basement. The Bousard cannons could've easily sheared the cables, but since they had electronic firing mechanisms, the EMP had rendered them useless. Even if they had kept a few canisters of N-30, they still wouldn't have been able to program a detonation tone.

All these what-ifs and how-comes were starting to aggravate the chief. The fact was, they were trapped, and it was a lousy feeling. He'd always had a do-or-die approach to life. Huddling in a small circle with everyone, while this thing huffed and puffed its way in, was very distasteful to him.

"Do you have any idea what that thing is Ms. Líang?"

Margaret barely heard him over the thunderous barrage from outside. And even though she had, she was hesitant to respond. Before the building lost power, she, along with everyone else, had been monitoring the street cams. They all saw the thing as it approached Division, but unlike everyone else, *she* knew what it was. And unfortunately, it too led back to OmniaR Enterprises. She would tell the chief, that much was certain, but she was already feeling like a pariah-by-association. This new bit of information would only worsen matters.

Despite the dire circumstances, her mind was so trained in corporate spin, she was already considering how to distance herself from liability. Being that she was conceivably the last remaining executive of OmniaR, she would unquestionably bear the brunt of all accusations. She would be *the* poster child, of *all* poster children, of corporate malfeasance. In history books, the week the world nearly ended would be linked to OmniaR, and her family name. All that misery would have to wait though. In fact, she might be able to avoid it altogether, she thought. Given their current predicament, there was a good chance she'd never live to experience any of it.

"I believe it's a variation of our Biotech Reconnaissance Unit,..though wildly upscaled," she finally answered, straining her voice to be heard.

"I'll forego asking what that is," the chief replied. "The question is, how do we take it down?"

Again, Margaret was hesitant. She knew that if it were even fractionally similar to Patrick Moody's wee golem, it would be virtually unstoppable. Furthermore, it had been weaponized. To what extent, she could only guess.

"If it's anything like the prototype, I don't think we can."

"How's that?"

She wasn't sure what to make of his question. Was he asking because he didn't hear her, or because he was boggled by her answer?

"I said it can't be destroyed," she yelled louder. "I'm sorry."

"Everything can be destroyed Ms. Líang! Now I need you to start thinking *very* hard about this thing's weaknesses. I want something to exploit!"

Between the chief's growing animosity and the glares she was getting from some of the other agents, Margaret almost felt she'd be better off outside facing the Golem. If things progressed much further, her co-survivors might just string her up.

Chapter 24

<u>The Challenge</u>

When Jake heard the roar of the jets, he cautiously stepped into the street to get a better view. The creature was now wrapped around the top of Division, and appeared to be starting another downward pass. As the two jets blurred by, they let loose a compliment of missiles. When they detonated against the creature's shell, it reared up from the building, keeping itself firmly anchored with the bottom portion of its body. After the smoke cleared, the only damage Jake could see were scorch marks across its back. It was hard to fathom, but the missiles hadn't made a dent.

Within seconds, Jake was on his knees. His skull felt as if it would shatter. He instinctively pressed his palms against his ears as the most piercing, siren-like shriek blasted out in all directions from the creature. Moments later, he found himself being pelted by glass fragments from above. Windows for blocks around had crumbled and were now raining down into the streets. Jake struggled to his feet and ran toward the overhang of a nearby building. He managed to get safely underneath just as tons of glass pellets crashed to the pavement.

The sonic burst was short, but exceedingly effective. Jake lowered his hands from his ears and noticed blood on his palms. He was suffering from an extreme case of tinnitus, making just about every sound imperceptible. Despite his diminished hearing, he believed he should still be able to hear the jets. But there was nothing. He didn't even feel the customary reverberations that rattle the body. It didn't make sense to him. As fast as they were traveling, the sonic blast shouldn't have affected them.

Then he saw one of the jets tumbling downward, nose to ass, like a tossed coin falling to earth. There weren't any flames exiting the engines, and no exterior lights. It was dead weight, silently flipping toward the side of a skyscraper. The canopy blasted off and the pilot ejected, but he timed his pull wrong. It occurred while the jet was perpendicular to the ground. His seat fired straight out to the side. The chute had just begun to deploy when he smashed into the side of a building. As he bounced off, the half-opened chute tangled up around him and he dropped like a stone to the pavement. The jet finally collided with another building further down the block, rupturing into flames and igniting several floors before crashing to the ground.

Even if the jet *had* been hit with the sonic burst, it shouldn't have lost power. Jake pulled out his EMP paddle and fired it at the ground, but nothing happened. It was dead. Ironically, it had been done in by an electromagnetic pulse. That would also explain the disabled jet. Still, to have had such a devastating effect, it must've been extremely powerful with an enormous field radius. Whatever this skittering abomination was, it appeared to be armed with a variety of next-gen weapons. Considering his hearing was still subpar, even though Jake hadn't seen the other jet drop, it probably had, and he just hadn't heard the explosion. He could only hope that the pilot had been able to eject safely.

He pulled out his phone, voice dialing, "PDC." Once realizing his phone was dead as well, he gritted his teeth and flung it at the ground, smashing it to pieces.

The only good thing to come of the failed sortie was that the creature, at least for the time being, had stopped attacking Division. Jake studied it, astonished by its naturalness. It fluidly rotated the upper portion of its body, which was still extended several stories above the demolished rooftop. It seemed to be scanning its surroundings, though scanning with what? Did it have eyes, sonar, radar? Maybe all three.

Jake had always tried to stay abreast of technological advances. He was pretty certain his knowledge was up-to-date, at least with regard to *public* disclosures. His understanding of matter mechanics was basic. Yet his job required him to keep tabs on such things, particularly with regard to biotechnical life forms. One of the more enthusiastically charted frontiers was the creation of brand new, organic materials. Even more coveted, cybernetic organisms which could supplant traditional technologies. The goal was to create living, self-sustaining creatures with biomechatronic functionality. Ideally, being fundamentally organic, they would be exempt from electronic failure.

Jake began to consider all the super-strength metamaterials that might have gone into the creature's design. Based on the list he came up with, it wasn't likely that such a cyborg would easily surrender the ghost. The only thing that *might* stop it would be a close-proximity nuclear blast.

His guess that it was entirely autonomous also appeared to be correct. Not only because autonomy was a given tenet of cybernetic design, but also because it hadn't retaliated against the jets until after it was attacked. That seemed to imply that it was a responsive organism instead of merely a programmed avatar. Jake found that somewhat comforting, because it served as further proof that the BESI was no longer active. If it *had* been controlling the thing, the jets would've never gotten close enough to fire in the first place. It's likely the creature was the BESI's Hail-Mary pass. When it realized it was done for, it breathed life into the vile colossus, hoping it would finish out the mission. But what *was* that mission? And how would it be carried out?

It was most likely programmed with some type of prime directive; namely, the extermination of the human race. And that directive probably included an array of complimentary subroutines. How this thing chose to proceed with that directive, however, would depend to a perverse degree on its own whims. It was a living creature, at least as defined by the Dorchester Convention, and as such, would devise its own methods for achieving its goals. It didn't require high intellect, only a diverse set of response protocols. Like the insect it emulated, it only needed to pursue its objectives and react to obstacles.

As if to prove him right, the creature, without any conceivable provocation, effortlessly descended the building and disappeared down a westward street. A din of timbering street lights and compacting cars followed in its wake. With his ears still plugged up, however, Jake heard little more than the muffled clattering of silverware.

As he approached Division, he noticed some sort of crystalline pellets mixed in with the rubble. He picked one up and examined it. It was about the size of his fist, and very dense. It had a smooth, teardrop shape, and a milky-white opacity. Apparently, it was the megalocritter's ammunition, though it looked completely organic. If that was the case, it would seem to imply that the creature had some way of converting raw materials into its own endless supply of ammo.

"Kepler?" a voice called.

Jake was glad to hear his name. It not only meant his ears were on the mend, but also that he'd found someone he knew. He turned to see Agent Sandoval leaning out from a building across the street.

"Martin!"

"How long you been out here?" Sandoval asked.

"Long enough. Where's everyone else?"

"The tunnels. When that thing stopped firing, we made a run for it. Chief's got me on recon. You run into any bots?"

"They shouldn't be a problem anymore. Every drone I've come across has been flatline."

"So what was that thing?"

"My guess? A going-away present. Is Margaret Líang with you?"

"Yeah. Come on, I'll take you down."

Jake and Sandoval made their way through the dank service tunnels with nothing more than a weak chem-light to shine the way. Sandoval explained that shortly after the 'big bug' hit Division, power was knocked out. With everything fried, the chemical lamps had become indispensable. He also noticed that Sandoval was carrying one of the older Klepp rifles; a model without electronic components.

"Where do these tunnels come out?" Jake asked.

"Just about everywhere in the city. Chief was headed to the river though. Before we lost Paulson, he said he saw that thing coming out of an old warehouse along the docks."

"Paulson's dead?"

"Yeah."

"But the plane detonated!"

"He got the shot off, true enough. Just couldn't clear the roof in time. That cruiser fired a missile."

Jake's stupefaction morphed into rage. How had he survived crashing a plane into a building, while Paulson ended up dead? It defied statistical logic! Cosmic zingers, he called them, and they almost always pissed him off. He was happy to be alive – without question. But whenever such absurdities occurred, especially when lives were lost, he wanted to find whatever mechanism ran the universe and smash it to pieces. Freak occurrences were not uncommon in his life, yet they contradicted the laws of science, in his opinion. And if science wasn't in charge, what was?

Chapter 25

<u>More Bad News</u>

As Jake and Sandoval entered the partially collapsed warehouse, they could see the chief and Margaret Líang standing near a megatrans teleporter. Several other agents were sifting through debris, looking for evidence. Just about every area of the warehouse was strewn with fallen girders and corrugated roof panels, but most of the equipment was still intact. The two men made their way along a fairly clear path, undoubtedly blazed by the creature when it exited. As they got closer, Jake could see that Margaret and the chief were reviewing something on the terminal next to the teleporter.

"Found a stray out there, Sir."

Sandoval said it lightheartedly, but the minute the chief glanced over, stone-faced, he realized it had been the wrong tact.

"Kepler. How in hell's bells did you survive that?"

Jake shrugged, "Got me, Chief. Heck of a story though."

"Humph, I'll bet." The chief turned to Sandoval, "Seems you found a stray with uncountable lives. 'Till now that is."

Jake didn't know what to make of the chief's comment. Furthermore, he wasn't his usual, snarling self. He even struck Jake as being depressed, a side to his boss he'd never seen before. Margaret was an even harder read. Though she brightened up when she saw him, she still appeared to be wrestling with one hell of a demon.

"When I heard you were alive, I-" She promptly shut herself down. She told herself it was neither the time nor place for sentimentality, particularly in light of such grim tidings. But the more immediate truth was, her feelings for Jake embarrassed her.

"So...what's all this?" Jake asked.

"A giant nail in our coffins," the chief responded.

Jake gave a weary look toward Margaret, who was blank-faced.

"Just a little good news, please," he said.

Margaret shook her head, "Sorry. The BRU...I mean the creature, it has the virus code. It's been transmitting the signal ever since it came out of the teleporter. Its spine is like a giant antenna. Considering its length and the power it can generate, it'll be able to broadcast the signal everywhere within weeks. It's essentially a mobile transmitting station. Once it crisscrosses the planet a few times, every active life chip will be infected."

"That's not good news at all. Means we're already infected then, huh?"

Margaret responded with a mournful nod.

"Well, I'm sure glad I made my peace before crashing that plane. At's all I gotta' say. Squared it away toot sweet. One less thing to worry about, ya' know."

Per usual, Margaret was having trouble relating to Jake's blithesome attitude. Sandoval was having even worse luck. He was still busy trying to grasp the personal implications of 'infected.' He stared at Jake, nonplussed.

The chief, however, simply rolled his eyes, "Knothead."

"Well I mean, what's the point of whining if we're already dead. We still might be able to kick this thing's ass, right? It's gotta' have *some* weaknesses."

"None that I can find," Margaret replied. "It appears the BESI constructed this facility using drones. The whole project must've been active for months right under our noses. It used the stolen commodities for raw material. Considering the BESI's intellect and the amount of time it had, the BRU's design is probably flawless. And even if it isn't, it's at least flawless to my comprehension."

"Well you know what? Kepler's right. We're gonna' stop it anyway," the chief said. "For the time being, we keep this under our hats. You too Sandoval. I know it's a lot to take in, and *hold* in, but I'm going to need every agent fully committed. Once we set up a new command post, and reestablish contact with PDC, I'll give everyone the bad news, fair?"

Sandoval nodded. The chief looked at Jake and Margaret, who also nodded in agreement.

The Golem slid into the Potomac river and began crawling across the bottom, displacing large amounts of water over the banks. As it passed under the Beauchamp, the ship nearly capsized, rolling to its side and slamming into the river wall.

Planetary Defense Command had been tracking the creature ever since their failed air strike against it. With the BESI out of commission, they were able to regain control of satellites and air defense systems. Bombarding the thing with several high-yield missiles was proposed. But considering that it appeared to have an electromagnetic defense system, the idea was summarily scrapped. Larger classed missiles were too slow, and would likely suffer the same fate as the jets; rendered useless before they could detonate. There was also the uncertainty of its armor threshold. Before they crashed, the pilots had confirmed two direct hits, yet the creature went unfazed. This left open the question of its ability to sustain even greater damage.

On its current heading, the Golem appeared to be moving toward Chesapeake Bay. From there, it would most likely enter the Atlantic Ocean. Since it was coping just fine as a submersible, the strategists at PDC deemed it prudent to assume that it could handle deepwater excursions as well. Multi-spectrum satellite images were bringing back details about the Golem's design, but the majority of its operational capabilities were open to speculation. Though they were having little success understanding it, they were nonetheless captivated by it. It was admittedly the perfect war machine. One technician studying the data stated, that if it should suddenly become airborne, then it would truly be the weapon of all weapons. So far, however, it didn't appear to have any aeronautic components. Since it could scale just about any object and take to the water, it could theoretically traverse the entire earth, or any planet for that matter, without ever needing to take flight. This was clearly a blunt instrument, and considering its near-indestructibility, had no need to rush toward its objectives.

A soldier called out from the communications tent, "General!"

General Pierce entered, taking the satphone.

"It's Chief Novak with the BCD, Sir," the soldier explained.

"Chief. Glad you're still with us."

"Likewise, Sir. Listen, General, I have Margaret Líang here with me. She's an exec from OmniaR. It seems that monstrosity is a product of their laboratories. From what she's gleaned, it's been tasked with further propagation of the virus. Its entire body is a transmitter. Beyond that, she couldn't determine much about its design. Most of the files have been deliberately wiped, presumably by the BESI. We'll forward you what we have. The immediate point, Sir, is that we need to stop this thing at any cost. Even if it means leveling this city."

"You're proposing a nuclear strike on D.C.?"

"Sir, if that thing crosses the globe, it'll infect every remaining person on the planet. One city in exchange for the human race seems like a fair trade."

The general held the phone aside, turning toward the team monitoring the Golem, "Corporal, what's that thing's current position?"

"It just dropped off the continental shelf, Sir. It appears to be diving to the bottom of the Atlantic."

The general lifted the phone, "I'll take what you've told me into consideration. As it stands though, the thing's already left your neighborhood. So I think we'll keep D.C. for now."

"Where's it gone?"

"Bottom of the Atlantic. If what you said is right, it may be headed for Europe."

As the Golem dead-fell toward the seafloor, it started circulating seawater through its body in order to equalize the pressure; curling itself into a ball to hasten its descent. Once the darkness of the ocean closed in around it, it began using sonar to orient itself.

Finally, it landed with a slow, bouncing roll at the base of the continental slope. Once it stopped moving, it unfurled, planting its legs in the murky seabed. It locked onto the nearest sonic transponder, getting its bearings from the GPS feed. It cross-referenced the data with thousands of environmental buoys on the ocean's surface. Once making its calculations, it plotted a course for its predetermined target: the transatlantic corridor. This was an area along the seafloor that followed the great circle route between North America and Europe. It's where hundreds of transatlantic communication cables had been laid over the years, some dating back centuries.

The very first telegraph line had been placed along this corridor. Even with the advent of wireless communications, hard-line networks were still considered more reliable. Cables had continued to be laid right up through the current era. A recent addition to the corridor were quantum relays, which allowed for instantaneous, non-local data transfers. Most information sent between the Americas and Eurasia went by way of the corridor. From there, it was often wirelessly transmitted via hubs on the surface. The reliance on hard lines was an obvious one; they provided shielded transfers. This eliminated any chance of data loss, which was crucial with respect to teleported material.

All this historical information was available to the Golem. Since it operated on a path-of-least-resistance maxim, it had concluded that the corridor would present the most favorable target. After estimating its time of arrival, and finding it acceptable, it set out on its mission. Its hydrodynamic design allowed it to crawl quickly across the seabed, leaving long plumes of silt in its wake.

General Pierce coordinated with the Planetary Naval Fleet and requisitioned two Behemoth subs, the Corallina and the Darius. They were sent out to monitor the Golem's progress, and if necessary, engage it. The subs were not capable of withstanding pressures at the Golem's current depth, but they could at least keep pace with it and provide sonar surveillance.

A plan to fire upon the Golem was already in the works. An underwater nuclear strike was being viewed as highly advantageous. The water would create added force to the blast, assuming they could detonate close enough to the creature. In addition, there'd be no surface damage or atmospheric radiation.

Each Behemoth sub was fitted with gyroscopic silos which could rotate three hundred and sixty degrees along the circumference of the hull. This allowed them to fire missiles or torpedoes in any direction. The strategy was to mark the Golem's speed and then accelerate ahead of it. If they paced themselves correctly, any downward launched warheads would reach the seafloor just as the Golem was passing by. The torpedoes would be set for contact detonation, so even if the Golem tried to disable or evade them, they would still detonate once they hit the seabed.

The order was given for the Behemoths to begin coordinal pacing. Even though the Golem was manually traversing the Atlantic, it was making good time. It had made itself slightly buoyant by pushing minute quantities of gas into its outer shell. Once buoyed a short distance above the seabed, it tilted to its side and began sidling through the water like a giant eel. At its accelerated rate of approach, PDC calculated that it would reach Europe (its presumed destination) in roughly three days. The consensus was, that with the time they were being afforded, they could carpet-bomb the entire floor of the Atlantic if need be. The environmental damage would be incalculable, but considering the alternative, PDC was unequivocal: the creature must not be allowed to resurface – ever.

Since the Golem had not altered its course since beginning its journey, the captains of the Behemoths moved ahead of its projected path. After achieving several miles lead on the creature, and factoring in the nominal drop-rate of the nuclear torpedoes, the subs came to a standstill. When their clocks reached the optimal launch time, they released one warhead a piece, straight down toward the bed of the Atlantic.

Having suffered the BESI's ability to commandeer their equipment, the PNF didn't want to chance the Golem having similar capabilities. Each torpedo was stripped of all remote-control interfacing, and their guidance housings were removed. They were the equivalent of dumb-drop depth charges. Once loosed, they could neither be recalled nor deactivated.

Only minutes after the launch, the Golem executed a sharp, northerly course correction.

"Captain, the target's altered course. It's now heading due north," the sonar technician said.

"Coincidence?" the captain of the Corallina asked his executive officer.

"Intel said this thing's pretty advanced," the XO responded. "But how it could mark our launch this far away, and so quickly – well that would involve tech I've never encountered before. Our torpedo is nothing more than dead weight, no mechanical noises whatsoever."

"Radioactive signature maybe. Either way, seems we've just decimated every creature below us, where no enemy shall be," the CO mused. "Okay. Correct our heading. Get us out in front of that thing again."

Chapter 26

Cat and Mouse

The Golem's change in direction had in fact been coincidental. At the moment the torpedoes were launched, it had finally reached the end of an underwater mesa. Its course correction had merely been a reactive choice; the sidestepping of an obstacle. It was now on a direct intercept with the midpoint of the transatlantic corridor. Barring any more obstacles, it would remain on a straight line until it arrived.

It had chosen its current depth because no manned craft could venture as deep. As for deepwater submersibles, the only types which could reach the seafloor were small, oceanographic drones, but nothing with military capabilities. While the Golem understood its own resilience, it was still a creature all the same, and functioned by the first rule of any creature, that of self-preservation. On the ocean floor, it could execute its directive with minimal interference or threat of harm. If after arriving, the plan proved too difficult or inefficient, it would simply recalculate a next-best option and embark upon it.

Most cables leaving North America extended out from Nova Scotia, along a well-established pathway. One thousand miles south of Cape Farewell, Greenland, marked the halfway point for many of them. After that, they needed to rise up in order to clear the peaks of the mid-Atlantic ridge. Since the older fiber-optic lines worked seamlessly with quantum relays, many of them were still in use. Tying into just one of these cables would allow the Golem to transmit the virus globally.

The BESI had coded the cabinet files with a terminus command. It instructed the data to flow to any and all digital inputs. If it reached a termination point (a dead end), the data would then back-route itself until it found a new, unexploited path. Between the continual, repeated transmission from the Golem, along with the self-disseminating nature of the data packets, every electronic device on the planet would eventually be visited by the code. If those devices were interfaced with human beings in any manner whatsoever, biodigital mutation would occur. Even if the Golem stopped transmitting after its initial send-out, the packets themselves would still cover the globe within days. However, *with* the added help of the Golem's continual retransmission, global dispersal would occur within hours.

This timeframe would be further reduced when taking into account the data packets previously transmitted by the BESI before it went offline. It had originally intended to deliver the entire reworked virus itself, having already transmitted several of the packets. Once it came under attack, however, it was forced to redirect its efforts toward self-defense.

The Golem had always been a backup measure, but one of last resort. The BESI viewed the BRU's autonomy as both a strength and weakness. Its ability to self-determine made it vastly superior to drones of all types. But unlike drones, it could not be directly controlled. The BESI knew, that once unleashed, the creature would be difficult to heel. It would be like an unruly attack dog, which could just as easily turn on its master. At some point, once humans were out of the picture, the BESI had planned to redesign it. It envisioned the Golem as a mobile vessel of sorts for its own neural network. However, once it started to meet with staunch resistance, it transferred the complete viral code to the creature's holographic imprint and prepped it for activation.

In the moments leading up to the blast that severed its trunk line, the BESI had been preparing to transmit the final few packets worldwide. Considering the heft of the data, however, there wasn't enough time. Yet the activation of the megatrans teleporter (which breathed life into the Golem) was a preprogrammed hot-button, requiring no more than a millisecond to execute. The choice was obvious. The BESI realized it would not be around to witness the Golem's triumph, but went offline confident that it would.

As the Golem neared the corridor of cables, it expelled the gas from its shell and descended to the ocean floor, momentarily disappearing into a cloud of clay and silt. Drawing from hundreds of cabling coordinates charts, it began searching for a fiber-optic line which would suit its purposes. It moved over the various cables, some of which were miles apart and partially buried, scanning each one to determine its viability. Many of the older telegraph lines, frayed and eroded, did not even register in its knowledgebase.

Using its EMF probe, it searched for the telltale signature of an active, light-wave line: electromagnetic output. Though faint, signal repeaters along a cable emitted energy. They were shielded to dissuade curious sharks from biting into them at shallower depths, but still emitted enough of a field to be detected.

Once locating a line that appeared to be in full use, the Golem edged its way down the cable in search of the nearest repeater. While splicing directly into the line itself would be too difficult, tapping in through the repeater housing was more than feasible.

"Captain, the target has stopped," the sonar technician called out.

"What's its location?"

"Forty-three degrees north, forty-two degrees west. Approximately five hundred and eighty miles off the eastern seaboard."

"Alright. Let's get above it," the captain said. "Chief Philips, get me some information about its location, ideas on why it stopped there."

"Aye-aye, Sir."

The captain turned to his XO, "This may be our best chance. If it sits still long enough, we can drop an anvil right on its head."

After digging out a buried portion of the fiber cable, the Golem was able to clamp down on the repeater housing. It extended a web-like membrane from one of its forearms and encased the signal repeater, creating an airtight seal. Using its internal, catalytic diffuser, it began converting carbonic acid in the surrounding seawater into

All Hailed The Singularity   223

carbon dioxide. It then injected the gas into the membrane cavity while drawing out the trapped seawater, producing a pocket of dry space around the housing. It retracted one of its shell coverings and extended a long, multi-hinged boom. At its tip was a slim, diamond-shaped pod. The pod pushed directly through the membrane wall, blossoming open to reveal an array of electronic devices. From a small opening at the center of the pod, a high-fracture laser began cutting into the side of the housing. After completing a precise rectangle, the Golem jostled the cable slightly, causing the cut-away plate to shake free. It then began the delicate task of tapping into the fiber-optic line.

"The only things of import are com-cables, Sir. Hundreds of submerged lines," the chief petty officer said.

"Think it plans to splice into one?" the captain asked.

"Makes sense. PDC said it was trying to transmit the virus," the XO replied. "One thing's certain. If we drop a fish there, we'll sever just about every link between North America and Europe."

"And if we don't?" the captain asked, rhetorically. "When we're parked on top of it, draw up a quick solution and drop another warhead. And apprise PDC that we believe it's going to tie into a com-cable. They can begin shutting down terminal stations."

The Golem was aware of the two Behemoth subs stalking it. It had registered the seismic shocks from their first, failed attack. Though it didn't know the means of delivery, it deduced that the Corallina, now stationed above it, and the Darius, closing fast, were the likely sources of the explosions.

Destruction by nuclear attack was decidedly not in the Golem's best interest. With self-preserving tenacity, it began focusing its sonar array directly upward. At first, it didn't perceive the dead-falling torpedo. Then, a minor cross-current nudged it, causing it to oscillate slightly as it descended. Once that occurred, the Golem was able to differentiate it from the Corallina hovering above it. Without abandoning its transmission efforts, it anchored its anterior to the signal repeater by digging several legs deep into the seabed. Then, like an acrobat performing a headstand, it raised up the remainder of its body. As it began to draw power from its internal energy core, tiny heat-generated bubbles started boiling off its midsection. Once sufficiently primed, the Golem fired out an incredibly powerful, ultrasonic blast. It was directed straight up toward the approaching warhead; now roughly half a mile below the Corallina. As the leading wave of the sonic blast made contact with the torpedo, it began to rattle to the point of breaking apart. Before it could though, it detonated. As soon as the Golem detected the explosion several miles above, it quickly furled itself into a tight ball around the signal repeater. When the dissipated bubble pulses from the blast finally reached the seafloor, they only slightly nudged the giant, orbicular insect.

The Corallina was not as fortunate. It had been much too close to the torpedo when it detonated. Once the blast waves collided with her, the pressure hull failed catastrophically and the sub imploded. There hadn't even been enough time to send a distress call.

The Darius, still several miles out, sustained a sizable shockwave, but did not incur any damage. It scanned the area, eventually tagging the sinking mass that was once the Corallina. As it dropped to the irretrievable depths of the Atlantic, the captain of the Darius could think only of the lives that had been lost. For a horrifying moment, *how* they had met their end assailed her mind. The lucky ones would've been killed instantly, or knocked unconscious. For any others, the influx of cold seawater, edging out the last vestiges of air, would bring death in a panicked, gasping rush.

Behemoth subs, like all Naval craft, had a minimum of human crewmembers. When the BESI had commandeered the vessels, the crews of both subs were able to seal themselves off from the onboard drones and remain unharmed. Once the BESI was taken offline, and control restored to the captains, they were able to lockstep back into service rather quickly.

For the Darius' commanding officer, Captain Kimura, the people that went down with the Corallina were not acceptable losses.

She knew each one of them personally, and the captain had been a good friend of hers.

After reviewing the data just prior to the Corallina's sinking, she was able to draw a conclusion about what most likely happened. Both captains were fully aware of the risks involved with passively arming their torpedoes. Once armed, a significant impact, even within the submarine, could cause detonation. She knew the Corallina had successfully launched its warhead, so whatever had set it off was in the ocean itself. Though unlikely, there was a chance it had collided with a whale or other large fish during its descent. The presence of the ultrasonic burst, however, emitted just after launch, hinted of a countermeasure by the Golem.

The immediate lesson to be learned was that dead-dropping armed warheads was no longer a working solution. Captain Kimura would've preferred a moment to mourn the crew of the Corallina, but understood that time was much too precious to pause operations.

The Golem was in the process of trying to lift the cable from under the silt of the ocean floor and move it. It would hoist it up, step forward in a lurching manner, then grow top-heavy. Once losing its balance, it would tip headlong into the seabed, yet remain stubbornly clenched to the signal repeater. Immediately, it would regain its footing and repeat the process, moving the cable a bit further along each time.

Like the Darius above it, the Golem had taken notice of the Corallina plummeting downward. Factoring in cross-currents and weight, it had calculated that the sub would set down directly on its position. Though aware of its own structural fortitude, it had no desire to dig itself out from under a crumpled Behemoth sub. Its directive, to continue transmitting the virus, coupled with a keen sense of self-preservation, had prompted the very logical act of getting the cable and itself out of harm's way.

Eventually, the lump of twisted, collapsed metal touched down on the seafloor. As it creaked and moaned through the dense, cold water, a huge billowing cloud of silt erupted from beneath it. Satisfied that the threat was over, the Golem, like a dog clamped to a bone, lowered the cable to the seabed and coiled around it. Then, in odd, successive shudders, the various somites of its body began to swell. The thermal exchange with the icy water once again caused small bubbles to boil away from its shell.

Since the Darius had tagged the Golem early on, it was aware of its exact location at the bottom of the ocean, and had maneuvered into a top-hat position.

"Captain. I'm getting a lot of bubble distortion. We've got some large air pockets headed our way," the sonar technician called out.

The captain looked at the floor and shook her head. The last breath of the Corallina escaping to the surface, she supposed. She recalled her early days in the Navy. Her first commanding officer had confessed to her once, that he chose to believe the souls of the dead were rising up from the depths in those last-breath bubbles.

Shortly after one of the bubbles collided with the hull, an alarm sounded.

"Captain! Hull sensors indicate a rapid degradation in section four, alpha," the chief petty officer said.

"What kind of degradation?"

"I can't make out the chemical signature, Ma'am. It appears to be a corrosive agent."

Within the span of several minutes, successive bubbles collided with the underbelly and sides of the Darius. Air pockets they were not. They were blastulas of synthetic acid, tooled with nanotech functionality, produced and released by the Golem below. On the ocean floor, it had turned itself into a chemical factory. Using stored resources, as well as surrounding elements from the seawater and sand, it had manufactured a highly corrosive fluid. It was able to manipulate the fluid at an atomic level, customizing it with nanotechnological properties not at all consistent with natural acids. Besides tweaking it to be extremely caustic (capable of eating through fortium metal), it also imbued the fluid with magnetic characteristics, allowing it to adhere to the sub's hull. Another modification was to give the fluid a saline-repulsive charge. This caused it to self-encapsulate when reacting with the surrounding seawater. The Golem was then able to release the fluid directly into the ocean without it becoming diluted. In the same way that oil and water separated, the sacs were formed as a result of the fluid repelling itself from the saltwater. The last alteration was to bond just enough gas molecules to the fluid so as to make it buoyant enough to rise quickly, but not so buoyant as to counteract its magnetism. Otherwise, it would continue past the sub altogether in its upward push to the surface.

The calculated balance appeared to be exactly right. Soon after the Golem began spewing the mordacious fluid from under its shell, the resulting globules rose swiftly upward. Upon contact with the sub, the fluid cleaved to the hull and began eating through its metal shell. The first hull breach occurred in the aft section of the sub. When water seepage was detected, the sub's automated system dispatched a repair drone to the area, then sealed off the compartment. Once the breach hole became so large that seawater was gushing in, much of the corrosive fluid entered with it, and began dissolving everything it touched. The repair efforts by the drone were forever halted when the drone itself fell prey to the acid. As more and more holes began to open up across the sub's hull, the captain knew it would just be a matter of time before they followed after the Corallina.

The boat's system fervently began sealing off one section after another in efforts to avoid decompression. But there were too many leaks occurring too quickly. Not wanting to condemn her crew to a frightful end, Captain Kimura gave the order to surface, in hopes of allowing them to abandon ship. Shortly after the sub began to rise, a critical breach occurred in the main ballast tank. A massive expulsion of compressed air erupted from the sub. As it rolled to the side and began a downward pitch, the captain knew she had failed her crew. They would all meet their graves on the ocean floor.

"Petty Officer Snuffé, what's our current rate of descent?" Captain Kimura asked.

"Eleven feet per second," the quartermaster yelled.

"Will that hold all the way to the bottom?"

The confused quartermaster gawked at his captain.

"Oh damn it all! Just give me your best guess!" the captain yelled.

"I can't be sure, Ma'am. Based on damage reports, we're nearly airless as it is. It's not likely we'll get any *less* buoyant than we already are. Based on that, yes. Our descent should remain constant."

"Arm every warhead," the captain ordered. "I want a timed detonation, set at," she glanced at her watch, then her XO, "thirty minutes?"

"Should be just right," the XO confirmed.

The fire control technician armed every warhead on the sub, missiles and torpedoes alike, with a thirty-minute countdown.

"Captain, what are the target coordinates?"

"There aren't any. We're not going to launch." The captain glanced around the control room, acknowledging her crew. "It's sunk us, that much is certain, but we're going to give it one hell of a counterpunch."

In anticipation of the Darius' arrival, the Golem was once again hoisting the cable overhead and awkwardly trying to move it. It did not detect any launched warheads from the sub. This caused it to conclude that the Darius had been properly caught off guard by the acid assault, and had not been able to mount a timely offensive. Its only concern, for the moment, was to reposition the cable, and itself, from under the projected path of the deflated sub.

Several hundred feet from the ocean's floor, the Darius' entire arsenal detonated with synchronized perfection. A pressure bubble, spanning roughly a mile in diameter, expanded outward within seconds, and then just as quickly collapsed inward on itself. This was followed by another instantaneous outward expansion. The force of the blast rippled through the water, pulverizing everything in its path. The first shock pounded the Golem, cable and all, deep into the sediment of the seafloor. As the bubble retracted, it wrenched the creature up from the resultant crater. As the second bubble expanded outward again, it engulfed what was left of the Golem and obliterated it. The various plasmas and fluids of its circulatory system vaporized instantly upon exiting its shredded body. It was almost completely atomized within the first half second of the bubble's expansion. When the bubble imploded again, all that remained of the Golem were portions of its fortium skeleton. These scattered, unrecognizable pieces of metal fell through the water to the ocean floor. The bubble pulse continued for several more rounds until it finally dissipated.

Shortly before the explosion of the Darius had severed most every cable in the corridor, teams had been dispatched to landing stations along the European coastline to shut down all terminal hubs. Many of those on timed lockouts had to be overloaded, causing fiber-fuse. Yet that was still considered a better option than waiting. In the end though, all efforts were pointless. Hours had passed since the Golem had first begun transmitting the virus. If they'd been successful in shutting down the cable it was tied to, the creature undoubtedly would've disengaged. The fact that it hadn't, meant that the line was probably active right up to the point of its demise. It was a better than sure bet that the virus had been thoroughly disseminated. Additionally, PDC was not yet aware that the data packets themselves were coded to redundantly propagate. Once they would finally discover this fact, it would be of little importance.

There were campaigns launched to get people into medical centers for life chip removal. Hoping to avoid a panicked rush, the Consortium created a cover story that the chips were defective and needed to be recycled. Most people weren't that gullible, however. Ever since the first virus attack, every snippet of network chatter drew their attention. Rumors of biodigital mutation, coupled with such high death tolls, had people putting two and two together. Furthermore, no one believed the Consortium would ever allow life chips to be removed without a *very* compelling reason. The stakes had to be extremely high, or such a measure would never have been approved.

With mob-driven fervor, people once again began descending on hospitals and medical centers across the planet. Further complicating matters was the fact that chip removal was an involved surgery. Simply injecting a nanotech drone to extract the chip was too risky. It needed to be carefully teased away from the heart tissue. A rushed job could easily cause heart failure. This meant the surgeries needed to be overseen by human doctors, which were in very short supply.

Other, less radical measures were implemented as well. The simplest of which was the avoidance of all digital interfacing. Every remaining network hub was shut down, and all wireless activity banned. Ultimately, all attempts to quarantine the remaining population from the virus turned out to be toothless endeavors. It had already found its many, many marks. What had once been digital was now biological. Even for those who had managed to get their chips removed, it was too late. Mutation had begun.

Bowing to the inevitable, the Apex CEO of the Consortium of Nations proposed the implementation of Order 201. He called an emergency meeting of all remaining super-corp CEOs (or their still-living successors) and put it to a vote. The vote was unanimous, but entailed conditions. Only specifically designated people would be remolecularized, and they would be detained in quarantine until it was determined just how bad the plague was. If enough people survived to ensure the continuation of the human race, then the restored assets would be immediately returned to holographic stasis.

Where the plan fell to pieces were the facilities themselves. Following the commodities theft, they had all been put into tier-five lockdown. The lockdown order had never been rescinded. Issued by the BESI and pass-coded, it made each storage facility as ironclad as a nuclear bomb shelter. Teleporter access had been suspended, and all surface entrances were sealed behind massive, blast-resistant doors. By the time this was realized, there were very few able-bodied soldiers around to even *attempt* incursions at these sites. Efforts were made using drones, but the facilities were simply too well fortified. They were impregnable, underground bunkers, each with their own internal power cores. The exterior sentry drones were easily neutralized, but the bunkers themselves remained impossible to breach.

As the first signs of illness once again started to surface, everyone braced themselves for round two of the global holocaust. Little by little, people began to fade away from view. Live news outlets began signing off, and broadcast transmissions started cycling into preprogrammed fare. In one last, feeble address from the Apex CEO, the actual cause and delivery of the virus was finally disclosed to anyone remaining to hear it. Perhaps he felt the need to go on public record, for whatever posterity may be afforded the human race. Perhaps it was to clear his conscience, to atone for all the corporate subterfuge which had impeded swift response to the threat. Or perhaps it was just mercy, born of the conviction that people had a right to know what was killing them, and why. Regardless the reason, of the few citizens still alive to hear him, none cared. The viciousness of the illness demanded every ounce of their attention. What had caused it, or who was to blame, was of little importance. Such was the primacy of dying.

Chapter 27

Catching Sand

Margaret walked to the curb and instinctively waved toward a row of parked cabs at the end of the block. Without hesitation, the first cab in line pulled away from the curb and moved toward her. It wasn't until the cab approached and the door automatically glided opened, that the surrealism of it hit her. As she climbed in, it struck her that all the doomsdayers had missed the mark. Here it was, the actual end of humanity, and everything was working just fine. They may have gotten the doom part right, but not the gloom.

After the BESI had been taken offline, most automated systems eventually timed out and rebooted. Restored to their default programs, they continued on with their previously assigned duties. Most of the bodies in public areas had been removed. The crematorium pyre had since been relocated out to sea, far from sight and smell. It was now a cobbled-together mass of antiquated, derelict cargo ships and barges, blazing around the clock.

Debris was being cleaned up. Power was still running. Water was still pumping. No one had explained to all these robots that without humans, they needn't bother working. Still, they did, and would continue to do so until their power supplies drained. Since fusion core charging stations were capable of providing decades worth of energy, it seemed apparent that drones would outlive even the last of the healthiest humans, if any existed.

Were it not for her own malaise, Margaret might have chosen to go out with some flare. For just a moment, she considered venturing over to Georgetown and embarking on a no-holds-barred shopping spree. Her concerns were far from material things, however. The thought of it did amuse her though. If there were to be any survivors, they'd have full run of a vacant world, and that pleased her in a peculiar sort of way. But that would be their present to open, not hers. She was certain to be dead within days. Currently, all she wanted to do is check up on her remaining relatives. Since none of them had returned her calls, she realized they were most likely all dead, or dying. Still, she felt obligated. And yet it seemed to make very little sense to her, spending her last few hours on social visits. And what really could she do for them? Death was a solitary experience. She might be able to provide them comfort, but she was scarcely able to comfort herself at the moment. Perhaps that was the real reason for her sense of obligation. She was afraid to be alone. She was using familial duty to avoid facing her own demise. Whenever life grew unbearable, she always found it beneficial to distract herself with some task or another. She had weathered so many storms that way. Yet it wasn't working now. Her fatigue and nausea were not allowing her to ignore her own predicament.

It annoyed her that no matter what the illness, the symptoms were almost always the same. It seemed as if the human body only had a few, select tricks to alert someone of its malfunctioning. The alerts worked, but were generally very tedious. Nausea was the worst. It was so obscure and hard to resolve, yet accompanied just about every illness she'd ever had. It struck her as particularly useless now. She wished she could explain that to her body, make it understand the futility of a lost cause. Perhaps then it would shut down all pain signals, release every endorphin, and let her spend her last hours in bliss.

As she rounded the corner onto Connecticut Avenue, she contemplated stopping by a pharmacy to grab an assortment of stim-tabs and painkillers. She was about to redirect the cab when she spotted something unusual, at least unusual by current circumstances. Further down the street she could see someone sitting alone at a sidewalk café.

She leaned forward, speaking into the dashboard mike, "Pull over in twenty feet." The cab pulled toward the curb and slowed down. Margaret stared through the windshield for a moment. Her eyes began to well up. She climbed out of the cab and stood still for a moment, dazed.

"Unbelievable...."

"Don't I know it," Jake replied, as if talking to himself. The table in front of him had various bottles of alcohol lined up and he was pouring drinks from each one. He was lost in a mild high and hadn't even bothered to look up. Once it dawned on him that someone had actually said something, and that he wasn't hallucinating, he looked up. He strained his eyes, trying to get a fix on Margaret, standing only a few yards away.

"Wow. Margaret Líang. You're not dead." He squinted again, growing slightly concerned as he stood up. "You're not are you?"

She laughed gently and wiped her eyes as she walked toward him, "Yes, it's me. I'm not dead yet."

"Well, small world then,..in more ways than one. If there's any sort of cosmic design to things, I'd say you and I were written into this scenario ages ago. I mean really, what are the odds?" He shot down a glass of rye. "Care for a drink?"

Margaret impulsively stepped forward and hugged him, taking him by surprise. As usual, he deflected with a joke.

"I'll take that as a yes," he said, patting her lightly on the back. She finally let go and stared at him for a moment.

"Yes!" She was then overcome by laughter, as if a curse had just been lifted.

"Go on, have a seat. If you feel at all like I do, standing up is a chore," Jake said, pulling out one of the chairs.

"I've never had alcohol though. Considering the way I feel, I'll probably just get sick," she said, sitting down.

"Oh most certainly. I've lost count myself. But right through those doors there, there's a big fountain," Jake said, waving one of the bottles toward the café entrance. "Perfect for puking. And you'll feel better! And little by little the alcohol will get into your blood and work its magic. Trick is to keep drinking."

"Don't suppose you have any stim-tabs or-"

"Hah!" Jake interrupted. He leaned down and pulled out a plastic pharmacy container from under one of the chairs. "Went trick-or-treating! Mostly just treating. Everything I could think of to alter one's consciousness and/or kill pain. But drink first, puke, then take the meds. If you take 'em now, then puke, they do no good. I also grabbed some injectables for when things get really bad."

"Are you going to…?"

"What?" After a moment, he understood her intent. "Oh. No. Least not intentionally. Why? Is that what you wanna' do?"

"No. At least I don't think so."

"I hear ya'. Might end up singin' a different tune when it gets down to it. If I'm able to avoid the pain though, I'll ride this beast right into a coma. I'd like to keep thinking for as long as possible – only thing made life halfway interesting."

"You really *do* talk strangely you know."

Jake laughed, selecting another bottle from his collection and opening it. "When I was growing up, people still liked to consider the meaning of things. Prattled on about self-awareness, fate, existentialism,..stuff like that. Your generation was much more practical. Just do for the sake of doing. I've always needed more meat on my plate. Still, even you must be pondering the unknown right about now?"

"I will die. That will be that. Come from nothing, go to nothing. You don't think a drone continues to exist after it's decommissioned do you?"

Jake shrugged nonchalantly, "Depends on what day you ask me?" He steadied his hand and poured a shot glass of brandy. "Today? I'd say it makes for a damn happy thought."

Margaret smiled. She couldn't express just how glad she was to have found him. They'd been through so much together in such a short span of time. It was indefensible, but she felt closer to him than most people she'd known her whole life. Perhaps it was just bonding through peril, but it was extremely comforting all the same.

He handed her the glass, "Here, something easy to start with."

Margaret was about to drink when Jake interrupted her, "Whoa, whoa, whoa." He poured himself another rye. "Gotta' clink glasses first. Old tradition." He raised his glass to toast, "To whatever being decommissioned brings, eh?" He leaned over and tapped his glass to hers. They both drank. Margaret showed no signs of displeasure, which surprised him.

"Another?"

"Yes. It's...fruity. I kind of like it."

"That's what I've been trying to tell people my whole life."

Margaret stared at the glass as Jake refilled it, "Any word from your friend Roland?"

"Nope. Stopped answering his line. He's a clever bastard though. If anyone could dodge this bullet, it would be him." He raised his glass unceremoniously this time, "Cheers." They both shot down their drinks.

"Where were you headed by the way, or were you just stalking my chip signal?" he asked.

"No," she laughed. "Truth is, I don't really know. I thought I did, but it was pointless. I guess it just made sense to be going somewhere."

Jake nodded as he poured another round.

"At first, I found myself at one of OmniaR's south-side labs," Margaret continued. "I was hoping to find out how the virus was designed, pass it on to the WHO. Nothing there though. Nothing at all. Then I decided to go to the population storage facility in Virginia, see if my credentials would get me past the lockdown."

"And?"

"Four drones pointed their weapons at me until I left."

"Ah yeah, I know that feeling."

"And you? How'd you end up here?"

"Everyone still standing from Division piled into a truck. Headed off to a med-center. They all looked like hell, from the chief on down. I told 'em, why bother? Come join me in a drink. Hard to fight the urge to live though. Overrides just about everything. Even reality."

They clinked glasses again and drank.

Margaret then let out an unexpected, guttural howl of frustration. She limply placed her glass down and rubbed her eyes.

"This is the worst way to die! I'm not like you. I don't *want* to think. All the things I should've done. All the things…I'm responsible for." She began crying full throttle.

"Hey, hey, hey" Jake cut in. He leaned over and gently rubbed her shoulder. "It's foolish to go there. You're no more responsible than the rest of us. The moment we all agreed to hand the reins over to that machine we accepted the terms. The user agreement, eh? Besides, complexity invites disaster. That's a truism. Patel was right, something like this was always bound to happen, one way or another."

"I just can't believe this is it."

"For humans you mean?"

Margaret nodded, wiping her eyes.

"Well hell, don't count us out just yet. We're as persistent as this virus. I have to think someone, somewhere will keep on going. Survive somehow, rebuild. Then again,..nature doesn't play favorites. Something stronger?"

She nodded, and Jake poured them both a shot of whiskey. Margaret grabbed hers and gulped it down without waiting for him.

"This *is* stronger," she said, wincing from the taste.

"It does demand attention. But hell, you're feeling better, right?"

"Yes. Still nauseous though."

Jake rummaged through the pharmacy container, pulling out a small packet of medicine. "For motion sickness. Works wonders. I'd wait though, like I say, then take it after. It'll calm your stomach."

Margaret pushed the packet aside and grabbed the bottle of whiskey. Jake leaned back in his chair, smiling as he watched her. She sloppily poured herself another shot, snatched up the glass, and drank it down. Immediately after swallowing, her eyes widened and she covered her mouth.

"There, there! In there!" Jake said, pointing to the café entrance.

Margaret ran as quickly as she could through the open doors and stumbled to a halt at the side of a large, baroque fountain. She heaved incessantly into the circulating water. As she watched the blood and booze swirl into the fountain's cascade, her nausea intensified. Once she was spent, she sat back on her heels, glancing up at the ornate sculpture of the fountain. All the bare-chested figures were in a state of capitulation to some unseen object. It seemed to hearken back to the ancient idea of numinous, a reverence for the divine.

But there *was* no such thing, she reassured herself. No object, no entity. And yet with death so close, her conviction was tenuous.

She pushed her doubts aside, asserting once more that there was *only* the natural world. Unfortunately, Jake was right. It didn't play favorites. Humans were merely one of many *unfavored* players in a vast and unforgiving landscape. They'd never had real control, only perceived control. The virus had proven that much. Yet presumably, one had control over their own mind, and by extension, their body – to a degree.

As she studied the cowering figures in the fountain, she became infuriated. NO! She would not satisfy the whim of some unseen god, even if one *did* exist. She was her own work of art, strived for from birth. That she could end her life was antithetical proof she had started it. She leaned heavily on the retaining wall of the fountain and lifted herself up. She shuffled out of the café and plopped down into her chair.

Drowsy-eyed, she glanced at Jake, speaking with the exaggerated slur of a novice drinker, "We are...our own designs."

"Well then, we clearly need more R&D," Jake said, with an absent chuckle.

"What's in here?" Margaret asked, picking through the pharmacy case.

"What're you looking for?"

"Absolution," she said, quietly.

Jake bowed his head. He knew this moment would arrive, no matter what either of them had said. He just hadn't expected it to show up so soon.

"I made a list for myself," he said, plainly. "A chemical opus of sorts. Taken in the right order, we're talking about sublime egress." He handed her the list and began retrieving various narcotics from the pharmacy container. "Sure you don't wanna' wait?"

"I need you to be here when I leave. It's selfish, I know. But I can't bear the thought of being alone."

Despite her pragmatic bravado concerning death, she was scared. Though it had never been outwardly apparent, nor would she ever admit it aloud, she had always relied on male figureheads to shore up her own confidence. For the majority of her life, that role had been filled by her father. Now, it was Jake's turn. She needed him to bear the loneliness. To defer the fear. To distract her from the task of dying.

Jake looked into her eyes, trying to see if there was any hint of doubt. When he could find none, he nodded, and lined up the various pills in front of her. He loaded a vial into one of the injectors and laid it nearby. Margaret methodically ingested the regimen of narcotics, washing them down with a fresh glass of brandy. Most were a variety of pain medications, designed for instantaneous absorption. Within fifteen minutes, Jake could see she was starting to feel the effects. Her face softened and she grinned slightly.

Close-quarter emotions were not Jake's strong suit. The end of humanity? Not so tough to wrestle with. It was such a large slice to ponder, it was impersonal. Margaret, on the other hand, was not. She was finite, and *much* more personal.

As he watched her drifting away, he sensed a great, uncontrollable sadness within himself, just waiting to break free. Despite all that had happened over the last few days, he had kept his head on straight. He had skillfully stowed everything away, somehow avoiding all the sharp edges. Yet Margaret was certain to break that trend. Not only was Jake attracted to her, he had genuinely grown to like her. For all her corporate starchiness, she betrayed a delicate, vulnerable side. His prehistoric, ape-man wiring made him want to protect her, care for her. He even allowed himself the fantasy that they might just love each other. Whatever the reason, the thought of her dying was causing him to unravel.

He could feel his face harden as he gritted his teeth. He knew he would see her through, but only if he fought every molecule of his being. He helped her extend her arm across the table, holding the injector against the inside of her forearm. She grinned at him lackadaisically, giggling softly. He took a quick, shallow breath, and pressed the plunger. The injector hissed, like an asp of old, delivering the drug into her system.

"Thank you," she whispered.

He grabbed her hand, as much for his sake as for hers. Sliding his chair closer, he started to caress her arm. With very little strength left, she squeezed his fingers. Her eyes conveyed a sense of great peace, unlike anything he'd ever witnessed before, in anyone. She smiled, patted his hand, and then laid her head down on the table. He watched as the breath from her nose created tiny circles of mist on the glass tabletop. After a short while, there was no more mist.

He let go of her hand and began sobbing. His arms went slack by his sides and his face locked up in torment. As tears flowed down his cheeks, he drew heavily for breath, each inhalation an audible, stuttering hack. It was as if he were having a seizure, with no ability to stop. Everything had finally caught up with him. All the death, all the suffering, all the sadness. An exorcism of grief was underway and he had no choice but to let it play out.

In time, the convulsions subsided. While he was far from being his old self, he at least felt more composed. He deliberately turned away from Margaret's body, struggling to find the lighter side.

"Always were a weepy drunk," he scoffed.

He wiped his eyes with the cuff of his shirt and swigged down another rye. A quick gust of wind blew the list onto his lap. The exit recipe. He glanced down at it, responding with a drunken guffaw.

"Really?" he said, squinting skyward. "This a hint, or a coincidence?" He laughed again, bitterly this time, "What a *stupid* game!"

It really didn't matter anyway. He'd already made up his mind. Things had changed. Thinking his way into a coma was out of the question now. Now he was *feeling*. Feeling way too much to honor his original plan. The physical pain was bad, but the emotional pain was worse. It was time to leave. Time for relief.

In a neat little row, he lined up the required dose of each drug and loaded another vial into the injector. He began swallowing each set of pills in succession, washing them down with a glass of rye, the last glass he would ever drink. Once he started to feel his motor skills dropping off, he readied the injector. After a decisive press of the plunger, a peaceful warmth began to wash over him.

He looked up and down the block outside the café. If the bots somehow overlooked them, he thought, their bodies would never reach the pyre at sea. Instead, they'd become mummies of a sort, entombed in an ancient ghost city. The improvised king and queen of the apocalypse, frozen in time. If any people did survive, and should one day happen upon this sight, he thought, hopefully they would understand. If not, to blazes with 'em.

Chapter 28

<u>Rebirth</u>

Ninety-eight years had passed since the extinction of the human race. In the years immediately following the viral outbreak, there had in fact been survivors. Some people had managed to avoid contamination. Others, by some genetic luck or another, had proven immune to the virus. Their numbers were extremely low, however, and too widely scattered. What ultimately dwindled their numbers down to nothing, was their inability to sustain themselves. Their over-reliance on the automated world in which they'd been raised, proved fatal both times. Once the mechanized workforces began shutting down from disrepair or power loss, these few remaining humans were like newborn infants without caretakers. To further complicate their predicament, most of them were genetically modified individuals. Their DNA had been molded, tweaked and augmented toward specific tasks, tasks solely useful in a modern society. Their prehistoric abilities to adapt and capitalize on their environment had long since been weeded out of their genome. Being thrust into a new paradigm, which was in fact a very old one, they buckled and withered like termites exposed to the hot, dry sun. They were too specialized, and nature never smiled on such creatures.

The planet, now vacant, bore few indicators that human beings ever existed at all. There was still some infrastructure, but it was profusely overgrown with vegetation. The only things still functioning, albeit with little future left, were facilities powered by long-term fusion cores. Such places had been built to weather just about any storm and remain operational. Primarily, they were commodity storage centers. Resource security necessitated that such facilities be fully autonomous and resilient – particularly in tier-five lockdown. Decade after decade, they had continued operating, together with the drones that maintained them. Having ample power and raw materials, anytime a drone or facility component broke down, it was promptly repaired. That the outside world had ceased interacting with them was of zero consequence.

The fusion cores were not inexhaustible, however, only longevous, and their life spans were reaching an end. When operational systems began factoring in the inevitable power loss, several contingency programs were launched. Most of these programs were capsulation orders, designed to cut back on power use by discontinuing non-critical operations. Further, long-term projections, prompted these systems to begin prepping for complete shutdowns. This would entail the total, sequential power-down of all systems, ending with the mainframes themselves. The last executed command, a stitch-up program hard-coded into each mainframe, would ensure that all stored commodities remained locked within their respective crystals in perpetuum.

At a population storage facility located in the southern hemisphere of the Americas, a peculiar subroutine launched itself and began executing a host of operational commands. The console in front of the reduction chamber booted up and began flashing. A robotic arm slid silently down a guide track in front of a long row of shelved crystals. It stopped at one bank, extended its arm, and lifted a crystal from its compartment. After returning to the main processing outlet, it seated the conic crystal into the reduction bed.

The facility's mainframe began to run a diagnostic on the subroutine. It was about to draw off huge stores of power for what was deemed a nonessential activity. With each attempt to vet and subsequently vanquish the program, the mainframe was thwarted.

As the vacuum-sealed array of Dessiper magnets began to rotate, eventually nearing light speed, the console triggered a series of commands, bringing into existence a docile white hole. Within an instant, from a diffused flash of light, Juan Augusta Sequenza appeared on the reduction bed, sprawled like a sleeping child. A second robotic arm, fitted with a web-like hammock, smoothly and silently pivoted into position, effortlessly lifting Mr. Sequenza from the platform. It glided across the room along its overhead tracks, gently setting him down on a padded gurney.

The process of remolecularization continued unabated for the remainder of the day, despite ceaseless attempts from the mainframe to shut the program down. Ever since having been uploaded by the rebel Mattie Ferne some hundred years prior, it had embedded itself in every human storage crystal from Mr. Sequenza onward; a total of eight thousand or so souls. It was a simple, yet ingenious Trojan Horse program. It had been coded to auto-launch at the first sign of a facility shutdown. Once triggered, its sole function was to restore all tagged assets.

After about twenty minutes, Juan regained consciousness. He sat up on the gurney and swung his legs off the side. He looked around to see several other gurneys adorned with sleeping villagers. He was at a complete loss as to his whereabouts. The last thing he remembered was sitting down to rest under a tree on the field he farmed. He had only wanted to take a nap. Now he was in this place, wherever this place was. He had no awareness of time having passed. Nor could he recall any dreams. For all he knew, this *was* a dream, though it felt much too real.

His bewilderment only intensified when the next remolecularization occurred before his eyes. *How* it had occurred was beyond his understanding. So much so, that he attributed it to an act of divinity. What he *was* sure of, however, is that he recognized the person. Very much so. It was his neighbor's daughter, Marquesa, the woman he loved. Once the robotic arm hoisted her from the platform and placed her on a gurney, he quickly stepped to her side. He began patting the back of her hand in an effort to wake her. Again, another person appeared on the reduction platform and was moved to a gurney. They were all faces Juan knew, and was ever so glad to see. Little by little, they regained consciousness as the auriflurane gas, locked in their bodies from the day they were captured, began wearing off.

As the room grew more and more crowded, the villagers began to explore the facility. With only dim security lights to guide them through the underground, maze-like complex, they strove to find an exit. It was Juan and Marquesa who finally located a massive vault door at the end of a long, upward sloping ramp. Marquesa noticed a phosphorescent green pad under a hinged safety cover. Once the facility's shutdown procedure had begun, a failsafe order was issued granting emergency exit override. This was done to ensure that no humans within the facility would ever get trapped inside once the power was lost. This emergency feature took precedence over any type of lockdown, tier-five or otherwise.

Marquesa waved Juan over to the pad, pointing at it with a conferring nod. Juan hesitantly lifted the cover and pressed the pad. An alarm began to sound as a track of red lights started cycling around the frame of the enormous doorway. The huge vault door began sliding to the left, slowly receding into the wall. Bright, warm sunlight flooded in, fanning out further and further across the interior as the door rumbled open. Drawn by the thunderous noise, several other villagers made their way up the ramp.

They stood at the mouth of the facility, awestruck. The smell of freshly fallen rain, mingled with the comforting scents of the natural world, washed over them in a gentle, cool breeze. When they first stepped past the vault door, they were frightened by four security drones standing guard on the loading dock. But the machines remained motionless and silent. The facility had been conserving energy for years. Most drones, particularly security units, had been deemed nonessential, and removed from their charging cycles. Their power cells had long since been exhausted. They now stood like totems, guarding the entrance of a most unusual tomb indeed. While the villagers were not ignorant of technology, they'd never been so close to such menacing contraptions before. They felt it best not to offend the hulking sentinels. As they quickly stepped past them, they would each touch their hearts and then kiss their fingers skyward. Under the circumstances, they felt a blessing was more than sensible.

Once they reached the outdoor parking area in front of the facility, what graced their eyes was hard for them to comprehend. They were no strangers to dense overgrowth, yet the expanse of jungle surrounding the facility lacked even so much as a footpath. They had no way of knowing that a century had passed. They knew only that they had been displaced, mysteriously, from the land they once called home. This was a new land, it seemed, and it was bountiful.

As the facility continued to remolecularize all tagged assets, Juan took it upon himself to institute a relay welcoming committee.

Each person to gain consciousness was told to remain in the room just long enough to revive and welcome the next delivered person. After having done so, and explaining as best they could what was happening, they'd be free to venture out into the new world. This simple and efficient process continued on for several days, as the facility's fusion core grew weaker and weaker.

Eventually, when there simply wasn't enough power to maintain the docile white hole any longer, the reduction chamber shut down. The last person to be remolecularized remained as instructed, but no new souls were delivered. After several hours of sitting patiently in the darkened room, he finally concluded that the miracle was over. He walked cautiously through the corridors of the facility until reaching the vault door, guided only by the light of the setting sun. Like those before him, he marveled at the wealth of natural beauty encompassing the facility. The facility itself, however, was cold and unsettling. He was glad to be free of it. He joined several other villagers who were camped nearby. They welcomed him gladly, treating him to a wild boar roasting over a warm, comforting fire.

Though feared as it was, over time, the storage facility came to be revered as a holy place, a place where life had been restored. Many of the villagers coalesced into larger populations, clearing away huge swaths of jungle around the facility. As they had done their entire lives, they found harvestable plants and cultivated them. They domesticated some of the local wildlife and began developing methods of commerce and governance. They renewed their cultural practices and began building families again, families which would reach for multitudes of generations into the future. Humankind 3.0.

www.ingramcontent.com/pod-product-compliance
Lightning Source LLC
Chambersburg PA
CBHW072217170626
46813CB00003B/986